cawnpore

CAWNPORE

by tom williams

jms books

JMS Books LLC
10286 Staples Mill Rd. #221
Glen Allen, VA 23060
www.jms-books.com

Printed in the United States of America

ISBN: 9781611522709

Dedicated to Lieutenant Michael Williams and the men and women who served with him in Afghanistan. Anyone reading about the history of British involvement in Asia soon comes to realise the more things change, the more they stay the same.

preface

IN 2010, JMS Books published *The White Rajah*, John Williamson's account of his life with James Brooke of Sarawak. Williamson had written the account as a personal record, not intending it for publication. It ended with him in Singapore, having left the man who had been his lover and mentor in Borneo.

Although much is known of James Brooke, I thought that Williamson had been lost to history after these adventures. About six months after *The White Rajah* was published, though, I received a package of papers from someone who has asked to remain anonymous. The papers had been in his possession for years and he had been uncertain what to do with them. He suggested that, following the success of the earlier book, I might like to see these published too.

The story follows on directly from the end of *The White Rajah*. Williamson apparently left Singapore and travelled to India. This book describes his experiences during the siege of Cawnpore in what was then called the Indian Mutiny. The siege of Cawnpore was one of the most comprehensive British military disasters of the 19th century and a source of fascination and horror to the Victorian public. One of the survivors, Captain Mowbray Thomson, published a book (*The Story of Cawnpore*) that was a best seller in its day. Williamson's manuscript suggests that he was thinking of publishing his own account. However, the work could never have been published at the time. Its open acknowledgement of his sexuality (when homosexuality was illegal), his ambivalent attitude to the rights and wrongs of the war and his failure to play the part of the conventional Victorian hero, all made publication impossible. Perhaps he intended this as a first draft and then realised that editing it for the public would have meant removing all the details that make it such a unique and fascinating record.

The Indian War of 1857 was probably one of the best-documented conflicts in history, although many accounts differ as to the details of events. Williamson's record is typical in this respect. Overall, Williamson's account seems reliable, although I have added some Editor's Notes discussing some of the apparent discrepancies in his account and a short bibliography for anyone who wants to check the details of what happened.

Like most authors of his day, Williamson's spelling of some Indian words and the names he uses for Indian towns are not the same as they would be nowadays. I have retained Williamson's spellings, although where these have been inconsistent, I have edited them so that they are at least the same throughout the book.

Williamson used chapter headings written in the long narrative style of the day. They were more like tables of contents than chapter headings and I have removed them. Other than that, I have tried to let Williamson's words speak for themselves.

chapter 1

IT WAS IN December of 1855 that I left Singapore. My time with James Brooke was generously rewarded and I found myself if not a wealthy man, then certainly in a position to return to England and live out my days quietly and in comfort.

I was by now approaching my middle years but I felt that I was still too young to retire to some country village. My time in the South China Seas had given me a taste for life in the Orient and James' stories of his experiences in India had left me curious about that country. So it was when I took ship in the *Swallow* I paid my passage just as far as Calcutta.

We celebrated Christmas at sea. The captain served a goose at his table and the crew entertained us with an impromptu concert that combined sea shanties and some carols, but otherwise there was little to mark Our Saviour's natal day. The sea looked much the same as the day before. There was a stiff breeze and, just before dark, there was a touch of rain.

We arrived at the red mud banks that mark the entrance to the Hooghly just as 1855 gave way to 1856. After three weeks at sea, I welcomed the proximity of land. Waking early, I joined the passengers clustered at the rails to watch the jungle passing in the pearly dawn light. For a moment, I felt myself back on the River Sarawak, seeing my first glimpse of Borneo. The Hooghly, though, was not the Sarawak. We were not feeling our way up an uncertain navigation. An East India Company pilot stood on the deck, alongside the captain, and we tacked our way confidently upstream.

When we arrived at last in Calcutta, no sooner had the ship docked than we were swarming with natives who hurled themselves up the gangplanks to inflict themselves on our poor vessel. Coolies, black and shining and naked but for a loincloth, came aboard, ostensibly for porterage. Most, though, seemed to squat idly or engage in animated but incomprehensible conversations with their fellows. Men claiming to be tailors, some armed with measuring tape and chalk as if to give proof of their profession, importuned any European who did not move rapidly out of their way, offering new suits at prices that would make a Singapore merchant blush. Other gentlemen, elegantly dressed in native drapery and turbans, glided toward me and, before I could effect an escape, they thrust into my face pieces of paper assuring me that the bearer had served this or that European as his khitmutghar or major-domo for so many months or years and that their services were in every respect satisfactory.

After I had assured several of my would-be servants that I intended to establish myself in a hotel before I made any decisions about my household, I decided to head for the shore and have my luggage sent on. Again, I found myself swamped with a crowd of natives. These were the boatmen, sinewy men, almost naked and so unlike the khitmutghars as to seem almost a different species. All offered their services at the top of their voices and all, on closer enquiry, demanded vast sums of money to paddle me the short distance to the shore.

When I had finally settled on a sum I suspect was scarcely more than twice that which old India hands would have paid, I descended the companion-ladder to an already over-laden boat and after a few nervous minutes, I was deposited safe and more-or-less dry on the soil of India.

Now I had to fight my way through yet another crowd who jostled and pushed at passengers disembarking on the quay. Arms reached toward me, clutching begging bowls; voices shouted offers of services of every sort; while what seemed like thousands of other figures seemed to be joining the pushing throng simply from some social desire to do as everyone else was doing. In truth, I had little idea what any of them were saying as, although I had made some attempts to learn Hindustanee in Singapore, not one word in ten was intelligible. In the end, I turned to one fellow who was, in some approximation of English, offering the services of a palanquin. This, it turned out, was essentially the same thing as the sedan chairs of old England and, once I was safely aboard, four bearers carried me in curtained seclusion to my hotel.

The hotel I had chosen, on the recommendation of acquaintances I had made on my voyage, turned out to be a splendid place and I was soon safely ensconced with a good meal in my belly. Now, sat in my room digesting a leg of lamb that seemed all the more delicious after shipboard food, I felt it was time for some belated New Year resolutions. The first (and without it this might not have come to be written) was to make a diary of my impressions. When I had come to write of my early days in Borneo, I realised how many details of my experience had become blurred by time and I resolved that I would commit my new life to paper while it was still fresh in my mind. I had no inkling then that I would find myself at the centre of great events and that I would be writing an account such as the one that you are now reading, but rather I thought I would keep some jottings in a commonplace book that might stimulate fond memories in my later years.

My second goal was to find myself some employment such as would enable me to utilise the experience of administration that I had acquired in Borneo. I remembered all James Brooke's complaints about the power and the manifest failings of the East India Company. Nonetheless, if I were to find employment in India, I would have to work for the Company which controlled the economy and government of the country with a grip no less firm for its being, to some degree, sclerotic.

I had feared that the Company would not be prepared to offer me any sort of position as most of their recruits were the children or close relatives of existing employees and those that were recruited in England were trained up in the Company's college at Haileybury. However, I was pleased to discover that, whatever his opinion of the East India Company, the Company held James Brooke in some esteem. Once it was known that I had been at his right hand in Borneo, doors I had expected to be closed to me were opened and I was soon being interviewed by a gentleman who declared that he was sure that a position could be found for me. His main concern seemed to be that I would find employment with the Company failed properly to exercise my talents for administration. I assured him that this was unlikely to be the case. Even quite junior officials in the Company's employ would be responsible for a population that might be greater than in the whole of Sarawak and I was more than happy to seek a post that would be supervised by a more experienced officer of the Company. As it happened, there was a vacancy for a Deputy Collector in the city of Cawnpore in Agra, part of the North Western Provinces. Thus, it was agreed that I should make my way there, to work under the Collector, a Mr Charles George Hillersdon.

The journey to Cawnpore was to take the better part of two months and my new employers were anxious that I should take it as soon as possible, for the cool of January was held to be the ideal time to travel. So it was around the middle of January (I look at my commonplace book and see that it was the 17th) that I set off from Calcutta. I had intended to travel light, but I was assured that no European could journey without servants. So, beside a man to drive my buggy, there was a separate groom to care for the horses and a personal attendant without whom, everyone told me, the natives would look on me hardly better than a vagabond.

Our caravan travelled fifty or sixty miles in a day, easing our way up the Grand Trunk Road. Each night we would stop at a Government post house or dak bungalow as they are called, where I would be settled into a comfortable bedroom while the servants were herded away to sleep, I knew not where. They seemed happy, though, such treatment being the custom of the country, and we progressed contentedly enough. At first, the journey was dull but, as the flat countryside around Calcutta gave way gradually to hillier terrain, I gave myself over to the thrill of exploration, finding excitement in the constantly changing vistas. At times, the road grew so steep that I had to abandon the buggy and move to riding horses. This was no great inconvenience, though, as arrangements were easily made at the dak bungalows to hire another buggy when the terrain allowed. Any difficulties that were caused by changing conveyance were more than offset by the magnificent views from the summits we ascended.

I was told that we might be bothered by tigers but I saw no wild animals other than the monkeys I would glimpse from time to time among the branches wherever the road passed through trees. Once we did come upon a bear sleeping on the wayside, but it woke and lumbered lazily away without making any move toward us.

We had left hills and jungle behind us by the time we arrived at Cawnpore. The town lay stretched out on the plain alongside the Ganges, a fantastical confection of towers, minarets and domes that promised the real India—an India that had remained tantalisingly out of reach in Calcutta where the Governor's palace and the offices of the Company dominated the town. Here the buildings of the European Station clustered beside the river to the South, leaving native Cawnpore gazing down on the sacred Ganges as it has for centuries.

The company had arranged a bungalow for me and I arrived there around midday. It looked pleasant enough. The building, with high rooms and a shaded veranda against the summer heat, stood behind a mud wall that ran alongside the road, surrounding a fair-sized garden. Little grew there, though, save for some patches of grass, survivors from the rains, which pushed their way through the red soil.

I walked up the short pathway to the door to find it opened as I approached. A tall Indian in immaculate white robes and a turban stood within and greeted me, bowing with his palms pressed together.

"Welcome, sahib. Mr Hillersdon has asked me to serve you as khanasaman."

A khanasaman, I knew, was almost like a butler. In Sarawak, James and I had been served by Freddy who had run our household with devotion and who had, on one famous occasion, saved our lives. Freddy had been short and always somewhat rumpled in appearance so about as different from the Indian before me as I could imagine but I hoped that, despite his almost formidable appearance, he might become as valuable an ally as Freddy had been. I decided to try out my Hindustanee and greeted him in that tongue.

"*Namaste! Maiṁ tumasē milanē se khuśa hūṁ.*"

Far from showing any pleasure at my effort, it seemed to me the khanasaman recoiled a fraction before ignoring my proffered hand and salaaming even more deeply than before.

"Mr Hillersdon suggested that you might like me to arrange the hiring of your staff."

I persevered with my attempt at friendliness, favouring him with a broad smile.

"I'm sure there's no hurry. We can get to know each other first."

The gentleman before me drew himself up and somehow looked even more formidable.

"It is essential that servants are hired without delay. I would have made the arrangements earlier, but Mr Hillersdon considered it appropriate to wait for your approval." Then, scarcely pausing for breath, he started to enumerate the hirings he had planned for that afternoon. There was to be an abdar who would serve my wine, a khitmutghar to oversee my dining room, a second khitmutghar to assist the first, a cook, a second cook, a man to wash dishes, another man to wash clothes and a third to iron them. In case these gentlemen should not ensure the eternal well-being of my wardrobe, I should hire my own tailor and then, as Indian servants come in pairs, a second tailor alongside the first. Beside these individuals, I was to employ various sweepers and gardeners and water carriers and, all in all, an establishment of some thirty or forty people. My attempts to explain that this was not necessary met, first, with incomprehension and then with dismay. "Sahib," he cried, "I have been employed by the Company to ensure that your establishment is such as is suitable to a man in your position. You will disgrace me if you do not allow me to make the proper arrangements."

It was pointless to argue. If I was to live and work as a Company official in India, I must maintain an appropriate style and that meant having servants—lots of servants. In order that I might give due honour to my position of Deputy Collector, I yielded as gracefully as I could and my khanasaman went off happily to engage this small army on my behalf. Only as he left did I realise that I did not even know his name. I think I realised at that moment that we were never going to become friends.

In the few hours of peace that I could expect before he returned, I explored my new home. The bungalow was a substantial building already furnished with such furniture as the Company considered suitable for a bachelor in its service—overstuffed armchairs and enough linen to make the most homesick of memsahibs feel that they were but a hop and a skip from London Town. I saw nothing that encouraged me to spend more time there than I had to so, after a quick wash and brush-up, I was ready to report for duty.

Finding the office where I was to spend my days was easy enough, for the Collectorate was an imposing building in the centre of the European quarter. It was built in a style halfway between the traditional Indian buildings and the offices of a

British merchant bank. The stone facade with its fine doorway was separated from the street by a veranda that offered some shelter from the sun and the windows were high and unglazed, the lower half screened with the rush screens called tattis which would be soaked in water to provide some cooling of any breeze that might pass through.

I announced myself to the babu guarding a desk at the entrance. He was dressed as a European and spoke to me in perfect English. In fact, he seemed almost more English than most of the Englishmen I had met in India. He was the ideal gentleman, from his stiff wing collar to his perfectly polished shoes. Only the colour of his skin and the lustre of his hair gave away his Indian origins for, like most babus, he was the child of an Englishman and his Indian mistress and the more he tried to ape his European superiors, the more they would despise him. His efficiency, though, was in no doubt and, minutes later, I found myself in the office of the Collector.

Charles George Hillersdon, who also held the position of Magistrate for the district, was a few years my junior, being in his early thirties. He was slightly above the average in height, but a sedentary life had left him somewhat corpulent and he tended to stoop, making him appear older than his years. His office was a large room, but, despite its size, it seemed cramped, for the walls were covered in shelves where books and ledgers filled every available inch.

Mr Hillersdon pushed his chair back and rose to greet me. "Welcome to my lair. See if you can find a seat somewhere and sit on it."

There was a seat and, miraculously, it seemed to have hardly any papers resting on it. I moved a sheet or two and sat while the Collector outlined the work that I was to assist him in.

"We collect the taxes, oversee tribunals, inspect public dispensaries, check the schools are up to scratch, make sure the jails are sound and the courts don't fall on the judges. A bit of everything really. As far as the natives here are concerned, I'm the Government. And you, too, now."

It was much as my work had been in Borneo, only on a grander scale. I admit, it sounded daunting and I imagine that some of my concern must have shown on my face for Hillersdon hurried to reassure me. "Don't worry. You won't be alone. There's a chap called Simkin who'll be as your right hand." He smiled. "I'll introduce you."

We left the Collector's room and walked a short way down a corridor. On one side, a row of doors stood open, revealing offices that faced out onto the veranda. "We never close the doors," Hillersdon told me. "It's hot enough with them open."

Internal windows allowed air to cross the corridor to a single large room on the other side. There I saw twenty or thirty babus at rows of desks, industriously scratching away at the piles of papers in front of them, but Hillersdon ignored them and gestured for me to enter the next office. I did so, but the desk that stood in splendid isolation on a patch of carpet was unoccupied. Hillersdon, following me in the door, paused, a look of irritation on his face. "Where the devil is Simkin?"

A note on the blotter, neatly centred on an otherwise empty desk, provided the answer. "Gone to lunch," it read.

Hillersdon sighed. "The man's got to eat, I suppose." He looked at me as if he had just that moment realised that the same was probably true of my constitution. "You'll be hungry yourself."

I assured him that I had breakfasted well—which was true for the food in the dak bungalows was generally excellent—but he insisted that he see me fed again.

We went to his Club, close by the Company's offices. "We must fix you up membership. Everyone here's a member and they do a good lunch."

I had never been inside a gentleman's club before. When I lived in England, my position meant that I would no more have dreamt of entering a club than of taking tea with the Queen. In Borneo there had been no need of such an institution, the gentlemen there all knowing one another and James Brooke and I keeping open house in any case. But I had heard of the London clubs and I had imagined what they might be like. The Club at Cawnpore was exactly as I had imagined gentlemen to repair to in London, though the height of the rooms and the slatted shutters over the windows were concessions made to the local climate.

Lunch in the club was obviously popular and the place was busy. Hillersdon introduced me to a dozen or more men in quick succession. All of them, like me, were respectably dressed in long jackets, high collars and ties which, even in the cool of winter, were far from ideal clothing for this climate. Perhaps that is why my impression was of a parade of red-faced, perspiring English gentlemen, most slightly overweight and, in the few moments of introduction each was allowed, all practically indistinguishable. Their names meant nothing to me nor mine to them, though several were anxious to try to place me.

"Are you one of the Surrey Williamsons?"

I had to confess I was not.

"Did I used to see you at Lady Forester's soirees?"

No, I had not had that pleasure.

"Did you know old John Marriot's lad?"

I feared not.

Hillersdon explained to each in turn that I had just arrived from Borneo and had worked there alongside James Brooke. At Brooke's name, one or two faces showed some sign of recognition but, for most, it seemed that my lack of any proper connections in English society was a grave disappointment.

Sensing my discomfort, Hillersdon steered me away to a quiet corner where we sat in stuffed leather armchairs in the reading room. Copies of 'The Times', shipped from London and filled with old news, were scattered around while the Indian papers lay pristine and neatly folded on the tables. We sipped gin until a native in a splendid white uniform came to whisper that luncheon was served. The food (roast lamb with mint sauce and potatoes followed by sticky toffee pudding), like the rest of the club, made no concessions to geography. Apart from the heat and the Indian servants, there was little to indicate that we were in India at all.

We lingered over coffee, but by three we were back in Simkin's office and Mr Hillersdon introduced me to a rotund young man with thinning fair hair, who at least had the grace to look embarrassed to learn that the Collector had been waiting on him. "I'm so sorry, sir…Most regrettable…My wife…new cook…"

Hillersdon waved aside his explanations. "Well, you're here now. Can you show Mr Williamson the ropes?"

The Collector retreated to his office and Simkin subsided into his chair. "Oh dear. I think I may have blotted my copybook rather."

I was not altogether impressed with Mr Simkin. "I'm surprised you have time to get away at all. There seems a fearful amount of work needs doing."

"Oh, yes. Fearful."

"I hardly know how you can cope."

"Ah hah!" Simkin tapped his nose with a wink. "Organisation. There you have it. The secret is organisation."

I sat, saying nothing. It seemed to me that young Simkin would expand on his point without encouragement.

"The natives are dishonest, feckless and lazy but over centuries they have built up a system where each class exploits the one below it. We have a good relationship with one of the local bigwigs—chap called Nana Sahib. We flatter him and go to the parties he gives and he makes sure that all the local landowners hand on the taxes that they're supposed to pay. I have a couple of native clerks and they handle most of the day-to-day stuff." He smiled with the confidence of one who had lunched well. "Organisation, you see."

I agreed that I did see and excused myself. I found my own way to my office and sat down with a weary sigh. Mr Hillersdon's intentions were good but I could see now why his office looked so busy. I had no doubt that mine would resemble it ere long.

＊

FORTUNATELY, SIMKIN WAS right about one thing. The babus were models of efficiency and, with their help, I was soon able to establish myself in my office and make a start on the tasks awaiting me. And if I could expect little help from below, I had Mr Hillersdon to aid me from above. For in an office where most of the Europeans seemed more concerned with following the fortunes of the runners in the famous Cawnpore races than in anything related to their employment, the Collector stood out as a model of conscientious behaviour. I soon came to admire him for his administrative skills and we seemed to rub along well enough together.

About a week after I arrived, he announced that now I had had a chance to settle down, I must dine with him at his home. "You'll have to dine with everybody eventually but you might as well start with us."

I think he realised that I was still not entirely comfortable in company. Dinner parties being one of the principal recreations of Cawnpore, I think he hoped to break me into the habit gently. In any case, I was the only guest of the Hillersdons that night, so just the three of us sat at table. Even with so small a party, though, we were waited on by no less than seven servants, one standing behind every chair, another to serve the wine, two to attend the table and a khitmutghar who acted as a sort of major domo. In addition, of course, there were the kitchen staff, who had prepared the food and Hillersdon's khanasaman who made an appearance at the beginning of the meal to ensure that all was in order.

With all the delicacies of the Orient at her disposal, Lydia Hillersdon had chosen to serve roast beef. I had tried, as tactfully as I could, to suggest that this might cause offense to the many members of her staff who were Hindoos, but she assured me that her cook was a Musalman and that he had no objection to our eating cattle.

Mrs Hillersdon was a pretty woman, barely more than a girl but already the mother of two children who were tucked away somewhere in the vast bungalow that reflected the Collector's status in Cawnpore. The meal, too, seemed designed more to astonish me with the profligacy of food available rather than to meet the needs of appetite. Besides the beef there was, as a concession to native cuisine, a chicken curry and then eggs and mutton chops besides a concoction described as trifle but resembling nothing I had ever eaten before. Mrs Hillersdon was particularly proud of the mutton chops. They were so tough as to be practically inedible, but they had the virtue of being the product of her very own sheep for, as she was quick to explain, she kept a small menagerie of animals on the grounds at the rear of her bungalow.

"I have guinea fowl, turkeys, pigeons, chicken and rabbits as well as the sheep. Alas! So many die in the summer heat, but I do enjoy looking after them and it is so rewarding to raise our own food for the table."

Mrs Hillersdon, resplendent in her wide skirt trailing the floor and her immaculate white blouse seemed an unlikely stockwoman. Then again, when she looked at me, dressed as a gentleman with my stiff collar and my cravat under a jacket of the latest pattern, she probably did not imagine that I had started life as a farm labourer in Devon. Relieved to find a common interest, I ventured to question her on matters of animal husbandry.

"Do you keep your own ram, madam?"

"A ram, Mr Williamson? Whatever for?"

"So you hire a ram to tup your ewes?"

"Tup, Mr Williamson? Pray what does that term mean?"

Mr Hillersdon saved me from further embarrassment by remarking on the charm of the lambs. "Our boy has made quite a pet of one of them. I hardly dare mention where his chops come from."

Lydia Hillersdon could not let mention of her son pass

without telling me all about his attachment to their flock and the shepherd's smock that her tailor had run up for him. The conversation moved on and the danger was passed. Fortunately, Mr Hillersdon was more amused than annoyed by my *faux pas*, explaining the next day that his wife's involvement with her miniature farm was limited to occasional inspections while her servants did the actual work. She employed a shepherd for the sheep and a murgh-i-wallah for the fowl and the rabbits. This seemed to me an extraordinary amount of care to lavish on a few animals for the table but Mr Hillersdon assured me that her efforts were, by the standards of many of the Europeans in the station, quite modest.

James Brooke had frowned on British women joining our community in Borneo, so dinners there were more relaxed, bachelor affairs. I had felt somewhat constrained before my misunderstanding with Mrs Hillersdon, and after that I fear I left Mr Hillersdon carrying most of the burden of conversation himself. He was a good host, though, with a store of entertaining stories that kept the table amused until more servants arrived to clear the meal. We withdrew into a parlour cluttered with furniture, much of which appeared to have been shipped from England, having no sign of native design or manufacture. In pride of place was a fine upright piano where Mrs Hillersdon sat to entertain us. The instrument was not entirely in tune, as the climate of India means that pianos have to be tuned almost monthly, but it was clear that she was a good player and I appreciated her attempts to entertain a stranger in her home.

I left at around ten, having found the evening trying after so many years of living in a bachelor establishment. The weeks that followed, though, made me realise just how pleasant a hostess Mrs Hillersdon was and how enlightened her husband.

I was invited to dinner party after dinner party. I would set off at around seven, leading a train of servants, for to arrive without them would be considered a grave discourtesy. I would take a vile sherry with the master of the household while my servants and their servants and the servants of the other guests all navigated themselves around the over-stuffed furniture and the occasional tables covered in sculpture chipped from the walls of the local temples. Our host's khitmutghar would announce dinner and we would traipse through to a dining room where we would be seated at a table that would not be out of place in a grand dining hall. An array of cutlery would be displayed, guaranteed to confuse me for all that I was now generally able to pass myself off as a gentleman, and dish after dish would be set before me in the confusion of over-spiced lamb and under-boiled beef that passed for Anglo-Indian cuisine. As a bachelor, I was invariably placed between two young women who would simper at me in the hope that I would relieve their parents of the embarrassment of unmarried daughters. We would struggle to make polite conversation, which, in these circles, meant empty chatter about English fashion and London Society. Sometimes the ladies would ask for advice on a horse they were considering purchasing. Here I thought I might impress, horses being, so to speak, in my blood from childhood. Unfortunately, I would barely have started on my enquiries on the finer points of their proposed purchases than I would see the light die in their eyes and I realised that they were no more truly interested in my views on horseflesh than my attitude to the latest colour for an evening gown.

I would stagger home from these evenings, my head aching from the heat and the interminable chatter and my bowels already complaining as they tried to digest the execrable food. I wondered what these people were doing here in India when they so clearly wanted to pretend to be in Surrey and to ride to hounds after the fox. (They did, indeed, ride to hounds in Cawnpore, but had to be content with chasing jackals.)

The contrast between these dinners and the quiet evenings spent at the Hillersdons (for there were to be many more after that first night) made me appreciate the virtues of the Collector's household. They kept a small establishment by local standards (though, even so, they must have had around forty servants) and they treated them kindly. They might eat beef at their table but they respected the religious sensibilities of their staff in their direct dealings with them and were generous with gifts on the many and various holy days that the Hindoos and the Musalmans celebrated. Indeed, in his role as magistrate, Mr Hillersdon was often distressed to hear of cases where Europeans had beaten their servants because a chop had been over-cooked or the leather on their horse's bridle had not gleamed from recent polishing when they chose to ride out unexpectedly. Although it was impossible, given the relationship between the races, for the Collector to side openly with the natives against their rulers, he would often take the delinquent master aside and speak so severely to him in private that his behaviour would be moderated for weeks or months to come.

In part, Hillersdon's attitudes seem to have been tempered by his relationship with Nana Sahib. "Old Nana," as Mr Hillersdon called him, was apparently a particular friend of the Collector as well as having the more general reputation of being well disposed to all the Company officials in Cawnpore.

"He's a jolly fine chap," Hillersdon assured me. "He heard that Lydia was a bit peaky last summer and said that if she ever needed a change of air, she was welcome to stay out at his guest house."

Nana Sahib lived something over ten miles outside Cawnpore and a visit to his guesthouse was viewed by the European community as a pleasant change from the dust and heat of the town.

"He's an excellent host and extraordinarily well disposed to Britain—surprisingly so, given the treatment he has received."

"We've treated him badly?"

Hillersdon had been explaining land ownership in the area, but now he pushed aside the books on property rights in Agra and reached for a bundle of papers tied in a green ribbon.

"These are copies of Nana Sahib's petitions to be recognised as Peshwa. That was his father's title, but dear old dad was a naughty boy. He raised an army down near Bombay and decided to drive the British out of India. We smashed his army and exiled him here with a pension to keep him quiet. When he died, Nana naturally assumed he'd get the title and the pension. The Governor-General doesn't agree. Poor old Nana is stuck here with hundreds of courtiers and retainers, all demanding pay and pensions and regular gifts. He even has his own little army to escort him around the place and let him play at being a great lord still. It's all very splendid but it doesn't come cheap. The old Peshwa left a fortune, but the well must run dry soon. Nana Sahib writes petition after petition and quite a few of us have put in a word for him but Dalhousie won't be moved. You can see why Nana Sahib might have it in for the British but far from it. I couldn't get things done half as easily if he weren't around to smooth things over with the natives when difficulties arise."

I picked up the petitions, almost without thinking, and spent the rest of the afternoon making notes on exactly who was responsible for the tax on the hundreds of farms in the countryside around Cawnpore. As I did so, I noticed how many were ultimately owned by Nana Sahib and, where they weren't, how often his name was mentioned as having adjudicated disputes on field boundaries or inheritance.

That night, after a dinner eaten alone but watched by four different servants, I settled to read through Nana Sahib's petitions. I wasn't surprised that the East India Company was no longer prepared to pay the eight hundred thousand rupees a year that they had used to buy off his father but some of the other measures—notably their refusal to recognise any of his hereditary titles—seemed cruel. Did the East India Company not understand how important titles and honours were in the East? And if they did, why were they antagonising someone who had shown nothing but good will toward their country and their Company?

By now, my understanding of Hindustanee was considerably improved. I would talk to my household servants in their own language (much to my khanasaman's disgust) and I would listen to the conversations I heard in the bazaar to try to understand the politics of the place. The Collector's offices were full of reports from European officials and native spies, but I felt that these looked only at the surface of things. I sensed deeper currents that would take events I knew not where—but I was sure that without understanding the Nana Sahib I could never really understand native politics in Agra.

Mr Hillersdon noted my interest and sought to gratify it by suggesting that we pay the man a visit.

"You'll have to meet him sooner or later. Everybody does—and, of course, he'll be interested to meet you as you're the new Deputy Collector. Why don't we ride out to Bithur tomorrow?"

WE SET OFF early. We had twelve miles to ride and we intended to take it gently. In the summer, we would have taken a carriage, but the winter chill was still on the mornings, so we preferred the possibility of some gentle exercise to sitting swaddled in blankets for the journey. We did not breakfast before we left as Hillersdon assured me that we would be more than adequately fed when we got there.

Our journey took us North, past the old town, nestling against the Ganges to our right. In less than a quarter of an hour, we had put Cawnpore behind us and we were riding across a wide plain with only occasional hamlets and the odd grove of trees to break the monotony of miles of open ground. Even here, though, were constant reminders of the sheer number of people living in India. We passed holy men who raised begging bowls, farmers carrying food to the Cawnpore markets in great baskets strapped to their backs and finely dressed men who Mr Hillersdon identified as the Nana's land agents, off to collect rents or adjudicate disputes with his tenants. Every mile or so we would pass fields scratched from the thin soil, a few straggling plants all that stood between the farmer and starvation.

Despite the plentiful evidence of hardship, the early light lent softness to the scene. It filled the landscape with a promise of romance so that the journey was as pleasant as I had hoped. It ended unexpectedly in a tree-lined boulevard that led to the Nana's palace. This was not as exciting an outlook as I had expected, for everyone who had visited it had told me what a splendid place it was. The whole compound was enclosed in a high wall which presented a dreary prospect to the arriving guest. At the gate, a splendid uniformed sentry leaned against the wall. As we approached, he recognised the Collector and hurriedly pulled himself to attention, giving an adequate salute as we passed through.

Once inside, we found ourselves in a pleasure garden with orchards and fountains as picturesque as anything I might have imagined. I relaxed after the ride and sat easily on my horse, admiring the monkeys that chattered in the trees alongside the path, when I heard a lion roaring nearby. I shortened rein, ready to gallop for my life but Hillersdon, seeing my alarm, reached out a hand to calm me.

"Relax! Nana has his own menagerie. The lion is far from the most remarkable beast there. We'll take a look later."

He rode on toward the house and, minutes later, servants were leading our horses to the stables while we entered the home of Nana Sahib.

Outside, the palace had little to recommend it architecturally. The long frontage was crudely coated with some sort of plaster. There was no decoration to speak of and, had I seen it in an English park, I would not have recognised it as the home of a great man. Once we had climbed the steps to the main doorway, though, the interior was another matter. We passed down a marbled corridor, lined with woven tapestries, the sound of fountains in dozens of tiny courtyards echoing on the stone. We were led to a dining room where, beneath a fine chandelier that had nothing of native manufacture about it, I saw, as Hillersdon had promised me, a full English breakfast. There was kedgeree, sausages, some fried eggs congealing in a chafing dish, devilled kidneys and mutton chops that looked scarcely more appealing than those produced by poor Lydia Hillersdon, ham on the bone and slices of greasy bacon on a silver salver.

I was hungry after our ride and if the food had clearly been cooked by someone who was a stranger to British cuisine and if it was served on mismatched (but expensive) china, it was still welcome. We set to with a will, while I admired the life-sized portraits of Nana Sahib's ancestors and tried to ignore the apparently arbitrary selection of paintings of European beauties that were mixed among them.

We had finished our meal and were relaxing with a cup of tea and a cheroot apiece when a young man in native robes entered the room and asked us to accompany him. His name, he said, was Mungo Buksh and he was a cousin of Nana Sahib, come to lead us to greet our host.

We followed young Mr Buksh along the marbled corridors, through more and more splendid rooms, some furnished like the dining room in European style, some with just cushions or daybeds on the floor. At last we came to a pair of ornate brass doors with guards, smartly uniformed in the style of Indians in the Company's army—that is generally like our own troops, only with turbans on their heads and the long curved scimitars that they call tulwars held at rest. As we drew up to them they came to the salute with their swords and unseen hands within opened the doors.

Our guide gestured toward our riding boots and I followed Hillersdon's lead in removing them before entering the room where Nana Sahib sat on a carpet waiting for us.

My first thought was that he seemed very young to be such a prominent personage. He was, I judged, not thirty years old, but already beginning to run to fat. He did not make a particularly imposing figure. To my surprise, he wore glasses perched on an aquiline nose, decorated underneath by a neatly waxed moustache. A small turban balanced lopsidedly on the top of his head—he was almost bald—and looked, frankly, ridiculous. Add to that the gold embroidered waistcoat he was wearing together with a pearl necklace, and the effect was as if a rather tubby child had been let loose on a dressing-up box. Still, he greeted us with a smile and a pretty speech of welcome which Mr Buksh translated for us (the Nana having not a word of English).

Hillersdon smiled in return and introduced me as one friend to another. Nana Sahib nodded and gestured to the carpet in front of him. "Do please be seated Mr Williamson."

I sat cross-legged like him and he smiled again, this time with more warmth. "You have been some time in India, Mr Williamson? You sit comfortably while poor Mr Hillersdon is still at a loss when deprived of his chair."

I looked across to where the Collector was, indeed, visibly struggling to settle himself on the floor. "Not in India, sir, but in Borneo."

"Borneo!" Nana Sahib's brown eyes sparkled with enthusiasm. "A land of mystery! You must tell me all about it."

So Mr Buksh was kept busy interpreting as we talked about Borneo and my time there and the work that James Brooke and I had done in Sarawak. Nana Sahib interrupted from time to time with intelligent questioning while poor Hillersdon fidgeted uncomfortably beside me. Nana Sahib was particularly interested in the basis of our rule in Sarawak.

"So the East India Company has no rule in Borneo?"

"No. Sarawak is independent of the Company and of Britain."

"And the titles of the native lords are recognised?"

"Of course."

Nana Sahib turned to Hillersdon, whose agitation was by now not entirely due to the cramp setting in in his legs.

"It seems to me," and his eyes glinted as he spoke, "that we could all learn much from the administration in Borneo."

Hillersdon stretched his lips into a smile. "Indeed. I am sure we will all benefit from Mr Williamson's experience."

At that, Nana Sahib appeared satisfied and our audience was over.

Mungo Buksh accompanied us as we left, expertly navigating the maze of corridors and hallways. He smiled comfortably when he caught my eye on him and, as Hillersdon's expression was much less encouraging, I concentrated my attention on our guide. He was, I guessed, in his early twenties; a good-looking young man with an open, friendly face. Although he had said he was a cousin of Nana Sahib, I could see no family resemblance and I asked him if he and his cousin were close.

"Close?" He looked puzzled for a moment. "Oh! Because I am his cousin." He smiled. "Nana Sahib has a hundred cousins. I see him only some days. I am useful to him because my English is good. He asks me sometimes to look after his English guests." He paused, looking between me and Mr Hillersdon. "I know the Collector has been here many times, but would you like me to show you around?"

For a moment, I thought Hillersdon's irritation at my apparently impolitic comments during our audience might make him object but it was not in his nature to be petty. He had matters to attend to in Cawnpore, he said, but he was happy to leave me in Mr Buksh's care.

We saw the Collector to the door and then my guide took me back into the building. "Saturday House was built by the Peshwa Baji Rao when he established himself in Bithur in 1819." He had obviously made this speech a thousand times before and he uttered it mechanically.

"Why Saturday House?" I asked. I had hoped to interrupt his rehearsed tour and elicit some more spontaneous response, but he had obviously been asked that question a thousand times too.

"It's named for the Peshwa's residence at Poona, which was also Saturday House."

"And why was that given such an unusual name?"

"Because the building was started on a Saturday."

I laughed. It seemed so ridiculous. Young Buksh, though, appeared quite indignant at my response.

"It is true. The building of the palace at Poona began on January 10th in your year 1730. It was a Saturday. It was a very auspicious day."

He made me feel as if I were mocking him and his beliefs in auspicious days and, as this had been far from my intention, I apologised. He smiled. "Most English people find the name amusing but they don't apologise when I explain it." He turned abruptly down a marbled corridor that we had passed earlier. "Come. We'll be just in time."

The corridor was something over twenty-five yards long and every yard along it there was a niche in the wall and each niche held a clock. Some were carriage clocks that sat on top of pillars; others were grandfather clocks, standing proudly on the floor. All were ticking noisily, the sound echoing on the bare marble. And all showed the time as two minutes before noon.

We walked to the middle of the corridor, my companion grinning broadly, while my ears seemed to quiver in anticipation of what I feared was coming next.

One of the clocks must have been badly adjusted, for it started to strike the hour while the others were still silent. A few seconds later, though, the others joined the mechanical chorus.

There were twenty-five clocks in that corridor and every one of them was striking noon. Carriage clocks tinkled, grandfather clocks tolled sonorously, one sounded the chimes of Big Ben, another trilled as if in imitation of a caged bird. All rang out at once in the marbled corridor, combining into an unspeakable din. For several seconds I stood dumbfounded and then, careless of the proper way to behave in such circumstances (for surely someone, somewhere must have decided what is the proper way to behave when faced with a potentate's clock collection) I put my fingers to my ears and waited for the assault on my hearing to end.

I looked toward young Mungo and caught him laughing heartily—though I couldn't hear him over the racket of the clocks.

One by one, Nana Sahib's horological tormentors fell silent and my guide, still laughing, led me onward.

"You didn't appreciate the chimes?" His face puckered into a mischievous smile. "Nana Sahib is very proud of his collection. Every one of them has been shipped here from Europe and then adjusted until they tell the time perfectly. He has three jewellers who have learned the skills of watchmakers and whose sole duty is to care for the clocks."

"I am sure the clocks are wonderful. But I can't help feeling that twenty-five clocks are not twenty-five times as impressive as one. Especially at noon."

"Ah, yes." He laughed again, a sound of sheer delight escaping his throat. "We were lucky to arrive in time. Imagine how disappointing it would have been had you arrived only an hour later."

I grinned back. My young companion was no longer the solemn guide and he led me through mirrored halls pausing to admire shrines with images of various Hindoo deities, many of which were garlanded with fresh flowers.

"This is my favourite." We were standing in front of a statue of a man-like figure with a monkey's face and tail. "This is Hanuman. He was always full of tricks and frequently naughty but in the end he was a brave warrior and he gained wisdom from the gods."

I looked at the brass face of the idol. There was, indeed, something in his eyes suggesting an impishness that I could see would appeal to the young man at my side.

"There are real monkeys outside," he said, and we were off to explore Nana Sahib's menagerie like a couple of schoolboys on a holiday.

There were indeed monkeys—and the lion I had heard when we arrived, and snakes. "A man plays a pipe to them and they dance," said Mungo Buksh, "but he isn't here now. Do you want me to have him come?" I assured him I was happy to see the snakes left peacefully asleep while I admired the birds in Nana Sahib's aviaries, the deer, the tigers pacing their cage and, in pride of place, a rhinoceros that stood like a statue on a patch of bare earth surrounded by solid iron bars.

"The elephants and the camels are kept separately because they are working animals. Would you like to see their stables?"

Of course I said, "Yes." The afternoon flew by as we explored Saturday House and its grounds but, all too soon, as children are summoned by their mothers' cries, so our afternoon ended as we remembered our duties. Mungo vanished into the palace and I set off back along the dusty road to Cawnpore.

chapter 2

THE DAYS THAT followed allowed little time to think about my visit to Saturday House or the friend I had made there in Mungo Buksh, for it was that February that the East India Company, having fenced around the issue for years, finally annexed the Kingdom of Oudh.

Cawnpore was not itself in Oudh, but one of the main reasons the Company had such a large presence in the town was to guard the gateway to that kingdom. The Ganges at Cawnpore marked the Western border of Oudh. Inevitably, the excitement occasioned by the imposition of direct British rule in Oudh led to tremors in the usual calm of life on our side of the river.

Alongside the administrators, merchants, engineers and men of business who made up the Civil Station of Cawnpore was an even more substantial military population who lived in cantonments on the outskirts of the town. My bungalow—like those of most of the Company's servants—was situated between the military settlement and old Cawnpore, so the sight of soldiers swaggering to and from the markets of the town was a common one. That February, though, there was more to-ing and fro-ing than usual. The native troops would gather in groups in the old town, while their European officers strode purposefully here and there or pushed their horses through the crowds blocking the roads to the bazaars.

I had no idea what the point of this martial enthusiasm might be. My own experience of the military mind in Borneo had left me unwilling to become closer acquainted with it. The view of most of the civilians working for the Company was not that different from mine. The Civil staff generally avoided the military as the military avoided the civilians, each considering themselves superior to the other.

Whatever led to the flurry of military activity, things soon quieted down on that front, for the annexation was achieved with not a shot fired. It created a deal of work for we civilians, though, as much of Cawnpore's business involved Oudh and contracts that referred to the government of the kingdom now all had to be re-written to take account of the new administration. There was also a positive storm of paperwork and regulation as we sought to harmonise the laws of Oudh with those of the rest of British India. The storm engulfed all of the Company but it beat hardest against those nearest to the kingdom.

For almost a month, I immersed myself in paperwork. For me, it was an invigorating opportunity to master the rules and regulations that governed every aspect of life in India and to understand how these were implemented in practice. I found myself arriving at my office early in the morning and often not leaving until the night watchman knocked worriedly at my door to enquire if all was well with the sahib. Mr Hillersdon did not need to spend as long in the office as I did, for his years of experience in India meant that he was able to digest the astonishing volume of memoranda, notes, policies, regulations and official advice with an ease I did not expect to be able to emulate for years. But he was thorough and conscientious with an unerring ability to go directly to the crux of any matter put before him. Although his grasp of the native tongue was limited, he had a real affection for the country and its people and he was quick to understand the implications of Company actions for the local people.

"Mark my words, John," he would say (for we were on familiar terms by now), "no good will come of this Oudh business. It's getting the natives agitated."

If Hillersdon had any intimation of the storm that was to

break on us, he was almost alone. For most of the Europeans in Cawnpore, the annexation was of importance only insofar as it interfered with the comfortable indolence of their regular lives. I was almost sorry for Simkin, forced to appear punctually at the office and work harder than he had in years. As the weeks passed and we moved into March, the weather grew steadily warmer and, by the end of the month, it was regularly over ninety degrees at midday. Most Europeans rose with the dawn, when it was still cool. While I welcomed the chance to make an early start in the office, I discovered that Simkin (like most of his colleagues) would start the day with a ride, claiming that the exercise was essential to his health. He would then breakfast ("I can hardly work on an empty stomach, can I?"), arriving at his desk—if all went well—by 10.00 am or thereabouts. He would make a vague attempt at dealing with his correspondence before announcing that the heat was insufferable and returning to his home to spend the afternoon lying on his bed being fanned by a native employed specifically for that purpose. When I raised the question of his behaviour with Mr Hillersdon I was assured that, unsatisfactory as it was, it was the custom of the station and there was little that could be done about it. The Company's servants, thousands of miles from home, could hardly be discharged from their employment. The climate did not encourage enthusiasm and a certain level of indolence had become accepted as a perquisite of the job.

Irritating as the behaviour of my fellows might appear, by April I had some sympathy with them. The mercury would often hover around one hundred degrees and I, too, would take to my bed in the midday heat. The pankha fan (an enormous construction some fifteen feet long) no longer seemed a ridiculous affectation. My khanasaman with his usual enthusiasm for increasing the size of my establishment, had already hired not one but three boys to act as pankha wallahs. They took turns day and night to sit in the corridor outside my bedroom pulling at the ropes that, by an ingenious system of pulleys, kept the fan turning and thus agitated the languid air within the room.

So life settled into the routine of the hot dry season. The flurry of activity that had marked our annexation of Oudh died away and was forgotten. The soldiers that we saw about the place, both natives and European, no longer strutted with self-importance but idled through the heat like mere mortals. The Company's servants and their families spent most of the day-light hours hidden in shaded rooms while any natives who could not emulate them would sit in the shade of the trees that grew on street corners or in the empty plots of dust that separated the houses of the Civil Station.

Only in the evening did the temperature drop to a point where I could work. The papers that passed across my desk were now, for the most part, routine but however many I dealt with, the pile brought to me every morning by my babu never seemed to shrink. There were requests for medicines to be supplied when outbreaks of this or that fever struck nearby villages, appeals from landlords saying that their tax had been wrongly assessed, requests that the Company involve itself with this or that dispute with a tenant, leave requests, accommodation requests, requisition slips for horses and camels and elephants and bills for feeding of aforementioned horses, camels and elephants. Matters serious and matters trivial—but all matters, apparently, that the Company must rule on.

Others had wives and families to distract them, but I had no one. I had left the only one I cared about over two thousand miles away in Borneo. I was invited to the evening picnics that the womenfolk organised and introduced to young ladies who had travelled to India from England apparently for the sole purpose of improving their matrimonial chances. These entertainments made me uncomfortable and I would excuse myself as often as I could, preferring to stay in the office about my business.

Hillersdon noticed the hours I was putting in and admitted himself concerned. "Take it easy, old boy," he said one afternoon as he set off to join his wife at a concert given by one of the military bands. "People are taking advantage of you. You're doing the work of half a dozen others while they rag about you in their clubs and laugh because it's known you do their work for them."

"The work needs to be done."

"It does indeed. And if you weren't here at all hours doing it, I could make some of the idlers on our staff pull their weight." He looked up from the papers he was tidying away and, seeing that I was making no reply, said, "Take a couple of days leave, John. Take yourself out to Nana's place. He'll put you up and the change of air will do you good."

NANA SAHIB'S GUESTHOUSE was a regular talking point in Cawnpore. Although the Nana never visited Europeans in their homes, he was a generous host. In the grounds of Saturday House he kept a separate building for his visitors and there was no one of any significance in our community who had not stayed there at least once. Mr Hillersdon had often visited the Nana with his wife and he insisted that a few days there would be good for my health.

"You've been overdoing it, old boy. You take a break from your toiling here and when you return you'll be able to work all the better."

So, with Mr Hillersdon's assistance, all the necessary arrangements were made, and on the last Monday in April I rose early so that I might make the journey to Bithur before the heat of the day became oppressive.

This time I travelled in a carriage. This was in part because the weather made riding, even in the early morning, quite exhausting, but also because Mr Hillersdon was emphatic that if I were to arrive as a guest I should travel in a style that would reflect my status. "Not to do so," he assured me, "will not only diminish you in native eyes but will be taken as an insult by Nana Sahib."

For the same reason, I was to travel with a valet to take care of my personal needs, a groom to take care of the horses and a coachman to drive me. I was perfectly capable of dressing myself and driving my own carriage and the horses would be stabled in Nana Sahib's own stables where his grooms would attend them as a matter of course but none of this was of any account. I was to travel in state because that was the way that things were done. So I bumped my way to Bithur (for Indian carriages are woefully inadequately sprung) and arrived hot and tired and very glad indeed that my journey was over.

As the gates of the compound opened, a servant, who appeared to have been waiting there for my arrival, ran forward to guide the coachman to the guesthouse in the palace grounds.

Rounding a bend in the carriage drive, we came suddenly upon the guesthouse, secluded in a rhododendron grove. I had not seen it on my previous tour of the grounds, so its incongruity struck me with a force that nearly made me laugh aloud. For here, in the Oriental splendour of the Nana's grounds, was a bungalow: a perfect replica of the houses that the Company had built for its servants in Cawnpore.

My valet, who had been riding alongside the coachman, carried my cases inside while I stretched myself after the ride and looked about me. To my delight, I saw, hastening along the gravel, the lithe figure of Mungo Buksh.

"Greetings, John," he called as he hurried toward me. "I am sorry I was not at the gate to welcome you, but I had matters to attend to."

My young friend was dressed today in loose trousers such as many of the better kind of Indian wear and an open jacket. Both were of red cotton, much embroidered with gold. Around his waist was a golden sash. He looked as if he had just stepped from a picture book.

"I'm so glad to see you." I stepped forward and embraced him.

He returned my embrace and asked, "Have you been inside yet?"

"No, I just arrived."

"Let me show you round."

He led the way through the door and introduced me to my home for the next few days. It was about the size of my house in Cawnpore but, rather than being crammed with furniture that aped European fashions, it was elegantly equipped with everything of the finest native manufacture. Beds and tables had been made high off the floor, rather than low to the ground in the native style (for Indians do not generally use chairs and prefer everything to be accessible to a man seated on the ground) but they were carved from teak and mahogany, decorated and gilded in the ways I had observed in the furnishings of Nana Sahib's own quarters.

"Your lord does me too much honour."

I spoke formally. Mungo Buksh should have replied with a similarly flowery phrase indicating that the guesthouse was not nearly fine enough for the use of one so exalted as myself but instead he just laughed. "It's a house, John, not a mansion."

I relaxed, taking my cue from him. "It's still remarkable. I'm impressed that Nana Sahib should have gone to such trouble for his guests. He must have a hundred rooms in Saturday House, yet he has had this built specially."

Mungo Buksh laughed again. "Do you really not know why it was built?"

I shook my head. My companion obviously thought my ignorance a huge joke but I truly had no idea why he was so amused.

"It's so that you don't pollute the palace."

My expression must have reflected my confusion so he explained the situation. Nana Sahib, being of the highest caste, would be polluted by intimate contact with those of no caste like ourselves. A bed we had slept in could not be used by any of his religion. Plates we had eaten from would have to be ritually cleansed before they could be used again. If even my shadow fell across a bowl of food prepared for the men of his household, the food would be unclean, fit only to be fed to animals.

The preparation of the guesthouse, which I had taken as an honour, in fact reflected the contempt in which Nana Sahib's religion held us.

I fear that the distress that this realisation caused me must have shown on my face for Mungo Buksh clasped me by the hand and, his young face suddenly very serious, said, "You must not be concerned, John. It is the rule of our Brahmins. It is like when your Brahmins say that they eat human flesh and drink human blood. It is a thing that you do in your religion. But I do not worry that you are going to eat me." He smiled reassuringly.

I was not reassured but I let him think that I was. It was not that I felt insulted, but that I was suddenly aware of my ignorance. I had come to live in India but, for all that I was learning Hindustanee and would speak a few words with the natives in the bazaar, I had no real understanding of the lives of the Indians around me. My khanasaman jealously guarded his domain over the servants, growing visibly agitated if I had any more dealings with them than were necessary to see my meals placed on the table and my linen cleaned and pressed. My babus insisted on maintaining the fiction that they were European and would refuse to converse in anything but English and so, though I was surrounded by natives, I was positively discouraged from coming to any proper comprehension of their lives.

I realised, with a start, that my hand still clasped that of Mungo Buksh and, in the same instant, came the realisation that I did have one friend who could help me understand the people who filled this vast country.

THAT AFTERNOON, MUNGO Buksh took me around the palace again. This time we didn't look at the animals or the clocks but concentrated our attention on the idols in their flower-bedecked shrines. We started by revisiting Hanuman and my guide tried to explain how Hanuman had led an army of monkeys to free another god who was imprisoned on the island of Ceylon and how they had been opposed by demons with necklaces of skulls. He spoke as if it was a story that everyone should know but, in truth, it seemed so long, confusing and foolish that I gave up trying to understand it.

Mungo took mercy on me and we moved on, finding idols everywhere we walked. Some dominated small courtyards, some were in niches carved into the stone walls of rooms or corridors, some sat on shelves high on the walls. All were, to my eye, alien and grotesque. There were human heads on animal bodies and animal heads on the bodies of humans. Some had four arms, some six, some eight. One had five heads. An elephant was depicted carried by a mouse.

While I struggled to remember their names, Mungo explained which each of these gods were and what they represented. At first, I tried to recall simple things about them. Lakshmi seemed easy because she had four arms.

"Lakshmi is the goddess of wealth." Mungo pointed to the coins in one of her hands. "She pours gold out, bringing blessings to the world."

We moved to another courtyard, where a statue showed a beautiful young girl, decorated with jewels.

"Who is this one?"

Mungo looked at me as if I were a particularly stupid child. "This is Lakshmi."

"But she has only two arms."

"That is because this image shows her as the goddess of beauty. Lakshmi brings so many good things." He bowed reverently to the statue, his hands pressed together. "She is the goddess of beauty and of wealth and fortune. When she brings wealth, she has four arms that she can distribute good things more generously."

"But in this statue she has only two."

"Of course. Would you think a girl beautiful if she had four arms?"

I hesitated, trying to imagine such a thing. "Probably not," I agreed.

"Then of course she cannot have four arms."

He bowed to the statue again and moved on. Clearly, there was no more to be said on the matter.

So the afternoon went on. By evening, my head was aching with the effort of keeping track. I was hopelessly confused, but intrigued. For the first time, I was looking at these idols not as exotic decoration but as the visible expression of the beliefs that permeated every aspect of Hindoo society, from their objections to the killing of cattle to the eighteen holy days on which they fasted; from the direction their houses should face to the way they styled their hair.

It had been agreed that I should spend four days at Saturday House, arriving on the first and leaving on the fourth. After my introduction to the Hindoo deities on that first day, I decided to devote the rest of my stay to trying to understand the religion. To this end, I prevailed on Mungo Buksh to spend most of the second day in repeating the stories of the deities while I made careful notes in my commonplace book.

"These stories have been written down," he said, as I asked him, yet again, to list all eight of the avatars of Ganesh. "Would it help if you were able to read about them?"

It would indeed, I replied. Like many who have come to reading late in life, I had an almost superstitious conviction that books contained the knowledge of all the world and that if I could only find a book describing these gods, then all would become immediately clear to me. So Mungo took me by the hand again and led me through corridors and up stairs and around courtyards and thus, eventually, to Nana Sahib's library, a gracious room with wide, high windows and reading desks arranged to best catch the light. He ran lightly to the shelves and returned with a book that he opened to a page illustrating ten avatars of Vishnu.

"Look," he said, pointing happily, "it's all explained here."

And it was. But it was written in Devanagari, the Hindoo script, and though I could by now speak the language passably well, the script was no more to me than a meaningless scribble across the page.

Again, I was forced to realise the depths of my ignorance. I knew that the Indians had a written language (or languages, for the Musalman script was based on the Arabic and looked entirely different). I had seen their writing on signs by their businesses but I had not thought of their having a literature and libraries to store it. It was not that I considered them ignorant—for I did not—but that I had not considered the matter of their literature at all.

It seemed that to understand their religion, it would be as well that I learn to read their script.

Mungo Buksh watched me sigh and turn defeated from the volume he had placed before me and he quickly divined the reason for my sudden gloom. He laid his hand reassuringly on my arm.

"Do not despair. I will show you how to read this."

And so my lessons started.

I could not help remembering the days I spent with James in Borneo when he taught me to read. Now I found myself struggling again with marks on paper that at first meant nothing to me. I would peer at them, trying to draw meaning from the scribbles and then I would look up to see the brown eyes of Mungo Buksh watching me and I would remember those other brown eyes that had watched over my earlier struggles.

Despite Mungo's best efforts, I could learn little in the time I remained in Saturday House, but I at least started to probe the depths of my ignorance and to overcome them with diligent study.

When I returned to Cawnpore I could hardly describe myself as rested, for my last two days at Saturday House had been spent hard at work with pen and paper, copying and pronouncing the letters of the Hindoo alphabet and my brain fairly ached with the effort. Yet far from feeling fatigued, I came back to work reinvigorated, to the delight of Mr Hillersdon who insisted that the break had so improved my health that I must make another visit to Nana Sahib as soon as my duties allowed me.

I was happy to fall in with this suggestion, for my attempts to master the ancient script were unavailing without Mungo Buksh to help me. So I got into the habit of spending every day that I could be spared from my duties out in Bithur and, slowly but surely, I began to progress in my studies.

I was helped by the relative calm of life in Cawnpore. The most exciting thing to happen was the arrival of a new commander for the garrison. General Wheeler arrived to take over the Cawnpore Division soon after the rains began around the middle of July. I recall meeting him at a formal dinner to welcome him to the town. It was given in the Assembly Rooms—a grand building but, I always thought, rather comical in those surroundings. The fine front with its Corinthian columns and the elegant interior with its ballrooms, the fine panelling and the chandeliers—all would excite enthusiasm in an English provincial town but here it was as ridiculous as if an Indian lord had set down a minareted mosque in Regent's Park.

Wheeler had arrived in a closed carriage but he insisted on standing in the rain while attendants hurried up with umbrellas to shelter his wife. I was waiting in the hallway with those who were to be the first to greet him and I was touched by the way this small, elderly man stood to attention, water soaking into his red jacket and pouring from the gold braid on his shoulders, while his wife slowly descended the steps that had been pushed against the carriage for her convenience.

I had heard about Lady Frances Wheeler, of course. The scandal was the talk of every station in India, though it had all been over forty years ago. It was almost certainly the reason that, nearly seventy years old and the most senior and experienced of the Company's generals, Hugh Wheeler was to see out his service as a Divisional Commander, passed over for further promotion. I don't know if people were more shocked by the fact that Lady Frances had been married to another man when she bore Wheeler the first of his nine children or that she was, with her dusky skin and graceful beauty, clearly the result of a union between a European officer and an Indian woman. Simkin had made it all too clear what was the prevailing view of such Anglo-Indians, as people generally referred to them. In one of his earlier (and more than usually misguided) attempts to ingratiate himself with me, he had suggested that we might call on some "ladies" he knew who might entertain us for an evening. When I asked what sort of unchaperoned ladies would entertain two men he explained, with a leering wink, that these "called themselves European but had more than a touch of the tar brush to them," and hence they were automatically viewed as little better than harlots.

Stories of the snubs that had been delivered to Lady Frances from the self-styled protectors of European morality in India were rife. Even as the wife of a man knighted by the Queen herself, Lady Frances was not received in many a Calcutta drawing room. The posting to Cawnpore, where the hospitality of Nana Sahib was typical of the easy relationship between the races, must have been a great relief to her, if a disappointment to her husband.

Although the General seemed at ease at the dinner and his wife appeared a lady of refinement, I did not expect to come across him in the daily life of the station, for civilians and military tended not to socialise together. The occasional officer might be invited if his family was known to the host but generally the swagger of the military men did not sit well with the administrators of the Company, though we all served the same masters. The distinction was maintained not only socially but geographically. All but the most senior officers were housed in military bungalows along the perimeter of the huge camp to the South and East of the town and I found only a couple of occasions a year to visit that quarter. I was, therefore, not a little surprised when Charles Hillersdon suggested, early in August, that I join him at an informal dinner they were hosting for the General the following evening.

"Just a few of us at home," he said. "Nothing special."

I was always delighted to receive an invitation to dine with the Hillersdons. I think Charles had some inkling of my nature. At least he did not seat me beside young ladies fresh from England and desperate to make a suitable match. Such girls, all coquettish charm and sly smiles, were the bane of my life and I suspected that suspicions about my immunity to their wiles underlay Simkin's proposal that we visit his Anglo-Indian "ladies." So it was that I hummed cheerfully to myself the next evening as I dressed in a dinner suit made by the tailor my khanasaman had insisted on hiring. I had decided to ignore the suggestion that the dinner was "nothing special" and to wear black-tie, and when I arrived at the Hillersdons it was clear that I had made the right decision. The place was rapidly filling with guests and Lydia Hillersdon, usually the calmest of women, was visibly flustered.

"John, thank goodness you're here. I asked the servants to borrow an extra two chairs from our neighbours because Charles has just explained that the General is bringing all three of his children." (The remaining six children, fortunately for Mrs Hillersdon's catering arrangements, had not joined the general in Cawnpore.) "Charles swears that he told me that a week ago but I'm sure he did not. And I fear he may have invited Simkin and now they're pretending not to understand and I know you can speak to them."

She was waving her hand in her agitation and I caught it up and kissed it.

"Don't worry, Lydia. I know Simkin isn't coming because I saw him just an hour ago sulking because he was not asked. And my Hindoo may not be up to much but the servants know better than to pretend they can't understand me. So you shall have your extra chairs."

She smiled prettily. She did everything prettily. She was a

sweet child and made her husband very happy.

I was a few minutes rousting out a servant and sending him off for the chairs. When I returned to the dining room, the General had just arrived. I almost could not see him: he really was quite a short man and he had chosen a dinner jacket rather than his red uniform, so he was nearly submerged in the throng of the Hillersdons' guests and the servants who accompanied them. I noticed Lady Frances before her husband. She was not much shorter than him and she held herself with the casual grace of the native women, which somehow made her seem taller than the General, for all that the he stood erect with the habits of a lifetime of military service. She was wearing a russet dress in the latest style yet, despite the conventional European clothes, she retained an air of the exotic which was visibly disturbing some of the other ladies present. Her daughters had inherited much of her beauty: the older girl seemed to take more after her father but the younger, Margaret, was almost as dark as her mother with a glint in her eye that suggested she was well aware of the effect her looks might have on the young men of the station.

The son, Godfrey Wheeler, was by contrast, quite severe in his appearance and his bearing was every inch that of a soldier. There was something in the half-protective, half subordinate way he hovered just behind the General that would have made me guess that the young man was on his father's staff even had I not known he was his aide de camp.

Beside the Wheelers, the most important guests were Thomas Greenway and his wife. The Greenways were part of a family whose commercial activities, from banking to indigo planting to running the general store, penetrated every part of European Cawnpore. The formidable Mrs Greenway oversaw the business but she was, she claimed, too old to enjoy dining out and so the company paid its respects by entertaining her son.

Some Company officials, wives and daughters made up the numbers. (Wheeler was the only man there to have his son at the Station with him.) With such a crowd sat at table, there was a constant bustle of servants. The Wheelers had, of course, brought their own people with them and the chaos caused by so many strangers getting in each others' way with every course made it difficult for me to follow all the conversation. Despite the interruptions, though, I was able to enjoy most of the General's anecdotes. He had built up his store of dining-out stories over a lifetime's campaigning and if some were so polished as to suggest they had been told a hundred times before, still they were fresh for me.

It was late by the time I came to make my way home and as I bade Hillersdon farewell, I congratulated him on the success of the evening. "You did well to bag the Wheelers so early on. I doubt they'll have a free evening the rest of the year."

Charles smiled at that but his eyes were wary. "I hope so, John. I really do."

I was puzzled by his response but I imagined it to be that he was tired at the end of the evening and I thought no more of it. But the weeks passed and I found myself joining Charles and his wife as he entertained the General almost weekly. It seemed that while Hillersdon enjoyed the Wheelers' company, there was, even in Cawnpore, a strange reluctance to entertain an Anglo-Indian in the home.

The prejudice was all the more incomprehensible to me as I would often meet my colleagues when I was staying at Saturday House. It seemed that, just as Nana Sahib was happy to have European visitors so long as they did not stay in his own house, so the Europeans were happy to meet with the better class of native so long as it was not under their own roofs.

In my case, I fear Nana Sahib's taboo was broken, though he was, I trust, unaware of it. The demands on the guesthouse were such that on several occasions Mungo Buksh was unable to procure accommodation for me. After two or three of our meetings had been prevented in this way, he suggested that I stay in his quarters. "There's plenty of room," he said. "No one need know."

I told myself that this was simply a sensible way to make sure that my studies were not disrupted but, in my heart, I knew better. Since I had loved James Brooke, I knew my true nature. Just as I saw no attraction in the vapid prettiness of the women who were so regularly pushed forward for my inspection, so I could not pretend that I was not moved by the beauty of Mungo Buksh. I have heard people talk of the Indians as black but Mungo's skin was the colour of a cup of rich chocolate. He was, like most natives, short in stature and delicately built. His cheekbones gave his face the shape of an angel and his eyes were huge and deep and brown. He moved with an easy grace, sometimes—when excited—fast, at other times lazily stretching into motion as if enjoying the pleasure of feeling the life in his own limbs.

I could not pretend that he could be my soul mate. James would be forever the man that I had truly loved. But Mungo had youth and charm and a laugh that lifted my spirits whenever I heard it.

Mungo's apartments were small, but more than adequate for a minor courtier whose needs would all be met by the palace servants. He had one room where he could read or entertain or eat, if he chose to eat in his own quarters, and one for sleeping. Generally, he would bathe in the grand baths that were available to all in the royal household, but there was an alcove off his bedroom where a tub and a ewer allowed him to perform his ablutions in private, should he wish to.

Latticed windows high in the walls gave light and air but allowed Mungo his privacy. The floor was of marble and the walls were tiled. The place was beautiful, but as I looked around, admiring the elegant furniture and the statue of Hanuman in a niche on the wall, I could not help but notice that there was no provision for guests.

We spent the afternoon in the library. My studies were going well and Mungo was even more than usually cheerful, constantly praising my efforts. We returned to his room to find fish and rice laid out for us by one of the ubiquitous palace servants. (When Mungo had said that no one need know I was in his apartments, I fear he had simply ignored the servants as being not worthy of consideration.)

We ate slowly and then talked about the gods I had studied during the day. As the light faded and we grew sleepy, I became increasingly conscious of how close we were sitting, the smell of his body, and the warmth of his breath on my cheek.

The feelings that had been creeping up on me as long as I had known Mungo were now too strong for me to ignore, but I resolved that I would not give way to my baser desires. I told Mungo that I would sleep on the ground. The night was very warm and I would need no bedding. But my young friend would have none of it. "Don't be foolish," he said. "My manjaa is big enough for two." He patted the string framework of the low day bed he was sitting on.

"Your charpoy?"

He laughed. He laughed so easily. "You call it a charpoy but truly it is a manjaa. The word is a Punjabi word and it is a Punjabi manjaa."

I shrugged. What he called it was scarcely the point. It was a bed, albeit a primitive bed, lacking mattress or sheets. And he was suggesting we share it.

I hesitated, but I knew what it was that I wanted. I nodded. I hope it looked like a simple manly nod of affirmation but inside I felt like I imagined a schoolgirl must feel before her first kiss. I confess my hands trembled as I shed my day clothes and donned the silk shirt and linen drawers that are the universal nightdress of the East. My nervousness was increased by the look of bemused amusement on my young companion's face. I fear I blushed for I was sure that to a youth the body of a man my age was bound to be a source of mirth. But it seemed his amusement was at the idea that I should dress for bed as, once I considered my toilette complete, he simply stripped off his trousers and tunic and settled down beside me.

Even now, I feel a stirring at the memory of that perfect body, the brown skin smooth and supple. He was almost hairless about his person and looked more like a living statue—one of those gods I had spent so long studying—rather than a mere mortal.

As he pressed his body against mine, and I felt the warmth of his flesh against my flesh, my desire almost overcame me. But he was so young and so beautiful that I felt that any touch of mine would be a defilement. And, in any case, surely he could not be offering himself to me—old, pale skinned, graceless with the ungainly ways of my race. So I smiled at him and turned away, lying with my back to him and hoping that sleep would come upon me quickly before I should yield to temptation and foolishness.

A moment later, I felt his arms around me. He pressed himself against my back and the warm of his body passed through my silk shirt as if I were naked too. His hands reached around my chest, brushing my nipples and he moved lazily against my buttocks.

I turned then and seized his face in my hands and kissed him. It was not like the gentle kisses that James and I had shared, but a hungry kiss, trying to consume him, as I was suddenly consumed with desire. It was the crudest form of lust that overcame me. I tore off the drawers I had just put on and thrust at him with an urgency that shocked me but he seemed unsurprised. Indeed, when I tried to regain control of my impulses and pull away from him, he reached for my organ and drew me back.

Later—how much later, I had no way of knowing—we drew apart. I was drenched in sweat but his body was just lightly sheened with perspiration, which seemed rather to add to his unworldly beauty than to diminish it. My mind was in turmoil. Everything that I had done with James Brooke had been sanctioned by love but I felt that I had no such excuse to offer now. I thought I should explain myself or grovel for understanding or at least say something of my behaviour but, though I opened my mouth to speak, I could think of no words to say. And then, while I sat in great confusion of mind, Mungo placed his finger on my lips, as you might hush a fractious child, and he drew me to him and I slept.

※

I WOKE LATE, to find Mungo sitting cross-legged beside the bed with a breakfast of fruit that he had cut up and prepared for me. As soon as I was stirring, he insisted that I eat and I was glad to do so for my eating avoided the necessity of conversation and I was still far from sure what I should say.

I think Mungo recognised my confusion for, while I was eating and in no position to discuss the events of the previous night, he started talking about Hindoo gods. At first, I scarcely paid any attention to what he was saying. I was usually more than happy to learn from him but, at that moment, the details of the Hindoo pantheon seemed of little importance. Then, as if I were waking from a dream, I heard a few phrases of his soliloquy.

"...many of our gods have both male and female aspects...any activity that brings joy is blessed...temple carvings showing two men engaged in carnal..."

I set down my fruit and concentrated on his words. Now that he could see he had my attention he began to speak faster and to concentrate on particular tales. He described the birth of Sabarimalai Sastha whose parents were both male deities. Vishnu had disguised himself as a woman and another god, Shiva, intoxicated by her beauty had had sex with her. The result had been the god Sabarimalai Sastha, born from Vishnu's thigh.

"You must remember, my friend, that our gods can take many forms, sometimes that of a man and sometimes that of a woman. Shiva often takes the form of Ardhanarisvara, neither man nor woman. Hindoos accept that all that is made by the gods is good. There are men and there are women and there are those of the third sex. In the South the third sex even worship their own god, Aravan."

His hand shot toward the tray of fruit and he snapped up two grapes. He threw one into his mouth and, as I opened my own to reply, he flicked the other into mine. "Let's not waste more time in talk. The library is waiting for us."

chapter 3

SO SUMMER PASSED into the cool of winter. Life in Cawnpore continued much as usual. Lydia Hillersdon was with child again to her husband's evident delight, but they continued to entertain. Every week they would invite the Wheelers to dinner until Charles' example began to have its effect. One by one, the ladies of the European community overcame their distaste for their mixed race sister and allowed Lady Frances into their dining rooms. General Wheeler approved plans to extend the military cantonment with a series of new barracks to the West of the main camp. More civilian engineers arrived from Bombay to survey the approach of the new railway that was planned to link Cawnpore with Allahabad. A tiger took to raiding some of the villages to the North and a hunt was organised: soldiers and civilians set off together, mounted on elephants, and returned bearing not one but two tiger skins as evidence of their success.

At Bithur, my command of the language improved to the point where Mungo swore that I could pass for a native. "I think perhaps in a previous life you were an Indian, for you speak the language so well."

"Good enough for you," I said. "But I think you are not a fair judge."

"Very well," he said and his eyes sparkled with mischief. "I'll put you to the test."

Commanding me to wait in his apartment, he whisked out of the room. I had seen that sudden enthusiasm before and it usually meant that Mungo was up to no good and so it was to prove on this occasion.

He returned almost an hour later bearing a bundle of red clothes wrapped around a sword.

"What in the name of all the gods do you have there?"

Proudly he unrolled the bundle, revealing a curved tulwar in its scabbard. The clothes he laid out carefully on the floor: a long red tunic, white britches, a black belt and a wide cross-belt to wear across the breast.

"I couldn't carry the boots as well. I'll have to go back for them."

"But what on earth is this?" I knew the answer, of course. I had seen enough of the Nana's sowars, his proud cavalrymen, to recognise their uniform when I saw it. "And where did you get it?"

Mungo tapped his nose, knowingly. "What do you English say, John? Ask me no questions and you'll be told no lies. Put these on while I'm away."

And, quick as a flash, he was out of the door again.

I looked at the garments spread before me. This was all too ridiculous. But then again, they were there: I might as well try them on.

I was dressed in this finery and trying to admire my turnout in the hand mirror that Mungo used for his toilette when he burst into the room again, carrying a pair of black riding boots, complete with clanking spurs.

"You look splendid," he said. "Turn around. Let me see it properly."

I did as he asked and he admired the fit of the uniform, insisting that it was perfect on me.

"But now," he said, turning his mouth down with a comically exaggerated expression of dismay, "you will have to take it all off."

"But why?"

He gave no reply. Indeed, he was already unbuckling the

belt. Laughing, I let him strip me. When I stood naked, he started to kiss me, but as soon as he saw I was aroused he pulled away, putting his hand to his mouth in mock horror.

"I've forgotten myself. There was a reason I had to have you naked and it had naught to do with my desire for your body. Stand still!"

From the pile of his own clothing (somehow that seemed to have been removed as well), he retrieved a bottle of dark liquid and a sponge. While I stood still, he carefully covered my hands with it, carrying on up my arm until well above where my sleeves would have ended, had I been wearing the tunic. Then he repeated the procedure with my face, working down my neck to the top of my chest.

"It's walnut juice," he said, anticipating my question. "Your skin is dark from the sun but I think that to look truly like a native of my country, you need a little assistance." He worked on, patiently.

"And to apply this to my face and hands, it was absolutely necessary to remove my trousers?"

"Oh, absolutely necessary." He grinned and slapped toward my buttocks. I tried to retaliate but he ordered me to stand still, lest I disturb his handicraft. "Though, truly, you need to take care not to get this stain on those lovely white britches. You'd best stay naked until it dries. And stand very still."

He took his time finishing the staining, all the while making me stand there while he took advantage of his insistence on my immobility to tease my body in a dozen ways that left me desperate to move, yet hoping that the stain might never dry.

"You can move now."

At once I made to seize him but he twisted from my grip. "Not until you've proved yourself."

"How?"

"Get dressed first."

Reluctantly, I pulled back on the clothes I had so recently taken off.

"One more thing."

Mungo produced a length of black cloth that he wrapped back and forth around my head, topping off the uniform with a fine turban. "I must teach you how to do that for yourself but I want to play this game out."

Taking me by the hand, he pulled me after him into the corridors of the palace.

Before long, we passed one of the tall mirrors that Nana Sahib had dotted around the place in what he imagined to be the latest European style. Had I not seen the strange figure reflected back at me still holding Mungo's hand, I don't believe I would have recognised myself. I must admit that I preened a little, much to Mungo's amusement.

"Wait here, my brave soldier!" We had reached the end of one corridor and Mungo vanished around a corner, leaving me wondering how I would explain myself if anyone were to come upon me standing there. I need not have worried, though. In less than a minute, he was back—but his face wore the grin I had come to dread.

"There's a guard in the next hallway. Walk past him and then turn back and criticise his turnout. There'll be something wrong. There always is. If you can't think of anything else, tell him his boots need shining. Tell him he's a disgrace and he should report himself to his havildar. Get his name and the name of his havildar and then we'll see tomorrow if he believed you to be what you seem or if he could tell you to be a white man."

"We won't have to wait until tomorrow. We'll know I've failed as soon as he draws his sword and skewers me with it."

"Be brave, John Williamson! And, in any case, if he does detect you, I will explain it was a trick of mine and I will bear you safe away."

I was not entirely reassured but Mungo was implacable and, a few minutes later, I found myself walking down the hallway with a swagger that perhaps over-compensated for my nervousness.

In the end, it was almost too easy. The sentry was apparently transfixed by the splendour of my equipage and, looking at the stains on his tunic, the missing buttons and (for Mungo had been right, of course) the unpolished boots, it was easy to see why. I found I had a real sense of grievance on behalf of Nana Sahib and I castigated the man at length before stalking off and leaving him quivering at attention in my wake.

After that, Mungo would often dress me in a variety of native dresses and he would set me challenges that tested my linguistic skills and my understanding of the world he was leading me farther and farther into. One day he decided I should beg as a mendicant in the streets of Bithur. I protested that it was a foolish jape, for were the mob to penetrate my disguise I did not see how he could have protected me and I was sure that it would take more than walnut juice to change me from a European to an Indian. But Mungo insisted.

"Do you not keep telling me that you would learn more about the ordinary people? And how better to learn than to go among them?"

I was far from confident, but there was no arguing with Mungo once he had an idea firmly in his pretty head. I was stripped of all my clothing and then Mungo shaved off my body hair. Fortunately, I am not a hairy man, but Mungo considered that I was, nonetheless, still too hirsute to pass as a native. After my barbering, Mungo covered me from head to foot with walnut stain before allowing me to wrap a loincloth about my nakedness. Then he thrust a staff into one hand and a begging bowl into the other and sent me off to fend for myself.

"You are a little too well fed to be utterly convincing," he said. "So you will have to take care to stoop and shuffle and generally try to look less the European gentleman and more the Indian mendicant."

I duly stooped and shuffled my way around the streets and alleys of old Bithur.

It was not a very prepossessing place. Before Nana Sahib had built his palace there, it had been just a fisherman's village on the shores of the Ganges. The fisherman's houses—little more than mud huts—were still there, facing the muddy foreshore of the river, which was still running quite high, it being not that long since the rainy season. The fisherman's village was quiet, most of the men being in their boats on the river, hauling their nets, casting their lines or dozing under canvas awnings while they waited for the fish to bite. On shore, there were just children running in the streets and women, most of whom kept modestly indoors.

Behind the old fishing village, further from the muddy stench of the foreshore, a new Bithur had grown up, full of shops to serve Saturday House and those who lived there, and houses for the families and hangers-on of the fortunate inhabitants of the palace.

Here was the bustle and noise that I had come to associate with all but the smallest Indian villages. Shopkeepers displayed their wares on mats in front of the shabby buildings where they lived and traded. Even fine silks were spread out for inspection where every footfall raised more dust to dull their vibrant colours. Samosas and chupattis were piled on plates ready to eat, while butchers hung carcasses from hooks on the front of their shop-houses. Hawkers wandered by, selling their own goods from bags slung over their shoulders or trays hung round their necks. Their cries competed with the shouts of the shop owners to raise a cacophony in which my plaintive cries for alms at first went unheeded.

The streets were thronged with the Nana's men, who were all-too-eager to demonstrate their wealth and status by purchasing luxury goods with an aristocrat's disdain for the price. Once these people had caught a glimpse of my begging bowl they were quick to buy food that they could give me. In the villages of India, at least, it seemed that no one gave money, preferring to honour the tradition that beggars should be fed. I was careful to mix the offerings together, honouring the equally ancient tradition that all the food I was given should be treated equally and I could not pick out the dainties to separate them from the poorer man's gift of plain boiled rice.

In all the bustle, no one seemed to notice that I was, perhaps, a little well fed for a beggar. Or perhaps Mungo had exaggerated the hardship of a beggar's life, for I found that my bowl was soon filled with a more than ample meal, which I took to the river's edge to eat with my fingers, as I now ate all my food when I was not dining with Europeans.

As I ate, I thought how differently the Indians viewed indigents such as myself from the way that they were viewed in Europe. Here, it was not unusual for a man of my age to retire from the world and spend his life contemplating the mysteries of philosophy while trusting to the kindness of strangers for his basic needs, while at home the parish beadle was always on the lookout to ensure that Christian charity was never extended beyond the minimum set down by law.

After my meal, I found shelter under a banyan tree and spent the hottest hours of the day in the shade, half-sleeping. With one lazy eye, I watched the passage of a sacred bullock making his privileged way to the river to drink. At this time of year, the days were still cool enough for a rest in the open to be pleasant. I realised why so many Indians spent the noon hours in this way, which the Europeans saw as 'idle', considering that a man should rest in the privacy of his home or spend his time in honest toil.

Refreshed, I returned to the market where, after the midday pause, people were already beginning to buy and sell again. My stomach well satisfied, I did not hold my bowl out for alms, but leaned on my staff and watched the ebb and flow of business. There was no school in Bithur and children ran amongst the adults, adding to the noise with their laughter. Occasionally I would hear a father call to a child to stop his play and come to help, holding this, counting that or just watching his father and learning from what he saw.

A knife sharpener appeared with his grindstone and suddenly the street was filled with women, flitting from their homes like a flock of birds in brilliant saris, chattering to each other in gentle voices.

I moved from the main street to a smaller alley that cut through to the high road back to Saturday House, ducking aside from time to time as people made their way to the market, sometimes bowed down by the weight of goods they were carrying. One man, presumably aware of the Nana's penchant for European furnishings, was somehow managing to carry an entire French bureau roped to his back so that he resembled a donkey more than a man. The alley was scarcely wide enough for some of the more heavy laden porters to pass but we all made our way well enough and, however burdened down they were, all found breath to exchange greetings with me as they squeezed their way by. Suddenly, ahead of me I heard a raised European voice.

"Out of the way, you fools! Make way there!"

Ahead, I saw, to my astonishment, a large man on an even larger horse. He was presumably one of the Nana's guests and had, for some reason, decided to take this path to the market, rather than follow the high road. Still, with everyone pressing themselves to any gaps they could find, he was able to push his way down. I was so astonished at watching his progress that I forgot myself a moment and failed to move aside as quickly as I should. He leaned forward, striking out with his whip and opening a cut across my shoulder. A man sheltering in a doorway behind me reached to pull me from his path and he was gone.

One or two of those who had seen what occurred looked at the cut on my shoulder and shook their heads in sympathy, but, within minutes, the interruption to the normal rhythm of life was forgotten.

I made my way back to Saturday House and slipped in past the kitchens, where beggars often came and went. A few minutes later, I was safely back in our apartments and Mungo was inspecting my wound and cursing himself for putting me in such a situation.

❀

We had regularly dined in Mungo's apartment. As I was usually at Saturday House for only a few days at a time, a bowl of fruit, a few chupattis or some nan bread and a samosa or two were quite enough to feed us. If we wanted to eat more, a servant would appear at the door and bowls of fragrant rice and spiced meat would be placed on the low table.

Now that Mungo had proved that I could pass myself as a native, though, he decided we should eat more often in the great refectory where food was supplied to any of the Nana's substantial household who chose to eat there. So, from time to time, I would dress as a scribe, with a cotton dhoti and a broad piece of white cloth swathing my upper body. Thus disguised, I would join Mungo, talking earnestly about the holy books I was studying as around us soldiers, servants, court officials and the hundreds of wives and concubines and cousins and assorted kin came and went, sometimes stopping to bow toward me on account of the learning they associated with my dress.

Never was I the subject of the least suspicion in Bithur, although, some of the Europeans in Cawnpore must have wondered at the change in my complexion. However much I scrubbed, some of the stain always seemed to remain, and I saw the odd peculiar glance at the Club. No one was so vulgar as to comment on it, and I imagine that most decided I had simply been spending too long in the sun. Hillersdon noticed, of course, but then he had always encouraged my visits to Bithur. I think he realised the reason for the change in my appearance and recognised, even before I did, that my ability to pass as a native might one day be of value to the Company.

As the weeks passed, what had started as a game came to have a more practical use. Although all seemed normal in Cawnpore, European visitors to the Nana became reluctant to leave the palace to explore the streets of Bithur. It was not that there were any positive reports of difficulties with the natives—just a general surliness that made the venture unpleasant. I went out one evening without first disguising myself and I found my horse's path blocked from time to time by groups of natives who ignored my shouts, responding only with angry looks and muttered curses. It was not until I struck out with my whip that I was able to proceed. When I told Mungo of what had occurred, his face took on an expression of unwonted seriousness. "I think, John, that it would be best if you wear native dress when you visit me. I think the days are coming when your pale skin will attract attention we could well do without."

I thought Mungo too cautious, but it cost me nothing to humour him. Indeed, I enjoyed the charade. I would insist on leaving my carriage in Cawnpore and ride out on the Bithur road in European clothes, stopping in a grove of trees to change into native dress for my arrival in Saturday House. The element of subterfuge added to the frisson of danger that made our illicit friendship even more exciting. A few weeks later, though, I was riding toward the palace in my disguise when a fakir threw himself in front of my horse and seized the bridle. I resisted the impulse to strike him, for though the fakirs are often frauds and beggars of the worst sort, it is as well to remember that they are viewed as holy men. I reached instead for my purse to throw him a few annas and be on my way but he showed no interest in my money, instead calling on the gods to bless me and repeating over and again, "*Sub lal hoga.*" "Everything is to become red." I shook my mount free of his grip and rode on and when I turned to look back, he was still standing in the middle of the road, his arms raised to heaven and chanting, "*Sub lal hoga. Sub lal hoga.*"

The incident, though trivial, worried me for some reason and I told Mungo about it. He did admit to having heard the phrase here and there before but insisted that it was simply a warning about the growth in power of the British and meant only that with the annexation of Oudh, it was but a matter of time before our scarlet uniforms were seen throughout the sub-continent.

I was unconvinced. The tone of the fakir had not been that of a man discussing the latest trends in Company policy and I wondered if the reference was to something thicker than water and of a deeper crimson than a British uniform.

My fears were reinforced as the days again turned cool and 1856 drew towards its close. I was studying alone in the library (this time dressed as a scribe) when Mungo came in great excitement to urge me to join the throng gathering in the Nana's audience hall—a great pillared court, half open to the sky, where Nana Sahib would sit in state.

That afternoon, Mungo said, the Nana's personal astrologer was to make a great prediction for the year 1857. I was intrigued, for there seemed no obvious reason why a Hindoo astrologer should see anything of important in our Christian calendar, so I squatted in the crowd, inconspicuous in sandals and loincloth, while the astrologer—a tall fellow in a red robe— came before the Nana.

With a great palaver, he produced a chart of the heavens which he pointed to and scowled over. The Nana's barely concealed boredom suggested he already knew what was to come but the courtiers around me seemed very impressed and excited by the whole performance. Finally, the astrologer wallah came out and told us that 1857 would see the hundredth anniversary of the Battle of Plessey, which had marked the start of British rule in India. "And on that anniversary," he declaimed (for he had worked himself into a state of considerable excitement by now) "the Europeans will be driven from our land and the rule of the British will end."

There was a deal of excitement at this, as you can imagine, and I could swear that I heard more than one of those around me mutter, "*Sub lal hoga.*"

I tried to convince myself that this was nothing, but by January I could not ignore the rumblings of discontent which, by then, had spread to Cawnpore. British rule in India depended on the army, but the army in India, though officered by Europeans, relied on local recruits. These sepoys, as they were called, were uniformed, equipped and drilled just as our British soldiers and, for almost a century, we had taken their loyalty for granted. The dark looks in the lines of the Native Infantry and the stories of seditious meetings in the hours of darkness were therefore a source of real concern. The immediate cause appeared to be rumours that the new cartridges to be issued to our Indian troops had been made using the fat of pigs and cattle and were hence offensive to both Musalmans and Hindoos. Yet something deeper was threatening our peace—something that affected civilians and soldiers alike. It was something that hung in the air like the wretched red dust that choked the city whenever the wind blew but, like the dusty air, it was intangible. I took to walking the streets of the Old Cawnpore, usually dressed as a beggar. With my wooden bowl held out for gifts of food, I could linger for hours without exciting suspicion and more and more often I would hear that ominous phrase: "*Sub lal hoga.*" Yet still there was nothing specific I could report to Hillersdon.

In the European Station, life went on as usual. The Collector was peevish because he had applied for funds to improve the embankment North of the town, where the Ganges would often flood some of the older houses where the poorer people lived, but the revenue board would have none of it. General Wheeler, by contrast, was kept in funds to build new barracks. I shared Hillersdon's irritation that money could always be found for the army while the civil authorities had to make do and mend but it had been ever thus and I could hardly hold it against Wheeler that he, at least, could expand his empire.

The 53rd Native Infantry arrived from Cuttack to reinforce our garrison in February, but the new barracks were nowhere near ready and they were billeted in the existing lines. I was concerned that this might lead to them being infected with the alienation we suspected already abroad amongst our troops. I did say something of the sort to Hillersdon, but he replied that in the absence of other accommodation it was not to be helped and there was an end to it. We could only hope that we might soon be sent a British regiment to dilute the predominance of surly brown faces in the cantonment.

February gave way to March and, with the coming of warmer weather, came yet more signs and portents.

On one particularly warm morning, I arrived at my office at the usual time to find a note from Simkin on my desk, asking me to look in on him at my earliest convenience. I was somewhat taken aback by the idea of his being at his desk before the appointed hour—or indeed within thirty minutes of it. But, on putting my head into his office, I saw him sitting there in a state of some agitation.

It transpired that Simkin (who had some small responsibility for the chowkedars, or local policemen), had been told by one of these men that he had been approached by a comrade who had run up and given him two chupattis before running off, apparently in a state of high excitement.

I calmed Simkin down, telling him that there was nothing in it and that making a gift of these unleavened loaves was a regular custom but, I admit, I lied. I had heard talk in the bazaar of waiting for the coming of the chupattis. No one seemed to know exactly what they signified but there was no doubt that, like the coming of a fiery cross, they indicated that some great mischief was planned. They seemed to be sent as a warning that men should prepare themselves for a day that was nigh upon them. I saw no advantage to having Simkin more agitated than he already was but, whilst affecting an air of nonchalance, I made my way directly to Hillersdon's office to see what experience he could bring to bear on the issue.

Charles greeted me in his usual cheery way but his face grew grave as I passed on the news and when I had finished he sighed, wearily.

"So it's among the townsfolk, too."

My expression must have made him realise that his response puzzled me.

"I'm sorry, Williamson, I should have told you. General Wheeler has informed me that his officers have reports of lotus leaves being distributed in the same way." I tried to remember what Mungo had told me about the symbolism of the lotus but, while I was still racking my brain, Hillersdon explained. "The leaves are a symbol of war. The chupattis could, I suppose, have some innocent explanation, but taken together there is no doubt that they presage some sort of trouble. I just don't know what."

So things continued as each day brought a rise in mercury in the thermometers and, less clearly visible yet all too real, a rise in the tension that pervaded Cawnpore. Servants were surly, mistresses more than usually ready to find fault and masters quick to lash out with fist or riding crop at any native they thought insolent.

Wheeler, though, was determined that the routine of life in the station should carry on as ever. The military band still took its place on the bandstand to entertain any who braved the heat to listen to them. The sound of marching feet could be heard in the still of the mornings, reassuring us that the Native Infantry still drilled obedient to their officers.

While insolence and petty pilfering might be rife, the courts were strangely quiet. Indeed, Hillersdon suggested that we close the local court on Wednesdays as, he claimed, the judges' dockets were almost empty and they presided over nothing but heat and dust.

In my own establishment, there was always a degree of petty theft. It was a regular part of any life where fifty servants swarmed around with little to do save plot mischief. Like every European, I pretended outrage but, in fact, tolerated the losses as part of the cost of maintaining staff. Now, though, silver spoons began to disappear at an alarming rate and the number of plates broken in a week necessitated new deliveries of china. I visited the servants' quarters, cursed fluently in Hindoo and dismissed on the spot the men I suspected of causing the most trouble. I blessed Mungo Buksh for the lessons he had taught me, for my confidence in dealing with natives in their own tongue was all thanks to him and my performance awed them into good behaviour.

Other households, though, were not so lucky. Noxious herbs appeared in the feed in Simkin's stable and his Arab, a rarity in those parts, died, foaming at the mouth. Poor Mrs Hillersdon hardly dared entertain, so often did she find the meat her butcher delivered was corrupted. Yet no one could prove these were not simply accidents or the result of the seasonal heat.

Europeans began to avoid the bazaar, promenading only on the Course, that stretch of road that ran up from the military cantonments and which, being straight and smooth and lined with trees, was favoured by those who would exercise their horses in safety and comfort. Now, to its other manifest advantages was added the fact that it was seldom frequented by native civilians and that the soldiers using it, being close to their camp, were generally well disciplined and polite. As the Deputy Collector, I shared their caution, riding up and down the Course and otherwise straying as little as possible from the concentration of European houses sandwiched between the military cantonments and the native town. But in my other life—the life I shared with Mungo Buksh—I spent increasing hours in exploring the lanes and alleys of both Cawnpore and Bithur and everywhere there were dark mutterings about a Red Year and old resentments of the British were being aired. Yet still all remained rumour and whispers on the wind.

Mungo swore that all would be well. "The rains will come in June and all the evil will be washed away." But, for all his soothing words, he would warn me to be careful in riding along the road to Bithur and, though he begged me to spend every day I could at Saturday House, he insisted that I never show myself there in my European clothes.

"But I scarcely ever do."

We were eating in his quarters. A palace servant had brought dishes of fowl and mutton served in sauces so different from what my own servants produced under the generic title of 'Curry' that I scarce recognised them as being even nominally the same dish. Mungo took some rice, rolled it into a ball with his nimble fingers, soaking it in the sauce and transferring the whole lot to his mouth with no mess, no spills and the merest trace of sauce on his fingertips.

"I wish I could eat as tidily as you do."

He smiled. "It's practice, John. It will come. But you're changing the subject." There was an edge of tension in his voice that did not sit easily with his naturally relaxed approach to almost all life's problems. "I know you seldom appear here in your European guise. But I think it best that from now on you never do."

"What's worrying you, Mungo? You can't believe that I would be in any danger in Nana Sahib's home."

"No, no." He took my hands between his, pressing them as he sought to reassure me. "Nana Sahib has always been a friend to the British."

"Then why your concern?"

"It is…" His eyes darted about the room, as if seeking an answer hidden among the cushions or behind the tapestry that covered one wall. "It is difficult. The Nana is loyal but there are those in his court who do not wish the British well."

"Don't be ridiculous, Mungo. The Nana is an absolute ruler within his court. If he is loyal, then I am as safe here as anywhere on Earth."

Mungo did not reply but his discomfort was obvious. I could not understand why he should have any fears. "The Nana is loyal, isn't he?"

My friend gave me a tired smile. "You speak our language so well and you understand so much of our lives, I sometimes forget that you are, in the end, an Englishman."

"Mungo, what do you mean?"

"You remember our gods. The ones that may have six arms or two? That may be a man or a woman? With skin of blue or of white?"

I said nothing.

"These are our gods, John. They are important. Their quality tells you something of our quality."

"That you can have six arms or two? That your skin may be blue or white?"

Mungo had been fidgeting, picking at the string of his day bed, but now he raised his face to mine. "Or that a man may be loyal and disloyal."

I stared at him in horror. As people had become nervous of taking the air in Cawnpore, so even more women and children had been sent to enjoy the hospitality of Nana Sahib. Only two days before we had this conversation, Hillersdon had confided in me that he was thinking of sending Lydia to Saturday House. "She'll be safe out there with Nana Sahib," he had said.

"I do not mean he is untrue." Mungo was, by now, wringing his hands in his agitation. "I mean just that nothing is certain. There are those who urge him to act against the British who have denied him his birthright and insulted his name. Yet he is a friend to many of the British officers and the men of the Company. He offers them his hospitality and it is honestly meant. He cannot hurt those with whom he has broken bread."

I forbore to point out that Nana Sahib did not, in fact, break bread with his European guests. Mungo's distress was painful to watch. Nana Sahib was his cousin and he owed him fealty: it was simply cruel to make him question his lord's integrity. But I took his advice to pass myself as a native whenever I was at Bithur. And I decided to keep a closer eye on the behaviour of Nana Sahib. The Nana's behaviour, though, was beyond reproach. Over the time I had spent in Cawnpore, I had seen him ride into town, parading himself on his elephant, surrounded by his own troops, half a dozen times and his visits were always well received by the native population. In March he made three such excursions, explaining to Hillersdon (whom he was careful to acknowledge with due ceremony on each visit) that his presence had a calming effect. There seemed to be some truth in this. As the Company's native troops became more sullen and disaffected, the sight of Nana Sahib's well turned out guard seemed to promise a security that I feared our own soldiers no longer offered.

The next time that the possibility of open revolution was raised at dinner, the circumstances were very different. Early in May, I was again invited to join Wheeler at the Hillersdons. The General was accompanied only by his son and he looked tired and old. Our meal was eaten quietly, the sombre atmosphere having its effect even on the usually lively Lydia. Her pregnancy was advanced by now and she tired easily. She was happy to withdraw as soon as the meal was over, leaving just the four of us (there were no other guests) to sip our port and chew nervously at our cigars.

Hillersdon waited until we were settled before broaching the topic that had obviously been on his mind for some time. "There's rumours all over the country that the native troops are on the edge of mutiny. As one gentleman to another, I'm asking you, Sir Hugh, if there's any truth in it."

"I'll not dissemble with you, Hillersdon." The General paused and turned his cigar, making sure it was burning evenly. "Things could turn very nasty. There's rumours flying about the new cartridges being greased with pig and beef fat and the natives don't like it. I think my chaps are reliable, but we could be in for a nasty couple of months."

I remembered Mungo's words. "Some of the natives are saying that the crisis will pass when the rains come."

Hillersdon pursed his lips. "That's all well and good and I trust you're right, but meanwhile I have the Treasury for the whole province here in Cawnpore and it's guarded by troops we can't be sure of. If there's even a chance they might be mutinous, surely leaving the Treasury in their hands is just putting temptation in their way?"

Wheeler nodded. "There's something in what you say, but I don't have a lot of choice. The only British regiment I have is the 84th Foot. There's only a hundred of them, and it sometimes seems that most of them are in the hospital with one thing or another. As far as the Treasury guard is concerned, it's Native Infantry or nothing."

"Not necessarily." Hillersdon picked up his port glass and swirled it round, watching the ruby liquid swill up the sides. "We could always call on Nana Sahib's men."

"You can't!" I spoke without thinking and the three other men stared at me in surprise. I blushed and started to mumble some sort of explanation. "I mean…If we're going to trust native troops, surely we should trust our own men."

Hillersdon was usually the most easygoing of superiors but my sudden outburst, in front of the General and his son, had clearly irritated him. "General Wheeler has intimated that our own troops are not entirely trustworthy. Are you suggesting that we cannot trust Nana Sahib either?"

That was, indeed, my belief, but I was reluctant to say so at Hillersdon's table.

Charles thought of the Nana as a friend and would take it amiss if I were to say that I thought him unreliable. In any case, what evidence did I have? Merely the remarks of Mungo Buksh, which I was hardly in a position to discuss. In any case, however much Mungo's comments had ignited my suspicions, he was himself convinced that in the end the Nana would be loyal. So I stuttered out some prevaricating nonsense about how I thought it a poor show when we stood down our own troops and put local soldiery in their place and generally played the part of a pukha-sahib, while the others stared at me and wondered if the heat had softened my brain.

"Well," said Hillersdon, when I finally stammered to a halt, "if there is no specific objection," (he laid an ironic emphasis on the word 'specific') "then would you have any problem with my approaching Nana Sahib, General?"

"In principle, I'd have no objection. But things are at a delicate stage now and I don't want to make any move that might precipitate disaffection amongst the men. Let us wait until the situation becomes clearer before we apply for local assistance."

Hillersdon did not press his point. The General had been generous in accepting the idea of having such an important task as guarding the Treasury transferred from soldiers under his direct command to those of a native ruler, however loyal. He had achieved all he could hope for at this stage and was quick to move the conversation to a broader discussion of the unrest now being reported all over the Northern provinces. Not that this topic was without its dangers. Wheeler had been an Indian Army officer for over fifty years and was reluctant to allow that his troops might rise up against the British.

"The sepoys can be foolish, I admit. Like children, sometimes. But they're loyal. I'd stake my life on it."

He did admit that rumours about the fat on the new cartridges and other, even more implausible, stories had led to a degree of discontent in the ranks. "I have never seen the men as nervous as some of them are now. But I don't blame them. The trouble is caused by the missionary societies interfering in matters they do not properly understand. These chaps come out from England and start telling the natives that their religions are all wrong and they should all convert to Christianity. You can see why they get suspicious. There's stories going about that the Company intends the forcible Christianising of the whole nation. One of my lieutenants swears he heard a sepoy explain that we were shipping our own army widows out to India where the native troops would be forcibly married to them so that they would be dragged to baptism by way of matrimony. It's madness and I rather agree with our friend,"—he nodded toward me—"that once the rains start, the wilder stories will be washed away in the flood and life will get back onto some sort of even keel."

So the port circulated and we exchanged stories of mutinies in the past (for here and there a regiment misbehaved every few years) and how all had blown over. As we puffed our cigars and allowed ourselves to relax after a good meal and sip our fine liquor, we convinced ourselves that this, too, would pass.

❋

THE WEEK THAT followed that dinner saw the temperature in the town edge its way past 110 degrees. As the mercury rose in the thermometer, so the tension in the town grew more palpable, but still the soldiers paraded and the band played, our sepoys smartly turned out, the European officers going about their business as usual. All seemed quiet in the province and life in the Company's offices moved even more languidly than usual.

Then, on Thursday 14 May, everything changed.

I had ridden out early when the temperature was barely 80 degrees, which we accounted cool in May.

I wanted to judge the mood of the population so, instead of having my cook prepare breakfast, I ate at the club. Simkin was there and he asked if he could join me. Generally, I ate alone, finding I had little in common with the other members. They, I think, sensed that I was not of their class and so I was left to my solitary meals, and arrangement which suited us all. Now that Simkin chose to break with this convention and impose himself on me, I could think of no reason to refuse his company. I was forced to listen to him droning on while I ate my devilled kidneys and bacon. He was full of rumours of the insurrection that was anticipated any day but he had no actual news. The bodies of Europeans, he said, had been seen floating in the Ganges, and for a moment I thought this might be real intelligence and I enquired as to where I might see these portents for myself. At this, Simkin admitted that the bodies, if they existed, were not at Cawnpore but at a village some distance away, the name of which he had forgotten, or had never known.

By the time I had finished my breakfast I was sure that the situation was just as it had been the day before and the week before that and the month before that. Wheeler was right; Mungo was right: we were starting at shadows. If we could but keep our nerves until the rains came, all would be well.

I made my way to my office, determined to make inroads into the returns required in Calcutta. How much tax had we collected? How many staff had we paid? How many hours had they worked? How many dependents did they have? Calcutta's demand for numbers, its appetite for neatly completed questionnaires was insatiable. I thought of Hillersdon's embankment and the peremptory refusal of funds for its construction and wondered, not for the first time, if joining the Company had been a mistake.

I was reaching for a ledger kept on a high shelf by the window when I heard Hillersdon call for me from the corridor. He was usually a carefully courteous man and calling for me in that way was unlike him. And I heard something in his voice that frightened me.

I remember pushing the ledger back into place and turning toward the door as Hillersdon entered.

"Williamson," he said, "we must see the General at once. I have terrible news."

THE SAME FOUR of us that had drunk port and smoked cigars together at that dinner party, now sat in Wheeler's house.

"It's best we talk here," he'd said. "It's more discreet."

His son grimaced. "Discreet or not, this will be all over the station by evening."

The old man nodded. "That's as may be, but at least we can discuss the news calmly before we have to deal with the panic." He turned to Hillersdon. "You're absolutely sure of this?"

"It's an official telegraph. I imagine the delay has been to give them time to confirm the truth of the story."

"Meerut." Wheeler shook his head, unbelievingly. "There's more European soldiers stationed there than anywhere else in the country. How the devil could they have let it happen at Meerut?"

He had rolled out a map on the table and we all looked at the point where a cross marked the garrison town of Meerut.

It is hard to credit now, when every schoolboy in the Empire knows its name, but until that day, I was scarcely aware that the place existed. Almost 250 miles North West of Cawnpore, Meerut was a base from which to protect the border with the Afghan tribes we had only recently defeated. Over 4,000 troops were based there, around half of them British and half natives. On Sunday 10 May, the native troops had mutinied, shot their officers, burned and looted in the town and marched on Delhi.

"You say this happened on Sunday." I turned to Hillersdon. "How could we not know of this 'til now?"

"They cut the telegraph." His tone was grim. "Law and order seems to have broken down entirely. The roads are unsafe. Messages are undelivered. What news we have is unreliable. But there is no doubt that Meerut has mutinied and that Delhi is now in the hands of what is, in effect, a rebel army claiming to be re-establishing the Mogul Empire."

We looked back at the map. Delhi was just 40 miles from Meerut, still over 200 miles from us.

"I think we still need to remain calm." Wheeler was on his feet, peering at the map and it struck me again how short a man he was, and how old. "The men here should yet prove loyal."

His son nodded in agreement. "We should take no precipitous action, to be sure, but I think that it would be wise to make plans for defending ourselves should we need to."

Wheeler nodded. "We don't have the men to defend ourselves against a full-fledged attack but, judging from what happened at Meerut, if there is a mutiny, we can expect a day of riot and then the rebels will march to join their brethren in Delhi. We should have a place of security prepared where the European community can gather with such protection as we can provide, to wait in safety while the storm blows itself out."

His son unrolled a plan of the military cantonment. "We could dig a protective trench around these two barracks here." He gestured at two buildings that stood between the main lines of the cantonment and the European part of the town. "One of them is in use as a hospital, which is a convenient type of building to have to hand if there might be casualties. The other is currently unused. There is a well, and a kitchen, some warehousing and the usual offices. If we dig a rampart around it, it will be as good a rally point as any 'til the natives have had their fun looting the town and make off to Delhi."

His father placed his finger at the point Godfrey had indicated, tapping at the paper with a preoccupied air. "It can do no harm to make ready, I suppose. Explain to the engineers what we have in mind and we can get coolies out digging. But I want no fuss. Nothing must be done that might alarm the troops and increase their concerns."

And that was that.

Hillersdon and I walked back to our office, neither of us anxious to discuss the meeting we had just attended. Godfrey Wheeler, I suppose, went off to instruct the engineers. The General had seen us to the door but his wife had come out of her sitting room to forbid him from walking out with us. It was too hot, she had said. "You must think of your health, dear." And so he had bidden us farewell and returned to his study.

The rest of that Thursday had an air of unreality. Hillersdon and I carried on as if we had heard no news, ignoring the rumours that, as Major Wheeler had predicted, were everywhere by nightfall. It was said that all of the country was ablaze, the Mogul Emperor restored in Delhi and his army, a hundred thousand strong, was setting out to sweep the British from Indian soil forever.

Friday brought an awful confirmation of the story Simkin had told me of Europeans in the Ganges floated downstream.

A body was caught in the current on the Oudh bank and it was decided not to attempt to recover it.

On Saturday, I was in my office, trying—and utterly failing—to concentrate on some correspondence about Hillersdon's plans for that wretched embankment, when Charles said that we had been summoned by the general.

"I fear it is unlikely to be good news," he said. "I am thinking that it might be best to get Lydia away."

"I know some people are trying to send their families to Allahabad but there are rumours that rebels control the river."

"No, travelling through the country in the present situation is unthinkable for Lydia, especially in her condition. But Nana Sahib has let me know that she would be welcome to stay with him until things calm down. She could take the children, too."

I had hardly seen the children, for Hillersdon was firmly of the opinion that they should be seen as little as possible and best heard never—at least when there were visitors in the house. Still, he was, I believe, a conscientious and caring father and the idea of his family being caught up in any untoward events in Cawnpore was a constant concern. The idea of sending them to Bithur seemed sensible. Lydia had been a frequent guest of the Nana and even if my suspicions of his loyalty proved true, I could not imagine that he would harm the family if they were left under his protection.

"It's worrying, of course. I don't like the idea of her being miles from a European doctor if she were to…"

"Absolutely." I nodded again.

So Hillersdon passed our walk to Wheeler's house worrying about his domestic arrangements and I spent it sympathising for, though I could not imagine ever finding myself in his position, it was clear that he was in an agony of doubt what to do for the best.

When we arrived and a servant had ushered us into the presence of the general, he wasted no time with conventional civilities. "I have new intelligence," Wheeler announced, almost as soon as we were seated. "I have it reported that yesterday one of the sepoys' sons was heard boasting to another child that he was in the secret of what his father's regiment was to do to strike a blow for his people."

I stared at him, astonished. "Is this our intelligence? Idle chatter in the school yard?"

"Mr Williamson!" Wheeler tried to sound magisterial but ended up simply querulous. "There has been seditious talk also from the sepoys. One of the Musalmans in the 56th has been spreading stories that we intend to gather the native regiments together at their next pay muster and blow them to kingdom come with mines we have been secretly constructing under the parade ground. The problem is that some of his comrades appear to have believed him. He's in irons now."

The General wiped his face with his hands, as if trying to wipe away his doubts and anxieties. The Indian Army had been his life and I realised now how desperate he was to believe that his men would not betray him. On the plain on the edge of town, a ditch and an earthen rampart was being painstakingly scratched from the baked earth. I had seen it that morning: a bank just three feet high, it would not serve to stop a child. Wheeler had to believe he would not be attacked, yet everywhere from the schoolyard to his own sepoys' quarters rumour spread—and rumour begat fear and fear was already giving rise to panic.

"Perhaps..." Hillersdon was speaking. "Perhaps now is the time to move the Nana's troops in to guard the Treasury."

Wheeler nodded. "I'll send for European troops from Lucknow. That may calm things. But if it gets any worse, we might have to use Nana Sahib's men. It will reassure the townspeople that there is still order in the place and it will show the sepoys that there are other troops to do our bidding if they are recalcitrant."

I was about to demur, but I knew Hillersdon was determined on the wisdom of this move and, after my earlier outburst, Wheeler was unlikely to respond favourably to any interjection by me, so I kept my peace.

My concerns remained, though, so as I walked back to the office with Hillersdon, I suggested that I should take some time away from my desk to take the mood of the people. Hillersdon was no fool and he knew that I used my facility with the native language to judge mood in the streets, although I took care for him not to learn how completely I was passing myself off as an Indian. I think, too, that while he would hear nothing said against the Nana, he welcomed the idea that I should satisfy myself that all was well.

That afternoon, I slipped away from Cawnpore and hurried to Saturday House.

If Hillersdon had hoped that I would be reassured by what I saw, he would have been disappointed by my reception at the Nana's palace. At the gate, instead of passing sentries slouched in their usual casual indolence, I was challenged by guards who had the air of soldiers already sensing battle on the horizon. Fortunately, Mungo's repeated urgings of caution had had their effect on me and I was immaculately turned out in the uniform of one of Nana's own men, so a sharp salute and a word or two of greeting was enough for me to gain admittance.

Mungo was not in his apartments when I arrived. I fidgeted, uncertain what to do with myself. I had, as usual, brought my commonplace book with me to Saturday House and I recorded the meeting with Wheeler. Reading my words again left me even more troubled. I picked up one of the books I had been studying with Mungo and turned the pages, reading the Devanagari script with practised ease. But I found that I could not concentrate on the text. I needed Mungo to reassure me that all would be well and that Nana Sahib's troops would truly keep the peace in Cawnpore.

I replaced the book on the table and opened the chest where Mungo stored his clothes. I found myself pressing my face into them, inhaling the lingering traces of his scent. It was not just his news about Nana Sahib I needed; I needed him. His presence, his youth, his vitality. With the ordered world of British India no longer secure, it was to Mungo that I turned as the one safe and certain point I knew.

He came in so quietly that he found me still sitting there with my face buried in his clothing. I should have been embarrassed, but he reached for me without a word and pulled me to him and the faint remembrance of his scent gave way to the heady reality of his presence.

He slipped off his tunic and unbuttoned my shirt and I clung to his body, kissing the soft, warm flesh while he stroked my hair, murmuring reassurance.

We made love slowly, as if both if us wanted to extend the moment and delay all talk of politics, mutiny and murder. But, at last, as we lay together, sated in each other's arms, we could prevaricate no longer. I explained that Wheeler was requesting the Nana for help and I asked Mungo to tell me if he was to be trusted or not.

"I would not ask so bluntly, but I have to know. At Meerut they killed women and children and burned the town."

Mungo lay quietly, looking up at the ceiling, where a gecko sat motionless above his head.

"Nana Sahib has been insulted by the British and they have refused him his pension. There are those who say that he should avenge the insults and seize the money that is his right. But when the British defeated his father, they did not kill him. They allowed him to live here. They paid him a pension. So Nana Sahib has always been a friend to the British. He entertains them here at Saturday House. He is polite to their wives and kind to their children. And he has shown respect to your Mr Hillersdon and to all the officers of the Company. This he does because the British treated his father honourably—and because he knows your army is strong and that when his father rose against your army, he was defeated."

I lay alongside him, thinking of what he said.

"Our army is still strong."

He turned from the gecko and propped his head on his

hand, looking at me as he spoke. "We are the people of this land. We do not need the telegraph to know what happened in Meerut."

"Meerut was one town. Britain has soldiers in countries all across the globe. Once her wrath is roused, she will crush the rebels entirely."

"Yes." His eyes gazed into mine. "I think you are right. And so do many in the court. And they tell Nana Sahib that he should stay loyal to the British."

"So he will send troops to assist us?"

"He will send troops."

"And they will be loyal?"

Now Mungo's gaze turned back to the gecko. "Why do you dig a ditch around the old barracks?"

"It's a precaution only. General Wheeler has a military mind, so he is preparing a defence in case one should be needed."

"A child could climb it."

"We hope it will never be needed."

"It should not have been done."

Something in his tone alarmed me. "Why not, Mungo?" I asked.

"Because it is weak. And Nana Sahib is loyal because he thinks you are strong."

I made no reply. The two of us lay beside each other on the bed, watching the gecko until, as if conscious of our gaze, it moved away.

chapter 4

I RETURNED TO Cawnpore the next day. Although it was the Sabbath, I decided that I should call upon Hillersdon and let him know how things stood.

Charles received me cordially enough, but Lydia was only a few weeks from her confinement and it was obvious that he did not want her agitated. So we sat and talked of the price of fish and whether they should buy a quieter horse so that Lydia might be able to ride out as soon as she was recovered from the birth and what the fashions might be for the ladies when the dancing season should come again with the rains.

Our increasingly desperate attempts to avoid any discussion of those events that were all that anyone in Cawnpore truly cared about created the very atmosphere of tension that we were trying to avoid. Fortunately, Lydia, who was as intelligent as she was pretty, had the good sense to tell us that her condition made it imperative that she take to her bed for a while and she withdrew, leaving Charles and me alone.

Hillersdon spoke immediately his wife was out of the room. "I take it you have news and that is why you have called."

"I do." I paused, for now that it came to it, what positive news did I have? "Do you trust my judgement, Charles?"

"You know I do."

"Then you should be careful of Nana Sahib. He is loyal for now but there are factions in his court who sympathise with the rebels. He will stand by us while he thinks the British will be triumphant but if he sees us weak, he can't be relied upon."

"Are you sure?"

"You said you trust my judgement, Charles."

He pursed his lips, his brow furrowed with concern. "Frankly, John, I'm not sure that anyone can be totally relied upon. The question is: is he safer than the troops guarding the Treasury at present? I have reports that natives who call there with all the proper papers are harassed and threatened and may be sent away with nothing unless they find favour with the guard. The sepoys there are becoming a law unto themselves." He rose from his chair and strode back and forth across the room, hardly recognisable as the affable administrator I had come to know. "The Treasury is my responsibility. There's upwards of a hundred thousand pounds in there. I have to know it's safe."

"Nothing is safe, Charles. Not now. You know that."

He stopped his pacing. "Very well. We have the sepoys, who are already semi-mutinous, and the Nana's men who may rebel in the future. As you say, nothing is safe. But the danger with the sepoys is already present, while the risk with the Nana is a problem for the morrow. I shall ask Wheeler to call on the Nana's troops as soon as practicable."

"And Lydia?"

"Do you think there is any possibility he would harm her?"

"I would doubt it."

"Yet if he were to declare for the rebels, she would be trapped in the enemy's camp. A white woman a prisoner of the niggers."

Although I had heard some men—Simkin came most readily to mind—speak of the natives in these terms, I had never before heard Hillersdon use that word and it was a measure of his distress that he did so then.

"No," he said. "I cannot do it."

We spoke a while longer but all that mattered had been decided. The Nana was to be invited to post his troops to Cawnpore but Lydia was not to go to Saturday House. I could see that Hillersdon was in great distress of mind about both these things and it seemed best to leave him.

I shared some of his agitation and felt I would not be able to settle if I went straight home, so I rode instead to see what progress had been made on the Entrenchment Wheeler had ordered. What I saw did not reassure me. The coolies had struggled to make any progress digging in the sun-baked soil and neither the ditch nor the mud rampart provided a convincing defence. The whole thing was a rough rectangle with bulges here and there to accommodate artillery, although, as yet, no guns were mounted in position. I feared Mungo was right: it looked like an act of desperation, rather than the military preparedness of a great army. I just hoped that things would remain calm until reinforcements arrived from Lucknow.

❉

THE DAYS THAT followed seemed never-ending. Each morning we woke in the hope that we might receive news that the rebellion was quashed or that we might see the promised reinforcements march into town. And then, as the day wore on and the heat became unsupportable, all pretence of work stopped. Men sat idly at their desks, or walked toward the cantonments to see what progress was being made on the fortifications. In their bungalows, the memsahibs took to their beds or berated their cooks with near-hysterical outbursts over the failings of the last day's dinner or this day's luncheon. Even among the natives, a greater than usual lassitude descended. Then night would fall and shadowy brown figures would move among the native lines or through the streets of the old town and any European abroad would be greeted with suspicion and disrespect.

On Thursday, Wheeler ordered all the women and children in the station to report to the Entrenchment. They were to sleep there, he said, simply as a precaution. Hillersdon chose to accompany his wife and children.

The next morning, he was rather later into the office than

usual. He explained to me that his wife, his two children and himself had been sharing a small room with two other families. There were only two barrack blocks into which all the women and children of the Civil Station were crammed willy-nilly.

"Wheeler was most insistent that the women and children shelter there for the night but there was no question of their staying in that awful place all day. So I had to arrange for us all to get home and then I had to settle the children, who were tired and fractious, and then I needed to perform my ablutions for there are no proper facilities in the barracks and, anyway, it's all made me a little behind."

I smiled, in what I hope was an understanding way. "It almost makes me glad that I have no family and was therefore able to spend the night in my own bed."

"Humph."

Hillersdon's expression left me thinking that perhaps my smile hadn't been as understanding as I had hoped.

Although his day had scarcely started well, Hillersdon was in the best of tempers, for that Friday the Nana's troops were finally to arrive in Cawnpore and, he felt, he would again see the Treasury safely under the guard of men he trusted. He was in and out of my room all morning, fidgeting while he waited for news. It was a considerable relief when, at about half past ten a brilliantly turned out cavalryman presented himself at our offices and announced that the Nana's guard was about to arrive in the town. Did Mr Hillersdon want to meet them at the Treasury?

Mr Hillersdon could hardly wait. Mr Hillersdon had had a groom standing by at the door all morning so that he could ride to inspect what I am sure he thought of as 'his' troops.

"Aren't you coming, John?" he asked. "It will be a fine sight."

Unlike the Collector, I did not have my groom standing by so I had to organise myself a horse. The Treasury was about three miles away and I had, in any case, no intention of being the only pedestrian surrounded by mounted officers both civil and military. Hillersdon was fairly bursting with impatience, so he rode off and I followed.

When I finally arrived at the imposing stone building that was, effectively, the European bank, I saw that Hillersdon had been joined by Wheeler and his son. Nana Sahib's state elephant was kneeling nearby and the Nana himself had dismounted and was conferring earnestly with the Collector and the General. The Nana had brought about three hundred men, both infantry and cavalry, and they even towed two guns with them. They were lined up in neat rows, as well turned out as our own troops had ever been and much better than the sullen sepoys of the 53rd Native Infantry, whose normally smart appearance was just a memory from happier days.

Hillersdon was smiling and looked more relaxed than I had seen him for weeks. If my warning had given him any temporary doubts about the Nana's loyalty, he had clearly put this behind him. The only one of the party of officers who looked unhappy was the colonel of the 53rd. I could see him gesticulating angrily and shaking his head as I approached. By the time I was in earshot, Wheeler was trying to placate him.

"The 53rd are not being relieved. Of course we trust them. It's just that the Nana's guard can share their duties, allowing some of the men to move onto garrison duty in the cantonment."

Colonel Gibbs was clearly still unhappy. "Look here, General, it's difficult for me to present this to the men as anything other than an insult. Even if a few of the 53rd remain here, most are being replaced by local troops who are not even under my command."

Wheeler had obviously had enough. "Mr Hillersdon has suggested to me that the men of the 53rd appear to be under your command only in the most limited sense. The troops of the Nana Sahib are well turned out, well disciplined and command the respect of the local populace and of me. The troops of the 53rd, sir, do not."

Wheeler beckoned for his horse and his son assisted him in mounting while the unfortunate Colonel Gibbs looked fit to burst with apoplexy. Indeed, given that the sun was approaching its zenith, I had some real concern for his safety in the heat.

I congratulated Hillersdon for having secured the Treasury, joined him in accompanying the Nana in a sort of informal inspection of the troops and then, the heat being intense, made my apologies and returned to the office. The place was almost deserted, most people having decided to retreat to the cool of their homes. I decided I would remain at my desk and await Hillersdon's return, for I was sure that he would want to record details of the new guard in his official paperwork.

I had almost decided that I was mistaken in my belief when, an hour or more later, I heard the thud of hooves on the dried earth followed by Charles' arrival in my office, mopping perspiration from his brow and complaining of the heat.

I agreed. "You shouldn't be riding out at midday. It's a recipe for heatstroke."

He shrugged. "I didn't really have a lot of choice. I had to stay and chat to the Nana and he said that he intended to remain in Cawnpore and camp beside his men. Showing the flag and all that sort of stuff. Can you get Simkin to make sure that it's all sorted out? I don't want complaints that he pitched his tent on Company property without a permit or any such nonsense. I did offer to pay for forage and provisions for his men but he wouldn't hear of it. Good man!"

And, with a smile on his face and a spring in his step, despite the heat, Hillersdon passed on to his own office and left me to my thoughts. The first of which was that it I was more likely to see a phoenix sat on my desk than to find Simkin in his office and as far the Nana's camping arrangements were concerned, I had best ensure that the proper formalities were observed myself.

It is remarkable how much paperwork a tent can generate—at least when it is accompanied by an elephant and three hundred troops. The job took me most of the day and involved another expedition to the Treasury, though I took care to wait until the worst of the heat had passed before I undertook that.

The Treasury was firmly situated in the Civil Station, though it was quite close to the army's magazine which, for reasons lost in time, was situated four miles or so from the military cantonment. The Nana had drawn up his army a mile or so back from the river, where there was open space in which his soldiers were bivouacked. The men were obviously expected to sleep on the ground under the stars but Nana Sahib himself had an elaborate pavilion erected in the centre of his force, with guards on piquet duty and his elephant resting nearby under the supervision of its mahout.

The whole arrangement, with muskets neatly stacked by each group of sepoys, the horses of the cavalry tethered in rows and the guns ready on their limbers all gave the impression of an army that meant business. But whether they were ready to protect us from our own forces or to aid in an Indian rebellion against European rule, I could not guess. I suspected that at that point, the Nana was not sure himself. I decided, though, that it would be best to ride out to Saturday House the next day and see what intelligence I could gather.

THE EXCITEMENT AND bustle that had permeated Saturday House when I was last there had vanished with the Nana and his troops. As had always been the case until the last few weeks, I was able to enter with only the most cursory of glances from a sentry slumped into a shady corner. Inside the palace, I made my way to Mungo's rooms, passing servants idly pushing brooms along passages that would usually be swept clean early in the morning.

When I arrived at his apartment, I found Mungo no stranger to the general air of idleness. As I entered (doors were never locked in Saturday House) Mungo was pulling on a tunic, his hair rumpled and his eyes still swollen from sleep. When he saw it was me, he simply pulled off the tunic and lay back on the bed, motioning me to join him.

"Lazy bones!" I chided, though I was taking off my own shirt as I spoke. "Do you have no duties to be about?"

He reached for me and pulled me to him. "Nana Sahib is away and we can play all day," he said. And then his mouth was busy with other things than words and we spoke no more.

Much later, as I held him in my arms and stroked his hair, I reminded myself that I was there to gather such intelligence as I could as to the Nana's intentions. I asked how long the Nana was expected to be away.

Mungo did not want to speak of it, which I felt ominous in itself, so I persisted and he grumpily told me that the Nana intended to stay with the army in Cawnpore.

"But what does he intend to do there?"

"It's his army." Mungo rolled away from me and started to pull on his tunic. "You understand so much about India that sometimes I forget that you do not belong here."

He was standing by now, pulling on trousers under the tunic, busying himself with tying knots and searching for his shoes—anything to avoid meeting my eye.

"Mungo, what have I said wrong?"

Now he turned to me and I saw the beginning of tears. "You ask why he is in Cawnpore. His father was a great man who ruled over an area of hundreds of miles, tens of thousands marched under his banner and millions acknowledged him as their lord. Nana Sahib has lost all this. You will not accord him his titles. You do not fire your guns in salute. His army is a few hundred men and his rule extends only over this palace. And now you need him, he is here for you and his army marches to Cawnpore, where your army is failing. And he rides with it upon his elephant for now he is as his father once was, leading an army in his own country. It is his country, you see John. And you ask, 'What does he intend to do there?' Is it not fairer to ask what the British intend to do, thousands of miles from their homes, their soldiers no longer true, hiding in their bungalows. It is not truly your country, John. It belongs to people like Nana Sahib."

I was still sat on the bed and I felt my head fall into my hands. "Then Nana Sahib will turn on the British and take the country."

"No." Mungo shook his head urgently, trying, I think, to convince himself as much as me. "The Nana will stand by the British and you will see that he is a good friend and when the rains come and all is quiet again, you will reward him for his loyalty."

I said nothing. Perhaps when Dalhousie had been Governor-General, this might have happened. But under Canning? The man who so adamantly refused to recognise the Nana's titles that letters that were signed with them were returned unread? The man who had annexed Oudh? All things, of course, were possible—but if I were Nana Sahib, I would not pin my hopes on Canning.

I think Mungo saw my doubts about Canning, just as I saw his about the Nana but we chose to pretend that all was well. And, indeed, for all we knew, the crisis might pass. The Nana could still preserve the European community in Cawnpore. He had the respect of the local people and troops at his command to keep order if there were to be unrest. Wheeler was an old India hand and could be counted on to do everything he could to calm the talk of mutiny and, meanwhile, European troops were promised from Lucknow. The rains could start in a month. Things only had to stay quiet until then.

That afternoon we explored the palace as we had the day that I had met him. We walked along the corridor of clocks and stood hand-in-hand to watch the lion pacing in his cage. We cooled ourselves in the waters of the fountains and our eyes were soothed by the green of the lawns.

That night we made love again, slowly, savouring each moment. It was as if we knew that something evil was coming but that we wanted to cherish what we had while we still could.

But we woke the next dawn to another day of calm. Mungo took me to the audience chamber where I had first met Nana Sahib. The door was open and there was no guard. He sat on the Nana's mat and told me he was ruler now and I bowed and called him 'Your Highness' and 'Great Majesty' and he laughed and then was suddenly pensive. "If only the British would do him honour and call him 'Your Highness'. It's all he wants."

I said I would ride back to Cawnpore and talk to Hillersdon and see if anything could be done that might ease relations. Mungo, sitting in the Nana's place seemed to weigh my words as if he really was a ruler, considering matters of high state and diplomacy and then, in a more than usually thoughtful tone, he said, "You should stay here. You can do nothing at Cawnpore now. Mr Hillersdon is a good man but he does not have the power to change things. I don't know that any of us can change things now." Then, with a flash of his old mischief, he was on his feet and almost running to the door.

I followed as fast as I could, hampered by the sword on the sowar's uniform I now wore more or less as a matter of course around the palace. ("It's safer," Mungo had said. "People will not challenge an officer.") Mungo, in his tunic and loose trousers, had almost vanished down the corridor before I was out of the door and he led me an undignified chase through the palace for most of the afternoon.

I thought I knew the place by now but it was vast, with separate quarters for different families related to the Nana by ties of blood or state and for the garrison and the servants. There were cellars storing food and cellars filled with bottles of wine (for the Nana's tastes had grown cosmopolitan over the years he had entertained the English). There were cellars with forage for the beasts of the place and one cellar Mungo hurried me through, muttering angrily that he had not intended to bring me there and where I saw pikes and muskets stacked neatly in racks against the walls. There were no attics but stairs led directly to the roof, marked off with walls protecting the ladies of the harem who might seek to take the air up there, while we wandered safely out of sight of them, looking across the parapets at the dusty countryside between Bithur and Cawnpore.

Mungo let me catch up with him there and we held each other as we looked out along the road.

"I have to go back," I said.

"I know." He slipped his hands beneath my clothing and held me to him. "Stay tonight," he said, "and then go if you must. But,"—and here he turned his face to mine and I saw real distress in his eyes—"if all you fear comes to pass, then come back here to Saturday House and I will protect you."

I returned his embrace. How could he protect me? He was little more than a boy. But I looked across the parapet and saw an alien country. Somewhere below the horizon was Cawnpore, where the European community relied for their protection on one hundred white troops and tried to convince themselves that this made them safe. As I looked down at Mungo's face, he gave me a smile of reassurance.

This was his country. He would protect me.

※

I RETURNED TO Cawnpore on the Monday, still no wiser as to what the Nana's plans really were. At the Collectorate, Hillersdon was in the best of humours. Nana Sahib's men had firmly established themselves at the Treasury and their presence did seem to be calming the locals.

I took myself to my office and settled to work as best I could. There was plenty to do. The end of the week would be Good Friday and work in the office would stop while the Europeans took themselves to church for a day of prayer and fasting.

That evening I did not return directly to my bungalow but, instead, called in on the Club. I was not a regular visitor for I never felt truly comfortable with the gentlemen there. Still I took care to call in often enough that neither my presence nor absence caused comment. This evening I wanted to judge for myself the atmosphere in the European community.

All seemed much as it had been on my last visit a couple of weeks earlier. The waiters moved quietly from table to table pouring more brandies than might have been expected in quieter times and the newspapers were tattered from the number of people reading them but there was no sign of panic. Indeed, the promise of Easter seemed to be calming nerves. The stately rhythm of the ecclesiastical year seems to promise that the present crisis would pass. The story of the Resurrection and Christ's triumph over death reassured believers (and none would admit to doubting) that the Lord would see them safely through their present travails.

So the days to Easter passed with no further excitement and, on Good Friday, I joined the faithful in St John's Church to repent my sins. I listened to the murmured prayers of the men and women around me and wished that I could share their faith and their belief but I could not and I left the service still weighed down by the guilt of all that had happened in Borneo. Every Good Friday since I had stood by and watched my friend destroy his enemies, I had repented my sin, that I had not stopped him. Yet I did not believe that God had forgiven me.

My spirits were lifted the next day when I dined again with Hillersdon. It was a quiet evening with Charles treating me almost as one of the family. Lydia suffered with the heat, given her condition, but was as bright and cheerful as could be expected and we parted with best wishes for Easter Day.

The service on Sunday went well. The bright red of the officers' uniforms enlivened the place and their voices covered for any weakness on the part of the choir. All the European families had turned out to celebrate and decorated eggs were handed to the children as they left the church. Listening to their laughter and seeing their mothers in their Easter bonnets, it was easy, for a moment, to imagine ourselves back in England and the air of menace that had filled every waking moment for so long seemed temporarily lifted.

The promise of redemption was short-lived, however. I woke on Easter Monday to find breakfast late and my khanasaman berating the boys in the kitchen. When the shouts began to be interspersed with the sound of breaking crockery, I abandoned protocol and went into the kitchen myself to find out the cause of the trouble.

One of the boys was on his knees gathering up pieces of a broken plate while the khanasaman was standing over another with his hand raised to strike him.

"What the devil is going on?" I looked about for the cook. "And where is Cook?"

The boys scurried to hide themselves in corners while the khanasaman explained to me that the cook was nowhere to be found. "He is a stupid man and is frightened by stories."

"What stories?"

No stories in particular, the khanasaman assured me. Just idle chitchat. He himself had heard nothing.

By now, I was becoming alarmed. Whatever had happened had been serious enough for my cook to flee. The khanasaman clearly knew what was going on and equally clearly had no intention of telling me. I decided to get directly to the office to find out the news and to breakfast later at the Club.

Instead of the normal morning calm of the office, I found almost every desk occupied but there was no sign of any work being done. I was accosted on all sides by staff—both Europeans and babus—who demanded to know the latest news. Unable to tell them anything, I made for Hillersdon's office, trying to look like a man who knew what was going on.

I was not surprised to find the babus so agitated, for they were prone to temperamental behaviour, but the excitability of the Europeans was a shock. Even men like Simkin would usually maintain some impression of *sang froid*, especially in front of the natives. The full extent of the panic only became obvious, though, when I entered Charles's office to find him rigid at his chair, pale as death under his tan, staring at the desk in front of him. When he heard me enter, he raised his eyes and gestured for me to sit.

"I fear the worst, John," he said.

"What on earth has happened?"

"Last night some damn fool subaltern was going home drunk. He was challenged by a patrol of native infantry. They were right to challenge him, there's no doubt about that. Instead of identifying himself, the damn fool took out his pistol and shot one of them." He passed a hand over his face. "You know, while you were away, Wheeler ordered that the guns should not be fired on the Queen's birthday in case the sound of the salute should alarm the native troops and make them think we were attacking them. And now some drunken lieutenant shoots a sepoy who is simply doing his job. It defies belief."

I sat silent, as horrified by his news as he was. We were sitting in a powder magazine and some young fool had dropped a lighted match.

"I'm taking Lydia and the children to the Entrenchment. I'm leaving you in charge here. I suggest that you tell all the men with families to go to their homes and get their women and children safe. Anyone else who has revolvers should bring them to the office. But tell everyone to be discreet. I don't want the natives to see us running around with guns."

He left and most of the men in the office left with him. A few of us bachelors remained behind with a handful of handguns to defend our files if insurrection were to break out. But the day passed in an awful stillness and in the evening I found myself, somewhat to my surprise, still alive.

I had heard no firing. The streets, when I ventured out, were quiet. Even so, I resolved to spend that night in the Entrenchment. I made a quick visit to my house to take a bath and eat an early supper, and then set off to Wheeler's earthworks. I decided not to ride, for I reasoned that there would be far too many horses there already and no provision for stabling. Instead, I walked the mile or so to where, on the edge of the great parade ground just to the East of the military lines, a crumbling embankment marked out the boundaries of our refuge.

I entered through a gap in the earthworks where a store-room had been adapted to make some sort of gatehouse. Some men of the 84th foot were standing around, almost lost in the mass of civilians who thronged around the entrance. It took me several minutes to get through. When, at last, I did, the place seemed scarcely less crowded than the gateway. The earthworks had been thrown up to enclose two long barrack blocks but these were almost entirely obscured from view by the tents and shelters erected haphazardly in the open ground around them. These were not the neat rows of army-issue tents that one might expect in a military establishment, but a shanty-town of canvas with which the civilian families sheltering under the army's protection sought to ensure themselves a modicum of privacy and shelter from the cruelty of the sun.

It was immediately apparent that the Europeans gathered in these shelters were those who lacked position or patronage and I made my way as best I could through their gypsy encampment until I reached the more Northerly of the two barrack blocks which, unlike the other, had a roof of tile rather than of thatch. Covered verandas ran along both sides of the building and the interior was broken up into a number of rooms which, between them, would probably have housed a company of a hundred men when they were in regular military use. Now at least twice that number were packed inside while as many again clustered onto the verandas which at least offered shelter from the sun and, being arcaded, some sort of privacy.

I found the Hillersdons sharing a room with the Greenways and two other couples whom I knew only vaguely. One of them had two children around the age of the Hillersdons' children and they were playing together rather lacklustrely in the heat. I stooped to pat their heads and congratulate Lydia on their good behaviour, for all around I could hear other children crying and whining and hers were really making the best they could of their situation.

Lydia rewarded me with a tired smile but Charles beamed his approval and, having established that I intended to spend the night in their encampment, he insisted that I find a space in the room with them. There was a certain amount of muttering from one of the other couples but the Greenways supported the Hillersdons and soon I was settling down on the floor.

I cannot say I slept well. There were no punkahs to stir the air and the windows were open with no wetted screens to cool it. All around were the sounds of men and women in uneasy sleep and the cries of children. After my years in Borneo, I did not suffer from lying on the packed earth floor but very few people had even camp beds and, for civilians used to the luxury of mattresses and feather pillows, the unwelcome novelty of their situation made repose difficult.

When Charles and I woke the next morning, we were in no fit state to go directly to the office. Fortunately, Hillersdon had arranged for his family to move temporarily into a new bungalow quite close to the barracks and he shepherded me with them to make myself presentable in his new home.

I must confess I felt guilty as I followed Charles to where I knew I would find a clean bath and all the other necessities of modern life. All around us less fortunate families were beginning to form queues for the two privies that served the barrack block and mothers were squatting on the ground trying to clean their children with cloths dampened from jugs of water.

Charles caught the direction of my gaze and misunderstood the look of concern on my face.

"Don't worry, John. There's plenty of water. We have a well over there." He gestured toward the space between the barracks but I couldn't see a well for the crowd and the tents that seemed even more closely packed now than when I arrived.

"Is there just the one well?"

"It's enough. It's never failed us yet."

I looked again at the mass of people who apparently relied for all their water on one well that stood in the open. I was no soldier but even I could see the danger inherent in this situation. If there were to be a mutiny, the Entrenchment would provide shelter from the first blast of the storm but, with no proper fortification and only that one exposed source of water, it could not sustain us against any prolonged attack.

I said nothing to Hillersdon of my fears. What good, I reasoned, could it possibly do? And by noon I was beginning to think myself a fool to have been so concerned for, at last, we received our promised reinforcements.

One hundred men of the 84th Foot and fifteen of the Madras Fusiliers arrived in a convoy of bullock carts. Tired and dusty as they were from the road, they dismounted on the edge of the town and marched into camp. Hillersdon closed the office for an hour to allow everyone to join the crowds cheering as they marched by. The babus made way for me so that I might stand near the front and I must admit to drawing comfort from the sight of those homely English faces under their uniform hats. They marched with a swagger that promised a restoration of the rightful order and we all convinced ourselves we had been saved. Small as the contingent was, the look on the faces of the native troops as they, too, watched the Europeans march into camp showed how much they felt the situation had shifted to their disadvantage.

Imagine, then, our shock as news came that General Wheeler had ordered that fifty of these men should be sent on immediately to Lucknow, where there were rumours that the European community faced dangers similar to our own. Simkin, on hearing that the fifty were already on the road, referred to General Wheeler as "a bloody idiot" in tones that were clearly distinguishable in the general office, where some of the babus started actually wailing. Hillersdon called me into his office and asked me to do what I could to calm their fears.

"After all," he said, "it is surely the strongest possible evidence of General Wheeler's confidence in the situation that he should sacrifice our defensive forces here to ease the concerns of our colleagues in Oudh."

I tried to persuade myself that he was right and I perhaps half convinced at least some of the babus. That evening, though, Hillersdon and his family again sought the shelter of the Entrenchment and I was not ashamed to join them. The crowding was, if anything, greater than that of the previous evening and there was a pervasive stench of unwashed bodies and, I fear, worse, as the privies were inadequate and the number of children in the encampment meant that small bowels were forced on occasion to empty themselves wherever was convenient. Yet things had come to such a pass that the squalor and discomfort seemed preferable to a night isolated in my own home.

I returned to my office the next day feeling fatigued and—despite again enjoying the hospitality of the Hillersdons in order to bathe—dirty.

The place was quiet. The European staff were all at their desks, though most looked tired and strained and I doubted that many were in any fit state to do anything useful. In any case, our paperwork relied on the efforts of the clerks and more than half of the babus had stayed away.

Like the others, I found it impossible to settle to any real work and sat in my office irritably moving papers around my desk. When one of the few babus there knocked at my door to tell me that there was a native soldier who claimed to have an urgent and personal message for me, I nearly told him to go to hell. Native soldiers seemed to me to be at the root of all our present troubles and I could think of none who had any proper business with me. Just in time, though, I calmed myself. I would not allow myself to be caught up in the hysteria that saw every native trooper as a threat. I would be as civil to this visitor as to any other.

My clerk returned a few minutes later and ushered in, not one of the Company's native troops, but an impeccably turned-out sowar of the Nana's force.

He bowed, his hands together in respect, and then held out a letter, heavily sealed with wax.

"I am instructed, sahib, to bring you this letter and to place it in your hand only."

I took it and he immediately bowed again and made to leave.

"Are you not to wait for a reply."

"No, sahib. I am to give you this letter and then leave."

"Well," I reached into my pocket for some coins and pulled out a rupee coin, "you should at least be rewarded for your effort."

The soldier shook his head. "I seek no reward, sahib. I have brought this message to pay an obligation to the sender. My obligation is discharged by its safe receipt and I require no other reward."

And with a smart salute he was gone.

Intrigued, I broke the seal. Inside was a short letter written in Devanagari script and, as I translated it, the soldier's behaviour was explained.

> *My beloved friend*
>
> *I send this message by the hand of one I trust. He has ties of blood and obligation. Even so, it is dangerous to write. But I have to send this message to you.*
>
> *It is dangerous for you to stay any longer in Cawnpore. I beg you, as you love me, come directly to Bithur. I beg of you that you do not tell your friends where you are going or why. You cannot save them and you will only put yourself and me in danger.*
>
> *I trust you, my beloved. And I wait for you here.*
>
> *M*

It was not yet noon but the day was too hot to contemplate riding to Bithur until closer to the evening and then there was every chance that night would find me still on the road. With the country simmering on the edge of anarchy, I was unwilling to travel after dark. Yet the message suggested an immediate danger.

What danger could Mungo know of? Was the Nana planning treachery? There was no evidence of this. His troops, I knew, remained camped out at the Treasury and, though there had been stories from some of the richer locals that the Nana's men had threatened them or demanded money, there was no evidence that this went beyond the misbehaviour of some individual soldiers. I could not even be sure that the stories were true.

Should I take the letter to Hillersdon? But what could he do if I did? It would simply be one more rumour in a town full of rumours. Anyway, Hillersdon and his family would sleep in the encampment again that night and that would be as safe as anywhere.

Perhaps Mungo's fears, like so many peoples', were simply based on rumour and there was no imminent danger? Yet, in writing to me, he had taken a real risk. No one of note knew of our relationship and Mungo was anxious to keep it a secret. Yet he had taken the risk of sending a message to me. Could I ignore his warning? And, if I did, would he trust me again?

There was nothing for it. I would have to ride out to Bithur.

I LEFT THE Collectorate soon after four. The afternoon was still blisteringly hot, but I did not want to risk delaying further. I had told Hillersdon that I had heard rumours that the European community might be attacked but that I needed to investigate further before I could give him any details and I intended to do so immediately. He took me at my word. He did not ask me where I had heard the rumours for he understood that I would not be specific. He shook my hand as I left and I think he suspected that I would not return.

I called in at my bungalow to collect the bundle in which I stored my sowar's uniform, hidden with some souvenirs of my time in Borneo and my commonplace book. I sensed that I would want to have a record of the days ahead of me. I warned the khanasaman that I might be away for a while and that he was to take whatever measures he deemed necessary to protect the premises in my absence.

I had two horses by then, in the small stables behind my bungalow. One was an Indian pony, quite large enough to carry me and tough and wiry. The other, a bay hunter. I had named him Kuching, in remembrance of my time with James and, though he was less suited to hard riding in the Indian climate, he was a thing of beauty and admired by both Europeans and natives alike. In the end, I chose to ride Kuching, arguing that he was faster and stronger.

Then I was off, heading North. I paused in the shelter of some neem trees to pull off my European clothes. I stood naked, staining my face and hands with walnut juice, working with the aid of a hand mirror bundled in with the clothes. Then I pulled on my uniform and stepped from the trees a soldier in the Nana's army.

I wasted no more time, proceeding alternately at canter and trot until my poor horse, eyes wild with the heat, finally came in sight of Saturday House. Only then did I feel safe to rein in, covering the last half mile at an easy walk that gave Kuching a chance to recover.

At the gate the guard stopped me. I worried for a moment that my hunter might be leading him to suspect that I was not the native I was pretending to be, though I knew that many of the sowars would ride a European horse if they could get one, as the animals made a brave show. To my relief, the sentry had stopped me, not to challenge my entry, but to ask what news there was from Cawnpore.

"Has the mutiny started yet?"

This was the first I knew that a mutiny was planned and that the plans were apparently common knowledge at Bithur, but I did my best not to let this shock show.

"There was no mutiny when I left," I said, "but it cannot be long now."

The sentry grinned broadly. "It must be soon," he agreed and waved me past him.

I left Kuching at the stables, where the Nana's grooms cared for all the animals of the household, and made my way directly to Mungo's quarters. The place was almost as deserted as it had been before, yet where my last visit had revealed ill-disciplined idleness, now the few servants I saw in the corridors moved sharply about their business. The Nana's apartments were guarded by sentries who stood smartly to attention and saluted as I passed. Even Mungo seemed infected by this new alertness, though in his case the tension visible in his lithe body as soon as I entered his room was more about his concern for me than the general situation.

"Thank the gods you are safe," he said, pulling me to him and hugging me until I thought I would not be able to breathe. "I think you escaped just in time."

"So a mutiny is planned and the Nana is involved?"

Mungo turned away from me, as if ashamed. "There will be a mutiny. It should start today. The Nana knows of it. Everyone knows of it. That does not mean that he has planned it or that it is of his doing."

"I should warn them."

Mungo shrugged. "And tell them what? That their army is on the verge of mutiny? I think, John, that they probably know that already."

"But people here know more than that."

"They know that the mutiny will start today. It has probably already started. There is nothing you can do about it now."

I sat on the bed with my head in my hands. If Mungo was telling the truth, what could I do?

He sat beside me holding me to him.

"I need to know what is happening."

"If there's news, it will arrive at the garrison first. We can go there and wait."

Mungo started off through the maze of passages. Fast as he

moved, I found myself passing him and striding ahead, for so many hours had we spent exploring the place together that I was now almost as familiar with it as he was and I was desperate to learn the latest intelligence.

Although from the outside Saturday House appeared one single building, inside the warren of passageways and courtyards created separate areas for the different elements of the Nana's enormous household. So it was that the garrison was quartered in dormitories that led onto the same open space where a statue with six heads held a positive arsenal of weapons—a spear, a bow, a sword and half a dozen more—in an improbable number of arms. I knew by now that this was Murugan. Mungo had pointed him out to me all those months ago when he had first been teaching me about the different deities—or (as I had come to learn) the different aspects of deity. Then the statue had been unadorned but now it was hung about with garlands of flowers and, alarmingly, lotus leaves like those that had been distributed among the native troops in Cawnpore. If I had had any doubts as to the seriousness of the situation before, the sight of all these offerings to the god of war made it all too clear that the Nana's soldiers were convinced they were about to go into battle.

The courtyard was arcaded but the centre was open to the air and, even at evening, the place was light and pleasant. We were obviously not the only people waiting there for news. When we arrived there were already knots of men gathering, talking and gesticulating excitedly together. As we waited, more people entered from the corridors that led from the rest of the palace. A few off-duty soldiers strutted about, enjoying the admiring glances of the civilians. One came over to me and asked for the latest news. For a moment I nearly panicked, convinced he would recognise me for an imposter. I would be torn apart and Mungo, who was standing beside me, would be compromised. But I kept my composure and told him that all had been quiet when I left, but that we expected to hear more shortly and he went his way satisfied.

We had been there for an hour and torches had been lit to illuminate the courtyard when there was the sound of shouting in the distance and word spread through the crowd that Nana Sahib was returning to Saturday House.

Now everyone was thrusting their way back through the halls and passageways, pressing toward the main entrance of the Palace. I started to try to push through the crowd, but Mungo plucked at my sleeve. "Don't waste your time. You'll never get through that way. Follow me!"

He darted off and I realised that there were secrets of the palace's geography that I had yet to learn. We darted down corridors of bare stone, up narrow staircases, across a roof, down a flight of wooden steps and finally emerged through a postern gate just in time to see the Nana's entourage arrive.

Indian elephants are quite small and not nearly such splendid beasts as they are usually depicted in pictures. Even so, the Nana, seated atop his State Elephant, was a commanding presence. The elephant towered over the crimson uniformed figures of his escort. From the howdah, the Nana waved regally at the few privileged courtiers who had been allowed to greet him at the door and then dismounted to be escorted by half a dozen of his men who marched beside him, swords drawn and held smartly at attention.

He vanished into the Palace without a word.

"Is there then to be no news at all?" I asked Mungo.

He shook his head, in disappointment, I think, rather than negation, and turned to go back into Saturday House. At that moment though, a havildar of the guard came to the entrance and, raising his voice addressed the courtiers who had made up the welcoming party.

"Nana Sahib, the Peshwa Seereek Dhoondoo Punth, desires that his loyal subjects should know and take cogniscence of the rebellion of soldiers of the 3rd Oudh Native Artillery, who have left the employ of the British."

That was all, though the cheers of the courtiers suggested

that they, at least, thought this an announcement of great moment. For Mungo and me, though, analysing every word of that brief statement back in his apartment, we were little wiser than before. I noted that Nana Sahib had said nothing himself and that he was here in Bithur, far from any mutiny. Mungo, too, was in no doubt what this meant. "Nana Sahib has not yet committed himself to the rebel cause. If the British stand firm, he may yet support them." On the other hand, the use of the title of Peshwa and his formal names, although not threatening in themselves, was sufficiently unusual to suggest that the Nana was at least aware of the possibilities that a mutiny might offer for him to consolidate his own position.

I slept restlessly that night and by the next morning I had almost persuaded myself to return to Cawnpore, but Mungo insisted that I wait until he had more news. "Stay here and eat. I will see what I can discover and then I will return and we can plan what you should do."

He kissed me and vanished out of the door. I lay on the bed, my mind running through all the possibilities over and over again. Yet however much I worried at them, every alternative seemed fraught with peril. An any case, whatever I did or did not do, it seemed it was now too late to avert mutiny.

I was still lying there when Mungo returned. His smile suggested he had good news but his first concern was that I had not eaten and he refused to tell me anything until I had at least nibbled at some of the fruit that he offered me.

"There has been no bloodshed. The men of the Artillery ran away from their officers. People say they crossed the Ganges into Oudh. That is all that has happened. Nana Sahib is returning to Cawnpore today. I think that which you feared may yet be averted."

Perhaps it would be alright. Perhaps the mutineers would drift away in the night and the 150 British troops would be left guarding an empty cantonment until this whole ghastly mess was over and some kind of normality was restored.

I looked up at Mungo who stood, his face unwontedly serious. Beyond the door, I could hear a sweeper cleaning the passage. A smell of incense wafted in the high window. This, I realised, was normality in India. European rule was a one hundred year old experiment that seemed now to be coming to an end. Could 150 troops really make any difference when we faced an entire nation who saw us as alien and who now might simply wish us gone?

"What should I do, Mungo?"

"Stay here. Rest." He paused a moment, and then added, "Pray to your God."

I took his advice as to staying and resting. I even tried prayer, but the words wouldn't come.

In the afternoon, I wandered the palace until I found a shrine to Ganesh. The elephant headed god was my favourite. He was a popular choice, bringing luck, and his shrine was heaped with offerings. I had begged a fistful of incense sticks from Mungo and now I lit them all, the acrid smoke rising from the courtyard to the heavens above. Somehow I felt that Ganesh might favour me with good fortune even while the God of my childhood turned his face from me.

Thursday passed and on Friday I woke to the prospect of another long, hot day. Mungo was nervous of my wandering alone about Saturday House. The tension that had pervaded life in Cawnpore for so many months was beginning to make itself felt in Bithur too, though here there was more a sense of anticipatory excitement, rather than dread. Still, Mungo felt that it would be safer for me to stay in his room while he found out the latest news.

Mungo had left me with a book about the history of the Peshwas and I found myself caught up in reading the story of the power that Nana Sahib's adoptive family had held before they were overthrown by the British. Immersed in the tale, I was able to forget my troubles for a while.

Then Mungo returned and my troubles with him.

chapter 5

THE MUTINY HAD started in the night, while we slept. The 2nd Native Cavalry had risen, firing their barracks and riding to the Native Infantry lines to call on their comrades to join them in revolt. In the confusion, with the weeks of fear and suspicion working on their minds, the British had fired indiscriminately on the native troops, driving any who had remained loyal to join their fellows in mutiny.

"The Nana opened the Treasury to them."

I looked up at him from where I sat cross-legged in native fashion. "Then he has made his choice."

"Your friends are in their fort." He meant the Entrenchment. I knew the Indians called it a fort. It was mockery: the Entrenchment was no fort and would never survive attack.

"There has been some looting. A few—very few, I think—have been killed. But the rebels say they will march to Delhi to join the Emperor."

I noticed he said 'Emperor'. So the King of Delhi was already seen once again as the Mogul Emperor his ancestors had been. This did not bode well for the Company.

Mungo was still talking, trying to reassure me. "If they march to Delhi, your friends will be left safe. I do not think you need to worry."

The native troops had mutinied, the Nana had thrown his lot in with them and the people were clearly ready to join a general uprising but, according to Mungo, I had no need to worry.

I tried to smile, but I felt my lips twisted with bitterness.

Mungo reached down to embrace me and I felt his tears falling in my cheeks.

"I am sorry, my love." His hold on me tightened. "Just stay here and I will look after you."

Now I found it easier to smile. Here was my Mungo—little more than a boy—promising me his protection. How could I not smile?

The wonder of our situation was that Mungo was, indeed, well placed to preserve me from the fate of those Europeans who had been caught out of the Entrenchment when the soldiers mutinied. There had already been murders. As the day went by and word came back to Bithur of events in Cawnpore, Mungo brought news of not only Europeans but the half-caste babus being killed wherever they were found.

Businesses which had supplied the European community were looted and the houses of rich Indians who had become too close to the British were broken into and robbed. But most people had slept for safety in the Entrenchment or fled there as soon as the mutiny broke out and there, it seemed, they remained unmolested.

I thought of the heat and the stench that I had experienced in my nights there and tried not to dwell on how things must be under the blazing noon sun. Poor Lydia, so close to her confinement and forced to rest on the hard packed ground, with no relief from the heat. And the children! Charles must be distraught.

I stayed in Mungo's apartments all day and I could not help but compare my situation with that of Charles and his family. I was sheltered from the sun, the marble floor cool to my naked feet, even at midday. Ewers of clear water were there for the asking and Mungo insisted on bringing constant delicacies for me to enjoy.

Still, I told myself, soon the rebels would be on their way to Delhi. The Europeans would return to their homes. All would be well. All had to be well.

By nightfall, I had convinced myself of the truth of this. At least, I had convinced myself enough to be able to sleep. I'm not sure that I ever really believed it.

※

THE MORNING BROUGHT confirmation of all my worst fears. I woke from an uneasy sleep to find Mungo already dressed. As soon as he saw me stir, he was on his feet, his face grim.

"Nana Sahib is returning to Cawnpore."

At first, I did not understand. The rebels were marching to Delhi. If the Nana was returning to Cawnpore, had he decided at last to abandon them and throw in his lot with the British?

I don't remember what I said. I must have asked some sort of question that made Mungo realise my mistake. He spoke gently, trying to ease the blow.

"He is leading the rebels back. He intends to use them as his own army, to take back the power of the Peshwas."

Gentle as he was, there could not really have been any doubting the meaning of his words, yet I lay there in his bed puzzling over them.

"Back to here?"

"Back to Cawnpore."

"But what can Nana Sahib have to do in Cawnpore?"

The anguish on Mungo's face should have told me all. I should have faced the truth on my own but I had to make him complicit. I had to make him spell out the detail of his master's treachery.

"They intend to drive the British from Cawnpore."

Still I pretended to myself that we were not utterly betrayed. "The British will be happy enough to leave. Men have been trying to get their families out for months but the countryside has been too dangerous. With the Nana Sahib giving safe passage, they'll be off like a shot and glad to see the last of the place."

"John…" There were tears welling in his eyes. "There will be no safe passage. They will attack the fort. They intend to destroy the British."

At the sight of his tears, for the first time I allowed myself to try to comprehend the horror that awaited the people I knew.

"Damn it, Mungo. There's women and children in there."

He said nothing, and his silence, more than his words, forced me to accept that this was really happening. Nana Sahib, at the head of his own troops and our disaffected regiments was to lay siege to the miserable earthworks that demarcated the refuge of every European man, woman and child left living in Cawnpore.

"I should go to them."

Mungo shook his head gently, like a mother comforting a fractious child. "It would serve no purpose."

""But I should go there. These are my friends."

Still Mungo shook his head. "Are they truly your friends? Mr Hillersdon—yes, I think he is a friend to you. But the others? If they are truly your friends, then why, now, are you here with me? Here you eat with me, enjoying the food of our people." He managed a wan smile. "You even manage to eat your rice with hardly any lost on the floor. Why are you not eating with the Europeans, if they are your friends?"

I thought of the dinner parties I had suffered through. The frightful women I would be sat between; the endless, pointless prattling about London fashion, London Society, and London theatres. I had never lived in London and I would sit almost silent, wondering what I was doing there. Mungo had scored a fair point.

"And you speak of Mr Hillersdon often and with affection. But of whom else do you speak?"

I closed my eyes and saw Simkin leering at me with his suggestion that we spend an evening with the Anglo-Indian women he had offered me. I saw the sun-reddened faces of the men at the Club, peering out from behind their London papers, complaining that their servants had been slow to come at their call, or had not checked the girth strap on their mount (God forbid that they should check it themselves), or had had the temerity to fall ill. Not everyone was like that, of course. General Wheeler was a decent man, but he was of a different generation and a different class and, though I admired him, he was not a friend. And the engineers up to plan the new railway were good sorts, but they tended to keep to themselves, there being enough of them to form their own society.

"You speak our language, you know our gods. I know you prayed to Ganesh, the other day. I saw the bundle of joss sticks and recognised the knot."

I shook my head but the gesture lacked conviction. Mungo smiled; a sad smile that made him look suddenly older. He pulled me toward him. "Here is where you belong, John. Here with me."

He held me. I felt his heart beating in his chest and I felt not aroused, but safe. He was right. I was where I belonged.

FOR THE NEXT day or two, I was able to convince myself that I should stay in Bithur with Mungo. However, by Sunday news was filtering back to Bithur of what the Europeans in Cawnpore were undergoing. Nana Sahib had decided not to sit and starve them out of their refuge but, rather, to destroy the Entrenchment and all within it. The mutineers had taken with them some of their artillery and, added to the Nana's own small field guns, he now had the firepower to bombard Wheeler's position day and night.

I thought of Hillersdon. I remembered Lydia, always trying to keep cheerful in the terrible heat of the barrack block and of the children. How were they coping, sharing that one small room with four or five other families, with no respite from the noise and the dust? How were they explaining the cannonade to the children? Did the barracks offer any shelter from the artillery or were they exposed to the enemy's fire?

I fretted all afternoon, desperate for information. By nightfall I could not sleep.

"I shouldn't be here, Mungo."

"We've talked of this. In any case, Wheeler's fort is surrounded. You could not enter even if you wished, and if you entered you would surely not leave alive."

"I need to know. I have to know if they are alive or dead. I have to see if there is anything that I can do to help them."

"There is nothing."

He spoke so calmly. I couldn't contain my own emotion any longer.

"I have to know! I have to go there. I have to know!"

I did not realise that I was shouting in English until I saw Mungo's calm expression give way to alarm. He wrapped his arms tightly round me. "Hush! People will hear. Calm yourself."

He tried to kiss me, but I pushed him away. I was quieter now, for the foolishness of my outburst was apparent even in my excited state. Even as I tried to calm myself, though, I was still determined on leaving.

"John! Don't be a fool. You can do nothing now but tomorrow I will see if there is anything I can do."

As suddenly as it had started, my outburst finished. I found myself weeping, clinging to Mungo for comfort.

"Can you really help me?"

He stroked my hair. "Yes," he said. "Yes, I think I can."

❋

MUNGO'S PLAN, WHEN he revealed it the next morning, was as simple as it was audacious. I was to dress in my sowar's uniform and simply ride out to the Entrenchment and see it for myself.

"You must be careful. If anyone challenges you, tell them that you have a message for Rao Sahib. He is not there; he is still here in Bithur. If anyone tells you this, say that you were told he was at Cawnpore but that if he is not, then you must ride immediately to Bithur. I do not think anyone will be sure where Rao Sahib is, though. So you may ride wherever you wish, to deliver this message." He handed me a parchment, folded, addressed and sealed with an impressive amount of red wax. "See. You even have the message."

I smiled, despite myself. "What does it say?"

"It asks him to dine with me tomorrow night. In the unlikely event that it is ever delivered, I will have to order in something exceptional." He laughed. It was a feeble jest but I joined his laughter. It was the first time I had laughed in too long.

Within the hour I was swaggering to the stables in my uniform. Kuching seemed pleased to see me, for I had not ridden out on him since the crisis had been upon us. The grooms had looked after him splendidly, but he was fretting from his days of inactivity. As soon as I mounted, he was as anxious as I to be off on the road.

We started at an easy trot for I wanted to get as far along the road as I could before the heat of the day made the journey intolerable. I soon realised, though, that the journey would take longer than in the past. Instead of just the odd farmer taking food to sell at market or a party of priests making their way to the Ganges, I passed people every few hundred yards and I was constantly forced to slow as I pushed my way through the traffic. There were cavalrymen like myself, carrying messages out or bringing word back, some with despatch cases strapped to their saddles. Some wore the same uniform as me, others sported the insignia of the Company's troops. There were soldiers, most in ones and twos, but every mile or two I would pass a group of ten or twenty marching in step, as smart as any I had seen drilling in Cawnpore. There were civilians too, rudely armed with whatever they had to hand—here a sword, there a scythe and a few with old muskets that I would not trust not to explode in my face like the pipe muskets of Borneo. I saw the look on their faces and recognised it from my time with Brooke, for it was the look I saw on the faces of the Dyaks who had joined with us to destroy the pirates. These were the faces of men who were taking up whatever weapons they could find to drive an enemy from their land.

I had never realised before how much the British were hated.

It was late in the morning and the heat was driving people from the road to seek shelter in the shade before I reached the town. At last I was riding down the road that separated the European quarter from the buildings of the native city. I passed on my left the offices and bungalows which, but a week before, had been the beating heart of a thriving community. Now, what a melancholy aspect these buildings presented. They stood silent in the noontide heat, an almost palpable air of desolation the more pronounced because here and there a swinging door or a broken shutter evidenced their rapid abandonment or the first signs of looting.

Moving South, there were more obvious signs that a mob had ravaged through these properties. Papers lay scattered outside opened doorways, the shutters on a dry goods store had been wrenched off and the interior, naked to the street, was in terrible disarray. From one or two windows, wisps of smoke betrayed the damage caused by carelessness or arson.

Now the eerie silence of the Quarter was broken by the distant sound of cannon fire. I had slowed to a walk but now I kicked Kuching on and, defying the heat, we trotted down to the military cantonment.

The stillness and emptiness of the European Quarter had been disturbing enough, but the sight that now met my eyes was one of horror. Smoke billowed from every side of the Entrenchment where cannon blasted in ragged volleys. I had to slow my horse to push through the throng of armed men who filled the road toward the cantonment. The bungalows of the officers were but ruins from which smoke still rose but the new barracks—still not yet completed—stood as they had been when I last saw them, forming a line of buildings to the South of the Entrenchment. They were the closest structures to Wheeler's position and the sight of rebel troops moving in and out of them suggested that they were being used as cover from which to fire into the British camp.

I headed my horse in that direction. Mungo had been right to suspect that I would not be challenged, for men were moving to and fro with no apparent order or direction. At first I thought this presaged well for the British force, as their opponents clearly lacked discipline, but then I saw a rifleman rise to stand on the half finished roof of one of the barrack blocks. He stood completely exposed, fired down into the Entrenchment, shooting over its pathetic little wall of mud and then calmly stood, still exposed, and proceeded to reload his weapon. I realised then that the lack of order was not a sign of weakness but came from the rebels' perception of their strength. They were treating the siege as a high holiday with the option of firing into Wheeler's position much as we might shoot at fowl on a hunting party—except that it would be considered unsporting to shoot fowl that could make no attempt to fly and escape the guns.

As I rode nearer, a sepoy reached for my bridle and urged me to dismount. "The English will not spend their shot on a man on foot," he warned me, "but they might fire at your horse." I offered him a few annas if he would hold my mount while I went forward and he was happy to do so. "Though you will not be able to kill them with your sabre," he grinned. "You will have to wait your turn. Now is the time for the infantry."

I forced a smile, promising myself that if I should ever see the man alone in Bithur, I would kill him.

I made my way across the open ground toward the unfinished barracks. For the first minute or two I had to steel myself to walk normally, as the multitude of other troops in the area seemed to be doing. I could not believe that at any minute there would not come the crack of a bullet to bear me away from this world. Yet the sepoy had been right. The only real danger seemed to be from the rebels' own artillery passing over our heads toward the enclosure beyond.

I decided not to walk to the furthest barrack but to move away from the line taken by the other troops and cut straight to the nearest building. As I tried to do so, urgent voices shouted to me in warning. "Away from there!" There was mocking laughter from the sepoys who liked nothing better than to see a cavalryman shown up on the field. "The British are in there."

Improbable as it seemed, I thought it best to take them at their word and to stay a safe distance from the barracks in the centre of the line and to make my way to the most Southerly of the structures which, coincidentally, were the furthest from completion. Arriving there I was greeted by a crowd of sepoys who, it seemed, were waiting their turn to climb onto the roof for the honour of putting a ball or two into the enemy position before giving way to the next man. There was much laughter and good-natured joshing, much of it aimed at me and the fact that I carried no musket. It was difficult to believe that these men were at war and engaged in the distinctly unamusing business of shooting into a crowd consisting in large part of women and children.

One man offered to lend me his gun so that I could join in the fun. Disguising my feelings of revulsion, I accepted his offer with a hearty smile. Not only was I anxious to do nothing to cause suspicion, but accepting the gun gave me reason to mount the roof and look down on the Entrenchment to see the state of things within—and though I would fire the wretched thing, I could take care not to hit anyone. So, after waiting a while for my turn and entertaining my fellows with tales of the British I had ridden down and killed on the road, I clambered up a rickety ladder and emerged on the roof beams.

The half finished building had offered shade at this, the hottest time of day. Now I emerged into the blazing sunlight and the heat struck me as if I had stepped into an oven. Coming from the shadows of the interior and suddenly emerging into the full light of day, I was dazzled for a moment and had to screw my eyes up against the sun before I could see anything.

The roof itself had hardly been started when the coolies had been ordered to abandon it to dig the defences that I now looked down on. From my precarious perch I had an excellent view of Wheeler's arrangements. The first thing I noticed was that a line of upturned carts and barrels now stretched from the fort to the barrack building I had been warned away from. In daylight, this would provide entirely inadequate cover, but I could see that at night a picket could move into or out of the Entrenchment, enabling Wheeler to maintain a sort of forward post. It was bad enough that I could sit on the perch where I now found myself but if the whole row were to be controlled by the rebels, it would bring their lines to within two hundred yards of the Entrenchment. Yet the defence of that barrack block must depend on just a handful of men, isolated from the main force. I could well see why they saved their ammunition to guard against a frontal attack and must perforce put up with rebel sniping.

The thought of sniping recalled to me the purpose for which, in the eyes of all those waiting below, I was up here. I raised my gun and made pretence of taking careful aim. This gave me every opportunity to look into the Entrenchment and what a miserable sight it was. The open space was littered with the wreckage of the shelters that people had made for themselves when they first arrived. Now no one ventured into this open ground. Here and there lay a body that showed what would happen to anyone foolish enough to try. Men, some in uniform, some civilians, but all armed, lay pressed to the earth, trying to shelter behind the rampart. But the miserable height of the defences meant that they were pathetically exposed and some already lay so still that I was sure they would never move again.

Driven from the open ground by musket fire, the women and children had sought shelter in the two barrack blocks but, as

I had seen when I spent my nights there, these were not nearly large enough to hold the mass of people trying to force their way into them. People crowded into the verandas, which offered some shelter from the sun but no protection from musket fire.

There was a constant jostling among the pathetic crowd as they sought to move away from the sides of the barracks which were exposed to my position, which was the only high point within musket range. But the women could not protect themselves from the artillery that boomed from every side of the compound. As I watched, the sound of a cannon came from the East and gunpowder smoke rose from the direction of St John's church. There was a crash as the ball struck home and a panicked rush of children from the cover afforded by the nearer barrack block showed where the round must have landed. A young woman braved the open ground to call the children back. I could not make out her features. Perhaps I had dined with her a few weeks ago. I may have seen her at the bandstand, calling her little ones not to stray too far from their picnic. What a desperate contrast was the scene before me! The woman, arms waving frantically, her mouth open in a scream I fancied I could hear above the gunfire. The children paused and turned and then scurried back toward the shelter of the building.

I fired my musket, taking care that my shot should fall well short but as I did so I heard another cannon sound. This time the shot came from behind me and the round struck the earth parapet, taking a chunk from the top of its already inadequate height. Slowing, it bounced across the open ground, falling just short of the barracks. To my amazement, I saw two troopers run into the open to seize the ball and carry it back toward the rampart.

I remembered that the Nana's forces at the Treasury had been based next to the Magazine so the rebels had been ideally placed to seize all the ammunition they could desire while Wheeler's men had only that which they had carried with them to the Entrenchment. And now they were reduced to salvaging the rounds that were fired at them to return against the enemy.

There were shouts now from below me that I had had my turn and others were waiting. Reluctantly, I started back down the ladder, pausing as another crash from the rear presaged a cloud of dust and plaster from the nearer barrack block as it was struck.

The sepoy grinned as I returned his gun. "Were you successful?"

"Truly I was. A woman ran from cover to save her child and I shot her." Remembering just in time that he would be able to see the bodies lying there, I added, "She dragged herself back behind the barracks but I think her wound is mortal."

The fellow clapped me on the shoulders. "A fair attempt for a sowar."

So it was that I was congratulated for the heroic business of killing a defenceless woman! And I had to smile and conceal my contempt.

I made my way back to where I had left my horse, careful to maintain the easy swagger that sowars affected though I wanted to stop and weep at what I had seen.

I found the sepoy and gave him a few more annas. He didn't expect to be paid twice but I had handed him the money without thought. Indeed, I seemed incapable of doing anything that involved mental effort. I did not even mount, just took Kuching by the reins and followed the milling throng.

The drift of the crowd carried me vaguely Southward to where I had heard the cannon sound behind me. Now it sounded again. I saw the smoke rise and heard the whoosh of the ball in flight. I imagined it crashing into the feeble buildings that were all that offered shelter to the wretches trapped behind those mud walls.

Ahead of me, something over a mile away, a small hill rose from the plain. I remembered it as an empty spot. There was a rather grand house built there, but it had fallen into disrepair and the place was now just used by the military to store unwanted equipment. Looking up at the hill now, though, it seemed a centre of activity. From where I was, I could not see the house, but I could make out some tents of gold and red fabric. These were by far the most distinctive structures on this side of the Entrenchment so, in the absence of any better plan, I made my way toward them.

The nearer I got to this encampment, the more splendid it appeared and, remembering that Nana Sahib had had a tent erected for his stay at the Treasury, I guessed that this must be his headquarters for the siege. I hesitated as to whether to approach it more closely, fearing that my disguise might be more carefully examined as I drew nearer the seat of power. Then I reminded myself that I had never been questioned, even as I roamed his palace. I was simply allowing the horrors of the battlefield to rattle my nerves. I would not skulk home to hide with Mungo.

I turned to pet my horse, stroking him, ostensibly to calm him but, in fact, as much to calm myself. Then, drawing myself up and trying to radiate the confident arrogance of a cavalryman, I carried on toward the tents.

The Peshwa (as he was now calling himself) had chosen the site well. It was far enough away for there to be no danger at all of being hit by a stray shot, yet its height above the Entrenchment allowed the Nana and his generals an excellent view of the action. Judging from the number of soldiers gathered around, he was keeping a substantial personal guard near at hand, though I imagine they may also have served as reserves, ready to throw into the battle if needed. Given the one-sided nature of the conflict, though, the reserves were unlikely to be called for. With nothing to occupy them, groups of armed men lounged around or squatted beside cooking fires. I noticed, though, that for all the apparent lack of order, piquets had been mounted and the soldiers on guard seemed attentive and alert.

I decided not to try to pass the piquets. I could see enough from where I was and there seemed no point in risking a challenge from the sentries. I mounted my horse, for a man seated on a horse looks as if he has a purpose in life while the same man standing beside the horse looks like a loiterer. From the saddle I looked down over the field. Cannon boomed at irregular intervals from all sides. Inside the Entrenchment there would be puffs of dust from the ground or from the walls of the barracks as the balls landed. From time to time a man would leave cover to make off with a cannon ball that could be recovered for the garrison's use or a child would dash from shelter pursued by a desperate mother. Once I saw a woman fall and her child turn to her as if willing her to rise again. There was another distant crack as a musket fired from the roof of the abandoned barracks where I had lately stood and the child dropped beside its mother.

I could watch no more and turned my attention to the tents. There was no sign of the Nana, though a regular coming and going of officers in smart uniforms of red or French grey, adorned with sashes and braid, confirmed that the tents were the centre of the Nana's command.

As the day grew hotter, I bypassed the guards on the tents and made my way around to the old Savada House (for such had the mansion been called in the days of its glory). In the strip of shade on the North of the building an elephant stood tethered by the leg, its presence confirming that Nana Sahib was still presiding over his troops.

At a safe distance from the royal transport, soldiers were also seeking shelter from the sun. It being time for tiffin, most were cooking. Only half an hour earlier I had felt sick to my stomach at the sights I was seeing, but suddenly the smell of spiced meats reminded me that I was hungry. The body knows its needs and will soon assert them. And would my going hungry achieve anything for those poor souls on the plain below?

I dismounted by one group of sepoys and sniffed appreciatively. Once I might have thought of their meal simply as 'curry' but my time with Mungo had taught me better and I was able to distinguish the scents of chilli and paprika, coriander and bay leaves, all mingling with the aroma of the lamb that simmered in their pot. There was even a sprinkling of saffron, suggesting that they had been busy looting in the town, as saffron was hardly a regular ingredient in a soldier's dish.

I had chosen to greet a group of mutineers, as I felt more secure from questioning than if I had approached men who, like me, wore the uniform of the Nana. I did wonder if there might be some awkwardness on account of our different loyalties but I was welcomed immediately as a comrade.

"You like the smell of our tiffin, eh?"

The speaker was a big man, with a thick moustache that curled down the sides of his mouth. He had abandoned his uniform trousers for the loose folds of a dhoti, leaving his legs bare below the knee.

I grinned at him without thinking, the simple response of anyone offered food and companionship by a fellow. And when I stopped to remember that it was a rebel who spoke to me, still the gesture seemed right. However much I hated the mass of Nana's soldiery as mutineers and rebels, I could not reconcile this hatred with my feelings toward the individuals making up that army. I had eaten alongside the Nana's soldiers in Saturday House. The man offering to share his meal now was probably a distant cousin of someone who had paused to salaam me when I was dressed as a scribe in Bithur. Perhaps he had tossed alms into my dish when I was disguised as a beggar. Besides, if I were to hate the Nana's soldiers, should I not hate his courtiers more? And was not Mungo kin to Nana Sahib and served him at Saturday House?

He pushed a tin dish toward me. "You'll have to share my bowl."

I smiled and bowed my thanks. Last week, serving the British, he was an ally. Tomorrow, I might have the chance to stop him from shooting a woman or a child and I would kill him as my enemy. But for now, he was a man offering to break bread with me and I would treat him as a friend.

One of the sepoys was crouched over a cauldron that bubbled gently above a small fire. He was apparently the cook for the group and now he ladled the stew into bowls and slapped unleavened bread onto a plate. My host tore off scooped food from the bowl between us. I followed his example and, for a few minutes, we concentrated on eating.

"Ahhh!" He gave a contented belch. "So what brings one of the Peshwa's sowars to mess with the common soldiery?"

"I'm just a messenger," I said. "I have a letter for Rao Sahib but no one can direct me to him."

"Don't they know over there?" He gestured in the direction of the tents.

"He's not there. I think he may be back at Bithur."

"It's possible." He paused and turned his attention to the food for a while. "There's people coming and going all the time."

"But the Nana remains here."

"Oh, yes!" He grinned. "Old Nana Sahib stays here. He's changed sides often enough. We want to know he's on our side now."

So Mungo had been right all along. Nana Sahib had been playing a waiting game, holding back until he was confident he knew which side of this conflict was going to come out on top. Looking down on the Entrenchment and the mass of men and artillery that surrounded it, I had to admit that he seemed to have chosen well.

The sepoy followed the direction of my gaze. "I'll say this for the British. They're stubborn and they're brave. We should have overrun that place in an hour but they're still there."

"Why don't you just rush them? That wall won't hold you back."

He grinned. "And you sowars can lead the charge, eh? Get all the glory while we have to do the dirty fighting in their camp?" Now the grin faded. "A charge will not be so easy. They have artillery and they lay their fire well. You do not see them fire because they are conserving their ammunition. But if a body of men were to rush at the fort" (and I noticed he used the word quite seriously) "then you would see them cut down with ball and canister. And the men you see lying waiting behind the walls—they took all the muskets they could find. Each man has two or three or four beside him, so they can fire again and again. Their women come from shelter and reload for them. I had never thought to see a memsahib do such a thing but they do and it means the men can fire repeatedly while we are in the open and can fire only once." He shook his head. "No, a charge will not be easy."

We returned to our food. Between scoops of spiced lamb, we looked out over the battle.

One-sided as it was, it was true that the rebel forces were not moving forward. Though the artillery kept up its bombardment and the snipers took their toll, it seemed to me that destroying Wheeler's position by attrition was likely to be a drawn-out affair.

"Are you planning to starve them out?"

He shrugged. "I think they have enough food. And there is water." He pointed to the one exposed well I had noticed when I was with Hillersdon in the barracks. "They have to show themselves to draw it, though. Then we can shoot them. But they generally use the well only at night now. Still, we can hear the windlass creak, so we can fire at them even in the darkness."

I thought again of the conditions inside the barracks. Out at Saturday House there was not the same obsession with the exact temperature that pervaded European life and I had not seen a thermometer for days, but I judged that it must be well over a hundred degrees. Here, on raised ground, the whisper of a breeze made the day just about bearable. But in the barracks below us, crammed together with the windows shuttered against the detritus thrown up by the shelling and the constant risk from musket fire, there the heat must be excruciating. The women and children now sheltered there were used to spending their days in elegant rooms cooled by pankah fans with freshly watered tattis to protect them from hot air through the windows. How terrible must they be finding their new habitation. And with every drop of water bought at immediate risk of death at the exposed well, there would be none for the luxury of bathing—even if the conditions allowed for the possibility of a bath. There would be hardly enough to satisfy the basic requirement for life. They must be continually thirsty, especially the children.

"Do you feel no pity for them?"

The sepoy shrugged. "I am sad that they must suffer so. But I never asked them to come to my land. I never asked that they should seize Oudh from its rightful ruler. My family have lived in Oudh for more generations than I can count. And now the British come and say it is theirs. It was never theirs. We are just taking back what was always ours."

"And the women? And the children?"

He shrugged again. "It is a war. These things cannot be helped."

We were both silent for a while after that. At one point, between the noise of the cannon, I thought I had the cry of a child carried on the breeze, but we must have been a mile from the barracks and it was probably my imagination.

When I spoke again, it was to ask about his family and his home in Oudh. He had a wife there, he said, and five children. "Three sons. One day they will be warriors like their father."

"And whom will they serve?"

He paused then, picking at some meat that was stuck in his teeth.

"The Peshwa now leads a mighty army. He is a Hindoo but the Musalmans follow him. The old King in Delhi may call himself Emperor but he is weak. The Peshwa is young and strong and full of cunning. I think the Peshwa will be a great lord in India and I will serve in his army."

Our bowls were empty and I felt it was time to be moving on. I smiled my thanks. "Perhaps one day we will be comrades in the Peshwa's army and I will be able to return your hospitality."

"Perhaps." As I prepared to mount, he rose to his feet and

clasped me to him as one comrade to another. I clasped him in return and then, with repeated assurances of mutual respect and affection, I was in the saddle and walking Kuching back the way I had come.

The sun had passed its zenith and the hottest part of the day was coming to its end. I passed slowly through the crowds of soldiers. There seemed no proper cordon round the Entrenchment but such was the number of those assembled to attack it that I could see little prospect of anyone smuggling themselves out. I supposed that I might make my way in by working my way along the abandoned barracks until I came to the pickets who kept vigil in the building that was linked to the Entrenchment by the line of carts. But once within, what could I do? I would be one more mouth to feed, one more person for whom water would have to be drawn from the well under the pitiless rebel fire.

Everything I had seen suggested that the situation was very different by night than by day. During the day, the rebels were unwilling to show themselves on open ground because they feared the fire of the enemy. But after dark, the Europeans' advantage of accuracy in fire would be negated. On the other hand, at night the Europeans would have freedom to manoeuvre around the Entrenchment in a way that was impossible when they were under targeted fire during the day.

I considered the possibility of waiting until nightfall to observe how things turned out under these very different conditions but I decided against it. By nightfall, I would be exhausted and I had promised to return to Mungo who, I knew, would not rest until I was safe home.

So I made my way slowly back to the town. It was still infernally hot and I walked Kuching easily to spare both the horse and myself. We ambled up the Course and I remembered the mornings I had ridden here for exercise in the cool of the early hours. I had been in Cawnpore less than 18 months, but my memories of those early days seemed like a dream now. Was it only a year ago that Company men had walked this land like the emissaries of the gods, the servants of the greatest power India had ever seen? And now they and their army cowered behind a mud wall and their homes and offices were abandoned to the mob.

As I approached the neat bungalows of the Civil Station, I decided that I should make my way through them to the river. It might be some time before my horse had another chance to drink and I felt I would benefit from the opportunity to cool myself in the water, even if I did not trust it for human consumption.

Here, walking past the tidy gardens and listening to the screeching of the swifts darting under their eaves, I was more than ever struck by the changes that so short a time had wrought. There was Mr Hart's place where I had dined just a few weeks ago; there was that couple with the sweet little girl with the big black dog. I wondered what had happened to the dog now. Somehow, it was easier to worry about the dog than the girl.

We arrived at the edge of the river. At this time of year, toward the end of the dry season, the Ganges here was very low and I had to lead the horse carefully down a flight of steps (which the Indians call a ghat) to get to the level of the water. Even then, there was an expanse of muddy shallows between us and the river proper, but at least there was enough for Kuching and, taking care not to get mud on my white britches, I was able to cool my face in water scooped from the ground.

The height of the banks here gave some shelter from the sun and the water passing by seemed to have some cooling effect, so I rested there awhile before carefully walking my horse back up the steps, his hooves slipping once or twice on the worn stone.

Back among the bungalows of the deserted colony, I mounted and, kicking Kuching to a trot, I set off along the road to Bithur. In the distance, I still heard the sound of cannon fire but I did not look back.

❊

I WILL NOT dwell on my dispute with Mungo the next morning. I had told him that I intended to return to Cawnpore in the evening so that I could see how matters fared in the hours of darkness. He called me a fool and said that I loved those in the Entrenchment more than I loved him and that I would die and that I deserved death and a hundred other things I know he did not truly mean. He was cruel but, I think, in the end I was the crueller, for I would not be shaken from my purpose. Late in the afternoon, having rested as well as I could in the face of Mungo's fury, I prepared to set out again.

I was still in the guise of a sowar for this had served me well so far but I knew that if I were to approach closer to the Entrenchment it would have to be on foot. My tulwar with its long, curved blade was an ideal weapon for fighting on horseback but not well suited to combat on foot. When Mungo saw that I was determined to go, he vanished from our quarters. I waited almost an hour for him to return and was about to depart, leaving just a note to assure him that I would come back safely, when he rushed in through the door carrying a pistol and a bayonet in its scabbard.

"Tuck them in your belt. If you must risk your life, at least these will give you a chance in a fight."

There were tears in his eyes as he spoke. I put them in my belt, as he suggested and, saying nothing, I held him and kissed him. He kissed me back and then pushed me from him.

"Go, if you must," he said.

I went.

With all the movement between Bithur and Cawnpore, the stables were a constant bustle of activity, but the men there knew their jobs and my horse was ready for me.

The road was even busier than the day before. More people were moving in the cool of the evening, either returning to their homes in Bithur or, like me, hurrying to join the army at Cawnpore. At one point, I was greeted by a group of sowars, who were heading to their barracks for the night, and who urged me to turn back with them. "There'll be no cavalry attacks tonight."

"I've despatches for the Peshwa," I told them and they waved as I passed.

The native town of Cawnpore was alive with movement and excitement, while the European quarter was even more desolate by night than during the day. No lights showed. All was silence.

I hurried past both, made my way down the Course, and then swung off the road toward the abandoned barracks. If I were to have any communication with the Entrenchment's defenders, the piquet they maintained in the middle barrack had to be the safest course. This outpost, well beyond the defences of the Entrenchment, was their most forward position. The British maintained their outpost in the centre of the row of unfinished barracks while the rebels controlled the buildings at either end.

It was full dark by now. The only light came from the fires of countless groups of soldiers spread across the plain around Wheeler's position, cooking evening meals or just keeping a fire against the fears that even brave men might feel in the darkness. The figures I passed now were just grey shapes and it took me a while before I found one who would tend my horse. I had no fear that he might steal it, for a poor Indian with a horse would be detected immediately and dragged before the Nana in the hope of reward—but I was concerned that I might be unable to find him again in the dark. I left him near one of the fires and, taking my bearings on two of the rebel artillery positions, which still kept up a desultory fire, I trusted that I would be able to retrace my steps to this point.

I moved forward, as near as I could tell along the path I had taken the previous day.

"Hush, you fool!"

The voice came out of the darkness on my left and hands pulled me off the path and down toward the ground. There, huddling in the darkness, were twenty or so sepoys.

"What are you doing here?" I could barely see the fellow's face but the voice was urgent.

"I'm sick of you infantry having all the fun. I came to lend a hand."

Light caught on his teeth, grinning whitely in the shadows. "Do you have a musket?"

"I have a pistol."

"Then you are welcome to join us. Now you will see some real soldiering. Move quietly!"

There was a stirring in the darkness and the men around me rose and moved, crouching to the shelter of the nearest of the barracks.

"Have a care. We don't know exactly where they are."

The building we had arrived at, though roofed, lacked doors and windows and we were able to climb inside with only the odd scuffling to reveal our presence.

The barracks were laid out with rooms leading off from either side of a central corridor. In the darkness, we slipped from one doorway to another, moving forward a room at a time, uncertain whether the enemy had sent out patrols which might be moving along the building from the other end. Our caution, though, was unnecessary. The British had not pushed out so far from the building they controlled and this barrack block was empty.

We gathered in the room at the far end and waited in silence.

In the distance, I heard the creaking of a windlass and suddenly cannon fire opened up from all the rebel positions and the crack of musketry came from the barracks ahead of us. I remembered what I had been told about the attempts of those trapped in the hell of the Entrenchment to draw water by night and how the creak of the windlass would betray them. I thought of a man crouched at the well while shot and shell ripped through the darkness around him.

There was a moment's pause in the firing and then I heard

it still: the steady creaking as he stayed at his post, drawing up the water that was life itself to all in that dreadful place.

"Move when the firing starts again."

The bombardment resumed and we were out of the barracks and running to enter the next, some by the door, some by the windows.

There was a confusion of sound against the gunfire from outside. Someone shouted a challenge.

"Just fire, you fool!"

The voice was in English and a moment later came a shot, echoing off the bare walls of the unfinished building.

"Corridor's clear."

The central corridor was, indeed, empty. At the first sound of voices, we had dived for the rooms that led from it on either side. Around me, I felt, rather than saw, half a dozen black bodies tense.

Booted feet moved cautiously toward us. In the room across the corridor, I heard the slap of a sandaled tread on the ground. In the dark, I was suddenly aware of how different was the sound of European footsteps to that of the natives. My own boots would sound as heavy as any of the Entrenchment's defenders, but would be all too easily distinguished by the jingling of my spurs. I cursed myself for not removing them but I could not do so now without making more noise than if I just stood still.

"No one in here."

Then they were in the next room. Some of our party were waiting silently and as soon as the searchers entered, they were on them. There was the sound of shots and then the clash of swords. Around me, men made for the door in the darkness, desperately pushing at one another as they ran toward the sound of combat.

I followed.

As soon as I passed into the corridor, all was confusion. There was even less light there than in the room we had taken shelter in, for the corridor had no windows. Though my eyes were already grown used to the gloom, I saw nothing but shadows. In the darkness, men had abandoned their swords for there was as much danger of cutting a friend as an enemy. Instead, they came in close, using all their senses to identify their foes.

I found myself struggling with one man whose lithe body suggested he was Indian. I kicked toward his legs and, as he sought to regain his footing, I heard the slap of his sandal. I knew then he was one of those with whom I had entered the building and who would have thought me a comrade. But now, fighting with Wheeler's men, the men I had come to help, I must see him as my enemy. My bayonet was already drawn and in the darkness I stabbed toward his gut, twisting as I withdrew it.

In the chaos, no one saw me.

Again, I heard the sound of sandals and another figure brushed past me. I seized his arm. "Wait!" I whispered the word in Hindustanee. He alone heard me; he paused. My bayonet swept across his neck.

An English voice shouted, "Ready!"

An instant before the light flared, I had realised what was to happen and I was already diving for the patch of grey that was a doorway. As I did, light burst forth from a shaded lantern, now uncovered. Three men, two kneeling and one standing between them, blocked the corridor, muskets levelled toward the Indians. As soon as the light allowed them to distinguish their targets, all three fired and two black bodies fell to the ground. The rebels now raised their muskets in their turn but already the lantern was shaded. Two or three shots sounded but there were no cries from where the British had been standing so I presumed that, in the darkness, they had missed.

I strained to hear any sounds in the room where I now found myself. The noise of deadly combat continued to dominate outside but in here all seemed quiet. I moved, as silently as my spurs would allow me, back toward the door.

Before I could reach it, I heard boots run down the corridor and into the room. I heard him stop and I imagined him listening, as I listened, peering intently into the darkness to see if he could make me out.

I concentrated on his breathing and, guided by the sound, I could just see his pale face in the shadows. I was still, taking care to breathe softly, and my face was stained, so I had the advantage of him. I could have killed him easily but I had come to help, not to destroy. My problem was how to convey this to him before he struck me down.

Slowly, taking care to make no sound, I crouched down on the ground. Only then did I say, as quietly as I could while taking care my every word was heard, "I am a friend. Stay calm."

His first response, as I had expected, was to strike blindly in the direction my voice indicated I was standing. The blow struck the wall above where I was crouching. I leapt up and grabbed his arm. "I'm a friend!"

This time the words reached him through the fear and the desire to kill.

"You're British!"

"Yes—but keep quiet. I came in with them and they must not know."

Even as I spoke, there were more shots, screams and the sound of running feet.

"I don't think you have to worry about them." The languid voice reminded me of a world that, in little more than a week, had come to seem impossibly remote. "I think you'd better meet Captain Moore."

Outside the room, lanterns now provided a steady light and I had my first sight of the men who had cleared the rebels from the building.

Their appearance was a terrible contrast to their voices. While their accents remained those of English gentlemen, the wretched figures I saw before me were scarcely recognisable as those of my compatriots. Their uniforms were filthy and torn. All showed signs of some injury or other, blood staining their tunics and filthy scraps of bandages showing through rents in trousers legs and sleeves. Their faces showed the strain of days and nights spent under constant bombardment. Above all, they stank as men without access to water for washing and inadequate facilities for the necessities of the toilette will stink after days baking in the Indian sun.

The tallest of the group, his badges of rank barely visible through the filth and blood, glanced over at me and spoke to the man at my side. "Don't waste time, Kirkby. Just kill the bugger."

"Beg pardon, sir. He's not a prisoner. He's one of us."

The captain turned and stared at me. "Don't be a fool, Kirkby. The man's a nigger." He held the lantern toward my face to make the point and I took the opportunity to speak.

"Captain Moore, I take it."

Moore's eyes, incongruously light blue in the filth of his face, widened in surprise.

"I have that honour, sir. And who the hell are you?"

"I'm the Deputy Collector."

For a moment, he looked nonplussed and then, without questioning me further he simply grinned, put out his hand to me and said, "Well, Mr Deputy Collector, you must have a tale to tell."

"And one I am to tell quickly." I sketched out the circumstances that had allowed me to escape the Entrenchment and hide among the rebels, skipping over the details and explaining simply that I had disguised myself and penetrated the enemy camp.

"I can enter these buildings at night and bring anything that I can conceal about my person. What do you have most need of?"

"Food is always welcome. Most of our diet now is gram." He wrinkled his nose in distaste—gram, or ground chickpea flour, was the basic food of the poor but featured only sparingly on European menus. "I fear you can't carry enough food in your pockets to make any difference. Bandages might make more sense." He gestured at the fabric visible through a bloodied hole on his sleeve. "We've been reduced to tearing up petticoats, as you can see. I fear the ladies are in rags." There was a rattle of musket fire against the wall and the lights were doused. "Look here." In the darkness, the Irish lilt in his voice was somehow more obvious. "What we really need is intelligence. News in and news out. Try to get word to Lucknow that we're in a jam. We can't hold out much longer. I've lost count of the dead and there's precious little we can do for the wounded. We've basic rations but nothing to cook with and that damn well is so exposed that we never dare draw as much water as we should. And we need to know what the rebels have planned."

"That last is easy enough," I said. "They will just stay round and about until they've killed you all. There's no organisation to speak of but they outnumber you by hundreds to one and they are in no hurry."

"They're not worried that we'll be relieved?"

"From where? The countryside has risen. Nana Sahib is calling himself the Peshwa. The King of Delhi is calling himself the Emperor. Every princeling in India will be Lord of this or that by now and they all want the British out."

Mr Kirkby was looking cautiously round the edge of the window and now urged that they pull back to the central block. "I'm not sure but that I can't see movement out there, sir."

"Two minutes, Kirkby, if you please. You may fire from the window if you are concerned."

I felt, rather than saw, Captain Moore turn his attention back to me as Kirkby fired out into the darkness. "Look, Williamson, things seem pretty dark. First thing is to get word to Lucknow. Second is to see if there's any way we can get safe passage out for the women and children. The men can hold out for as long as it takes, but this is no place for families. Find out what the rebels plan and let us know. Write it down and leave it in the room we are in now. If you can, bring in bandages and any medicines—iodine would be especially welcomed. Food if you can bring it safely."

Kirkby fired again and was joined by two of the others.

"Time to go, I think," said Moore. "Good luck!"

There was the sound of running in the darkness and they were gone. I waited a few minutes and then made my way back the way I had come, slipping quietly through the doorway and, bending low, across the open ground back to what passed for the rebel lines.

I had worried that my solitary return might lead to awkward questions but I need not have been concerned. In the darkness and the excitement, I had not been aware of my own appearance but, back in the company of the mutineers, I saw myself by the light of their torches. My uniform was covered in blood, which I was quick to assure them was that of our British foes and I was treated as a hero for my endeavours.

I had an unpleasant quarter of an hour while I struggled to find my horse, for all the care I had taken in marking the spot, but, once I had done so, I was safe away back to Bithur.

As I rode, the horror of the night's events returned to me and I swayed uneasily in my saddle. Fortunately my horse was steady and, by then, knew the route to take so I arrived back at Saturday House without mishap. The sentries, bleary eyed as they were, still noticed the blood upon my clothing and saluted sharply but otherwise my return excited no attention.

Two hours before dawn, I was back in Mungo's rooms to find him trying to read by the light of an oil lamp.

"I couldn't sleep."

"Am I forgiven, then?"

He said nothing but opened his arms and held me, bloody clothes and all.

I HAD THOUGHT that the hardest part of the tasks that Captain Moore had set me would be to get a message through to Lucknow. I was sure the roads would be sealed and, in any case, with the populace hunting down and killing any Europeans that they found, who would be foolish enough to attempt to carry a message on behalf of the hated foreigners. To my astonishment, when I explained my problem to Mungo, he said that he would be able to arrange this with no difficulty at all.

"There are messages being sent to Lucknow all the time," he assured me. "Every foreigner who has gone to ground anywhere within a hundred miles is desperate to get word to Lucknow. And every Indian who ever served them and who sees no possibility of employment in the future is desperate to take their money to see these messages delivered."

"I'm sure they take money but do they really see the messages delivered?"

Mungo shrugged. "There are thieves everywhere. I'm sure you have some in England too. But remember that though people say they hate the British that does not mean that they hate each and every person from that country. I'm not too fond of the British myself but I would do anything to save you."

All that remained was for Mungo to find a messenger, which was but the work of an hour or two. Following his instructions, I spent the time that he was away in writing a concise account of the situation of Cawnpore and transcribing this in letters a small as I could manage onto a thin sheet of paper which was rolled into a tiny cylinder to be secreted in the clothing of our courier.

That afternoon the message was on its way and Moore's first commission was completed.

Finding out what Nana Sahib's plans were proved more difficult. The chaos in the rebel ranks meant that all Mungo's attempts to discover their intentions were producing nothing. When my frustration led me to complain that he was not exerting himself enough, he pointed out that I had actually fought in the rebel army and I still had no idea what their strategy was.

The confusion was in part, I think, because the Nana lacked good generals, but was also an inevitable consequence of the nature of the rebel force. Although all the troops besieging

Cawnpore owed nominal allegiance to Nana Sahib, it was less a single army than a ragtag coalition. There were mutineers, the Nana's own troops, local Musalman troops and local Hindoo troops—the last two being almost as likely to attack each other as the British. Added to this confusion of loyalties were thugs with no loyalty at all. One of the first acts of the rebels had been to open the jails and the rogues that were released saw the opportunity for good pickings in the confusion of war. There were few rich merchants who did not have some connection to the British and many was the household broken into and looted for no better reason than that they were rich and had once done business with an Englishman.

The one thing that was completely clear was that the rebels intended to show no mercy to any foreigner who fell into their hands. In the days immediately following the mutiny there was regular news of Europeans who had been away from Cawnpore when the trouble broke out being rounded up here and there throughout the area. These were not soldiers but businessmen, engineers or, like myself, Company servants. The storm took the lowest and the highest. Even the Eurasian clerks were liable to be dragged from their homes and killed while the matriarch of the Greenways survived as a prisoner with her immediate family. "They have promised a ransom of 10,000 lacs," Mungo told me, awed at the vast sum that was to buy their lives. "But I am not sure it will save the men."

For those without the wealth of the Greenway family bank behind them, the end was at least quick. They were taken to Savada House and led before Nana Sahib. In almost every case, the women were imprisoned but the men were executed on the spot.

I seized on the fact that most of the women had not been killed. "If he spares the women, then perhaps he might let them leave the Entrenchment."

"I don't think so, John. His father's widows still live here at Saturday House and they are a power in our land." He gave a wry grin. "I think that Nana Sahib would as soon that they were not. He was adopted, remember. His father's widows have no reason to love him. And it is the widows who have insisted that he spare the women he has captured. He gives them their way on this because there are few women prisoners and it is easier not to cross the widows. But I do not think he will want to have scores of these women. What will he do with them?"

"He could offer them safe passage."

"To where? All India is aflame."

"When last I heard, Lucknow was safe."

"After Cawnpore, Lucknow will be next."

Mungo saw the look of horror on my face. "John, it is known. It is decided. I cannot pretend to you that this will not happen. The Peshwa has cast the dice and now he is committed to fight. War will continue until all the British are forced out of India. Already there is an Emperor at Delhi. Here, the Peshwa will extend his power and Oudh will acknowledge him as their liberator. The old kingdoms will rise again and all will be as it was."

"So my people have to die so that Nana Sahib can show that blood can be spilled as easily in Cawnpore as in Delhi?"

For the first time, I saw Mungo angry, his chocolate skin darkening with emotion.

"Your people? Are these truly your people? And, if they are, can you dare to complain that they are driven from this land by force of arms? Did the Peshwa choose to live in Bithur or was he dispossessed by British armies? Did the Emperor resign his power voluntarily to live half-mad in Delhi under your guard? Or did you seize his lands from him?"

With a visible effort, he calmed himself. "I know you, John. I know you are better than that. In Borneo, you ruled with the love of the people and they accepted you because they knew you cared for them. And here you have tried to understand our ways and to see our people fairly treated. It is not by chance that you are here and not trapped with the men of General Wheeler."

"And the women? And the children?"

Mungo shrugged. "It is sad. Truly, it is sad. And I will help you pack food and medicine to relieve their suffering as much as I can, though I know it is very little. But this is India. There are countless women and children trying to scratch a living in this country. And every day, thousands of them die. When you confiscate lands, do you make sure that all the pensioners of those you have dispossessed are provided for? When you build your roads and your barracks and your grand buildings, do you worry that the land you are taking may have supported a household? When the Europeans of Cawnpore dismissed a servant who had not pleased them, did they concern themselves with how the man's family was to live? For a hundred years, the British have ruled in India and Indian lives have been held cheap. Now, we take back what is ours. Should we hesitate because the innocent may suffer alongside the guilty?"

Now it was my turn to shrug, for what words could I say?

chapter 6

THE NEXT AFTERNOON, I was again on the road to Cawnpore. Mungo and I had spent the morning thinking what were the most useful things I could carry with me. I would not be able to take any sort of bag into the barracks for a sowar carried his kit upon his horse and any pack would excite curiosity. Nor did my uniform have any pockets. There was a small leather pouch on the belt and iodine went in that. Otherwise, all that I carried had to be concealed beneath my tunic.

We slung two bags, such as sepoys might carry, across my shoulders, sewing the straps short so that they lay across my chest. Not much could be placed in them without my chest taking on a swell that might remind a literary observer too much of Falstaff. So chupattis and slices of dried meat that could lie flat against my body made up the bulk of my supplies. Bandages, such as a medical orderly would have about him, were not easily come by in Bithur but we cut cotton into strips and wrapped it around my waist.

I spent an hour trying to compose a letter to Captain Moore. Telling him that I had sent news to Lucknow was the easy part, though even there I felt I had to caution him that other messages had probably got through and had no effect.

Then, though, I had to admit that I could offer no intelligence as to the rebels' plans beyond their intention to maintain the siege until all were destroyed and that the women and children could expect no mercy.

I drafted and redrafted my note until, at last, I told the simple truth and, with a heavy heart, I placed it in one of the canvas bags, alongside the pitiful provisions we had assembled there.

The cotton and the canvas against my skin meant that the journey to Cawnpore was even more unpleasant than usual and I was covered in sweat when I arrived back at the siege. Little had changed, though the number of vultures that glided in lazy circles over the field of battle had increased. From time to time one would brave the firing to drop to earth and feed on the remains that lay around the Entrenchment's defences. I recognised some of these pathetic remnants as horses but other shapes were smaller and I took care not to look too carefully at what they might be.

The Nana's cannon had been joined by two new pairs of mortars and the weight of artillery now being brought to bear was such that the crash of firing echoed across the plain every few seconds. Even the brief interludes of quiet were interrupted by the crack of muskets as snipers kept up their fire into the compound. Most of the Indian troops, though, just lounged in such shade as they could find, waiting for the defenders to die without the necessity to engage them in open fight.

I joined the loungers, grateful for a chance to rest and allow my body to cool. We talked idly of our homes or the women who waited there or the possibility of a good supper. I noticed that people did not talk of the siege or of the Entrenchment, as if these things had already become simply part of the background to their lives. As the darkness drew in, though, these men drifted away and a few others gathered—quieter fellows with a grim look about their faces. One or two looked at the bayonet which I again wore tucked into my belt and they nodded quietly, recognising that there could be one reason only why I should carry such a weapon.

The oldest man there, wearing the uniform of a havildar in the Company's army, was recognised by the sepoys around him as their natural leader and he set out our objectives for the night for all as if he was still fighting for the Company and briefing his men there.

"Tonight we shall move forward together until we make contact with the enemy and then defend our position. We do not try to drive them out. We will hold our position until daylight. If we are still in the barracks when the light comes, then we will be able to overrun them. They are few and in the daylight we can defeat them."

His thinking was sound. Captain Moore and his men had succeeded by being better organised in the dark. They shot a disciplined volley when the lantern was uncovered and moved to new positions while the native force was divided and confused. The havildar might well lead his men to success. The implications of this could be disastrous, for if the British were driven from their outpost in these barracks, the rebels would command a line of buildings where they could muster men for an attack less than a hundred yards from Wheeler's defences.

The havildar's strategy was also a direct threat to my own plans for the night. I was relying on separation and confusion to allow me to take off my jacket and leave the supplies I was carrying safely in some dark corner to be found once the attackers had withdrawn.

Fortunately, I had an excuse to separate myself from their plan.

"I fear, comrade, that I cannot remain all the night in the barracks for I have not stabled my horse but have him in the charge of some ragamuffin I am paying two annas to guard him until my return. But I am happy to scout ahead of you. When I encounter the enemy, you will know that you must prepare to defend your position. Then I shall withdraw, leaving you the glory of the field."

There were mutterings of appreciation at this, for the idea

of one of the Nana Sahib's own cavalrymen leading an action on foot was seen as most gallant. My desire to withdraw after the fighting was done for the night was thought of as just another aspect of my heroic nature. The only problem with the plan, from my point of view, was that it involved my being in the forefront of the attack when I had good cause to know the deadly efficacy of the British fire.

I had little time to dwell on my predicament for the dusk is short in India and with full dark, we started across the open space toward the barracks.

Our adventure at first followed the pattern of the previous night, though this time I had the forethought to remove my spurs. We crawled through the darkness, slipped into the first building and made our cautious way along its length. The havildar's strategy meant that the force moved as one group, slipping silently from doorway to doorway, invisible in the dark but their breath warm upon my neck as I kept my promise to take my position at the front.

Again, we waited for the noise of firing before we slipped from the first barracks to the second. Again, the group moved forward as a single unit. Silently we slipped into the first two rooms, either side of the central corridor.

We paused for a moment and then I felt a gentle push from the havildar. I stepped cautiously through the door and started up the corridor. After I had gone a few paces without challenge, I felt the stirring of the air and heard the barely perceptible sound of footsteps following me.

I moved forward in the darkness, step by careful step. My fingers felt along the wall for the next doorway. Surely we must have reached it by now? I seemed to have been walking forever.

Now I felt the door and slipped inside. Half of the rebels followed, half entered the doorway opposite.

Again, a brief pause and then I was out and moving again. This time, the rebels were slower to follow and I was almost at the next doorway before I sensed them behind me. Obviously they, like me, feared that we were moving ever closer to the British and that at any moment we would come under fire. Not yet, though—we had gained the third doorway.

Now we paused a little longer, but, all too soon, I was once more in the corridor.

Something ahead of me moved. I felt a whisper of a breeze and threw myself to the floor at the very instant that the corridor filled with the thunderous crash of musket fire. Behind me, I heard a single cry. Had the rebels all been following me, I would have heard more. Almost all, I guessed, were still in the rooms, leaving me exposed alone in the corridor.

Already I was scrambling to my feet, throwing myself forward to the shelter of the next doorway. I could not see it but I knew it must be there.

There was a sudden light as, just as they had done before, the British opened their dark lantern and those who had not fired in that first volley took their aim. But the light showed me the doorway and I threw myself through it as the musket balls flew past.

The lantern was closed and it was dark once again. I heard the booted feet in the corridor.

"There was one ran in there."

I flattened myself against the wall but stayed as far as I could from the door, which I could just make out as a fractionally blacker rectangle in the darkness. There was the sound of boots and there was the slightest deepening of the shadow of the doorway.

My ears told me that two men had entered the room and now stood in the centre. My guess was that if I remained silent the next step would be for someone to enter with the lantern. I decided not to wait for that.

I spoke as softly as I could. "I'm British. Get Captain Moore. And clash your swords together so it sounds as if you're fighting me." As I spoke, I was already pulling off my jacket and pulling the canvas bags over my head.

Fortunately, my two unseen compatriots were quick on the uptake. They clashed swords most convincingly while shouting for their captain and a light. The rebels hiding in the next room in the corridor would have every reason to think that I was putting up a desperate struggle.

Moore came in at a run, accompanied by a man in civilian clothes who carried a musket in one hand and the lantern in the other.

By now the bags, my letter and the iodine were on the floor and I was unwrapping the bandage as fast as I could.

"Captain, don't speak. You can scream if you want."

Moore looked at his men, still striking each others' swords with vigour and immediately understood the situation. He gave a bloodcurdling yell.

"They're all in the next room and the one across from there. Pull a couple of your men back with a lot of noise and the rest wait here. I'll lead them to you."

Moore gestured the two men who were still enthusiastically clashing sword on sword. One broke off and ran into the corridor followed by the other.

Their screams and yells moved into the distance while the rest of Moore's men assembled around their captain. The lantern was closed and they remained in darkness while I made my way back into the corridor, yelling imprecations in Hindoo.

"Cowardly dogs! Come back and fight, you scum!"

For a moment, I thought that the rebels were not to be fooled but then I heard them leaving the rooms behind me to start down the corridor. They moved without caution, confident that I had cleared the way ahead and that the British had fled.

As they passed the room where Captain Moore and his men waited, the British fired into their flank and followed this up with a furious charge. Shocked and confused in the darkness, the rebels never had a chance. In a few minutes, it was all over and Captain Moore's outpost was safe for another night.

I had sheltered in another room, anxious not to be caught up in a battle where I could easily have ended up killed by either side, but now the lantern was lit again and I presented myself to Moore. My pathetic gifts were enthusiastically accepted, though my summary of the contents of the letter was received sombrely. I asked how things lay in the Entrenchment and their grim looks told me more than they were prepared to say in words.

"We pray for relief from Lucknow, but your intelligence suggests our prayers will not be answered."

"I fear not, but the situation changes daily. Lucknow may yet come to your aid."

"Then we will stand and fight until all hope is gone. But you must stay safe. Don't come here again unless you have intelligence we can use. Every time you come is fraught with danger and you may yet have something to tell us that could make a difference. Stay safe, John Williamson, and watch for news that may aid us in our plight."

"And if I ever do, how will I get it to you?"

"I'm sure you'll find a way." He grinned. "You're very resourceful."

I took his hand and shook it. "Then I must be off."

"Not just yet."

I was puzzled. The longer I stayed with them, the more chance of being discovered as a spy.

"All the others are dead and you are unmarked."

He was right of course, and his solution to the problem was right as well, but I could wish that his men had not been so damnably enthusiastic about it. Still, I was convincingly bloody as I recovered my horse and started yet again on the road to Bithur.

❋

I HAD PLANNED to spend the next day—the 12th—resting, but word came to Saturday House that there was to be an assault on the Entrenchment that evening. I could think of no way to warn the defenders in time but I reasoned that they would be able to see the preparations for the full-scale assault that was planned. I decided, though, that I should once again journey to Cawnpore to see how the Nana's ramshackle army behaved when ordered into action.

In the event, I had to admit they acquitted themselves rather well. They dug a trench from a drainage ditch that passed by the opposite side of the Entrenchment from the empty barracks and used this to enable themselves to advance under cover. At the same time, other rebels moved forward on the blind side of the unfinished barracks. Every ruined wall was used for shelter as some five thousand rebels closed from all directions on Wheeler's two hundred men.

The Nana's artillery now set up a concerted firing, such as I had not seen them do before and which I would have thought beyond their organisation. Alas, it was all too clear that it was not. For almost two hours the bombardment continued. It was as if some infernal thunderstorm was rolling across the plain with musket bullets sounding like hail between the claps of the artillery.

Artillery and infantry were both being thrown against Wheeler's defences, such as they were. The cavalry, though, was being held back so I rode to the promontory where I could observe the efforts of the defenders.

Looking down into Wheeler's position, I was struck again by how inadequate these defences appeared. Men lay in depressions scratched into the ground, offering no real protection against the mass of shot that fell into the compound so thickly that it was visible even from where I now stood.

For the first time I saw Wheeler's artillery in action. There were no proper breastworks to protect the gun crews and the pathetic wall of dried earth that the soldiers sheltered behind offered no protection at all when they stood to fire their field pieces. There were fewer than a dozen guns in the compound and every time a crew rose to their feet to load and aim, the intensity of musket fire increased. Again and again I saw men fall at their posts to be pushed roughly aside as others crawled to take their places, the air above them thick with lead.

The defenders' cannon did not fire that often, but, when they did, the skill and training of their European crews showed in the accuracy of their shots. While most of the Indian fire was wasted, often falling short and sometimes overshooting the compound altogether, the Europeans were deadly accurate. When a group of rebels found a strong position from which to fire, it was only a matter of minutes before canister shot would drop around them. I saw black bodies shredded as the canisters burst, spraying metal in all directions. Sometimes the screams could even be heard over the racket of the firing.

The musketry of the defenders was also impressive. There were few rifled weapons in the garrison and the secret of success with musketry is not accuracy but rate of fire. Each of the figures lying behind the earth bank had several muskets beside him and fired each in turn. From where I sat I saw women, their dresses torn and filthy, crawl across the open ground to take the empty muskets and bring reloaded ones. Some loaded lying beside their men: a difficult exercise when it was impossible to kneel to drop in the ball or wad down the charge for the rebels were quick to fire at any exposed person of either sex.

I thought of the silly chattering wives I had known, and could hardly believe that these same women now lay in the dust alongside their men, doing what they could to hold off the enemy's advance.

Every minute I expected to see the Nana's forces rise from cover and charge forward, overwhelming the Entrenchment by sheer weight of numbers. Yet they never did. Now and then one rebel, braver than the rest, would rise to his feet, gesticulating to his comrades to follow him, but every time he would be cut down by musket or artillery and his fellows would once more sink to cover to consider the danger of exposing themselves to European fire.

As darkness fell, I was sure that the natives would use the

cover of night to accomplish by stealth what they had so signally failed to achieve by open assault. Yet this was not to be the case. The coming of night seemed to quell their spirits and the firing fell away. Wheeler's tiny force had survived an organised attack by the full might of Nana Sahib's infantry. I left that night wondering, for the first time, if the garrison could, against all the odds, survive the siege.

WHAT CAN I say of the days that followed? I spent much of my time with Mungo, who listened assiduously for every scrap of gossip he could gather. His efforts yielded rumours aplenty. Nana Sahib was to march to Delhi to take the throne of the Emperor; the British had sent an army from London but the fleet it was travelling in had been intercepted by the Turks and utterly destroyed; a group of Musalmans had killed a cow and roasted it in the rebel lines. There was, it turned out, some truth in this last story. For a few hours, it seemed possible that the Hindoos might turn on the followers of the Prophet and the Nana's army might have disintegrated in an orgy of fratricide, but the Nana restrained his co-religionists and passions were calmed.

The welter of confusion and lies, contradictory report after contradictory report, moved us no further forward. I did my best to add to the confusion. When I was seized by the arm by some inhabitant of Saturday House anxious for news from the battle, I would purse my lips and say that the troops feared to approach too close to the enemy because they believed the area to have been mined. Or I would say that I had smelt the odour of roasting flesh from the defenders and I feared that they had more provisions than we had believed.

In such petty ways I did what little I could to undermine the morale of the rebels but when I rode to Cawnpore, day after day I saw the same sad spectacle with only minor alterations. The barracks where Captain Moore maintained his piquet sprouted a strange construction on the roof—a sort of crow's nest where a man could sit concealed from hostile fire but himself shoot out at anyone approaching the building. These efforts made an assault across the open ground that much harder and reduced the amount of sniping from the other buildings but the rebels continued to fire sporadically into the compound. The rebel artillery, too, kept up a steady bombardment, despite desperate sallies by night that had seen some of the nearer guns spiked. It seemed now that every time that I climbed that accursed promontory, there were more corpses lying exposed in the Entrenchment and the vultures had taken to landing at the centre of the camp, pecking at the flesh of the dead until a weary hand heaved a stone in their direction and they flapped ungainly away.

I did wonder why the open ground was not piled with the European dead but a rebel sepoy explained to me that at night the bodies were dragged to a well outside the Entrenchment and deposited there.

"We hear them doing it," he said, "and sometimes we fire toward the sound but…" He shrugged. It seemed that even in this ugly battle, there were limits to what most of the sepoys were prepared to do.

For all the casualties inflicted by the rebels' fire, the most deadly enemy of the Europeans was the heat. It was the hottest time of the year. Every day we waited for the weather to break but the monsoon rains held off. Even the natives began to feel the effect of the heat. After my years in the tropics, I was as inured to its effects as anyone, but by midday, the least exertion was intolereable. Even a short walk involved an enormous effort and the idea of undertaking any strenuous activity was impossible. I would sit sweating in the shade, remembering stories I had heard of men struck down by heatstroke; fit and healthy at breakfast and dead by noon. The natives were as helpless as I in the hottest hours of the day. Even to load and fire a gun taxed their strength and there was always an easing of the amount of fire at noon, which must have offered some relief to Wheeler's men. It might have gone some way to make that time of day just bearable, for the tortured souls in the Entrenchment had no relief from the sun beating down on the hideously over-crowded barracks that were the only shelter remaining.

Wheeler's promise that the well would provide enough water to sustain life seemed to be being kept. By now, the brickwork at the top of the well had been completely destroyed by the artillery that rained upon it whenever a creaking in the night betrayed the unfortunate at the windlass. The sepoys told me, though, that they would still hear the rattling of a bucket against the bricks of the shaft as the garrison was supplied with the liquid it needed to stay alive. With every drop drawn at terrible risk to the men at the wellhead, there would be none to spare for bathing or to splash on hot children. No dampened towels might cool the fevered brows of ladies used to sitting in the airy shade of their drawing rooms while a pankah wallah worked to keep a cooling breeze. Here the air was disturbed only as cannon shot tore through the walls of the building, bringing terror and death to all those huddled within. I saw those shots smash into the old barracks and, remembering the families packed in there when I had shared their shelter less than three weeks before, I saw in my mind's eye the trail of blood and entrails that would follow the ball as it carved its way through the interior.

The kitchen block still stood but by now there could be lit-tle left to cook in it. The desperate state of the garrison's sup-plies was reflected in the way they opened fire at any sowar within range, even if he posed no threat to the Entrenchment. Short as they were of ammunition, they would always try to hit a horse. The sepoys warned me of the danger. "If they can kill it, then when it is dark, they will sneak out to cut off the flesh for food."

"I CAN'T JUST stay here and do nothing."

Mungo sat cross-legged on the floor while I paced around the room. He didn't speak.

"Say something, for God's sake."

He shrugged. He had a very eloquent shrug.

"They're dying there."

"We're all dying, John."

"I should do something."

"You cannot help them."

"If I could save just one person...If I saved just one, I would feel that I had not been entirely useless."

Mungo rose to his feet in a single graceful movement.

"Not everyone made it into the fort."

He was right, of course. Europeans had been rounded up here and there and either killed on the spot or hauled off to the Nana and killed there, except for a few of the women who had been spared to appease the old Peshwa's widows and one or two men it was rumoured were being held for ransom.

Mungo stood in front of me and held me by the arms, stopping my pacing. "John, you can do nothing for those trapped with General Wheeler. But you might, perhaps, save some of your compatriots who are hiding in the country."

Mungo's suggestion showed how well he had come to know me. Riding the countryside, searching for fugitives would give me an outlet for the nervous energy that was eating me up. And he was right—I had more chance of saving lives out in the open country than in Cawnpore, surrounded by Nana Sahib's army.

I started that very afternoon, making a wide circuit North and West of Bithur. The country was, by and large, open fields, but there were occasional stands of woods and ditches where a man might hide. I was handicapped by my appearance. I had to wear the Nana's uniform to guarantee myself free passage but I knew that any Europeans who saw me approach would take care to conceal themselves. So I had to search as thoroughly as if I were truly an enemy come to destroy them.

That day, and for days to come, I pushed my horse through the woody groves, branches scratching at my face and tearing my clothes. I dismounted to clamber into dusty ditches that proved empty as far as the eye could see. I demanded peremptorily of villagers if they had seen any feringees, as the foreign devils were called. Each day, though, I returned to Bithur hot, tired and covered with the grime of a long ride but without having seen any Europeans. I did come across evidence that there were refugees surviving somehow in that hostile country. A villager, anxious to please, denounced a fellow as having sheltered a family a few days previously but further enquiry would reveal that they had left the district and no one knew where they might be now.

A ruffian walking along the road was carrying a pocket watch, clearly stolen. At first, he denied it but I drew my sword and made to strike him with it and he admitted he had found a man hiding in a ditch and he had robbed him.

"But he wept and pleaded that I should spare his life, saying he was a merchant and had never cheated the Indians he had traded with, so I left him." He paused to spit. "It was no matter. He had no food and no water. He will be dead by now."

I had him tell me where he had found the man and I rode there and searched but I saw no sign of him.

Once, beside a shrine, I saw the ground disturbed with a new grave. Dogs had scratched at the turned earth and part of a red coat showed through. No native would have been buried thus, so I knew I had found one of those I was searching for but too late, too late.

About a week after I had started my quest, I was riding in the later part of the morning across open land where ditches separated the poor fields. The heat was near insufferable. I had just turned toward a cluster of huts some mile away, where I planned to rest in the shade, when a movement drew my eye to the ditch ahead of me.

Heaped in the red dust was what I first took to be a pile of clothing but, as I drew near, I saw it to be the huddled body of a man. He had scraped a hollow at the bottom of the ditch and sought to shelter from the sun with his jacket draped over the shallow declivity.

When I first saw him, he was lying motionless, as if hoping to avoid detection but, as I approached, he must have realised that he would be seen and he started to scrabble desperately along the ditch. I called to him in English and, at last, he stopped and turned to me. From the look of terror on his face, I think he stopped only because he recognised the futility of his attempts to escape, rather than because he was reassured by my words.

The ragged remains of his clothes showed that he had once been a man of substance but now, it seemed to me, he was scarcely a man at all. His shirt and trousers were torn and filthy. His face was burnt by the sun and his hair a wild tangle. I dismounted and walked slowly toward him, holding out my water bottle. Judging from his cracked lips, he must have been desperate for drink and I think that is all that made him face me.

While he drank, I explained that I was English and was there to help him. I had chupattis and dried figs in my saddlebag and he seized these ravenously.

"You are safe now," I said. "I will protect you."

He made no reply, as if unwilling to draw breath for explanations until he had eaten and drunk all that I could offer him. Even then, he said little and much of what he did say made no sense. As far as I could tell, he had been a week on the run with scarce anything to eat and drinking foul water in any place that he could find it.

"They spill it from the wells when they water the cattle in the evenings and it may lie puddled until dark," he said. "And once I stayed two nights beside a river but there were people and it was not safe."

I learned his name was Mr Ashley and he had been a telegraph engineer. He spoke of a woman but whether this was his wife, lost in India, or some English sweetheart, I could not ascertain. It seemed that the heat, the hunger, the thirst and the constant fear had addled his brain.

I was so thrilled that I had at last found a survivor of these outrages that it was some time before I started to worry about the practicalities of helping him. It was possible, I knew, that a combination of threats and bribery might buy him shelter in the village to which I had been heading. However, this was far from certain and I was reluctant to reveal myself by riding in with him under my protection until I had sounded out the disposition of the inhabitants. If they seemed to me unreliable, I could move the man to shelter in the woods nearer to Bithur until such a time as Mungo and I could between us make some more secure arrangement for his safety.

Looking back at it now, it seems obvious that I should have made some proper plans for how I was to deal with such a situation before starting my search. At the time, though, finding some survivors seemed so urgent a goal that I had concentrated all my thoughts on that, confident that once I had found somebody I would be able to develop a plan to succour them. Even faced with the immediate problem of providing shelter for Mr Ashley, I was confident that I could secure his safety. Convincing Mr Ashley of this proved, though, immensely difficult. His troubled mind had seized on the notion that I was his saviour and he clung piteously to my legs begging me not to go and leave him. In vain did I assure him again and again that I left only to secure a safe place in which to shelter him and that I would return to bear him away.

At last, he seemed to understand the situation but he said that he feared to be left alone and defenceless. Could I leave the pistol he had seen holstered on my saddlebag? Armed, he thought he would be able to wait for me with some confidence.

I was reluctant to part with the weapon, especially to one whose mental state seemed so uncertain, but it did seem the easiest resolution of the situation. So I handed the pistol to Mr Ashley and, mounting, turned my horse again toward the village.

I had ridden no more than a hundred paces when, behind me, I heard the sound of a single shot. I did not hurry my return, for I already knew what I would see. There in the ditch lay the mortal remains of Mr Ashley, my pistol gripped in his fist and his brains a mess of blood and grey matter, already drying into the parched soil.

❋

I RETURNED TO Saturday House in the blackest of desperate moods. Mungo sat cross-legged and silent while I poured out the story of my failure.

"I thought it would be alright if I saved one person. One person, Mungo. Is that so much to ask?"

At last, after I had raged and wept, he rose to his feet and kissed me. "You are a good man, John. We will see you save one soul yet."

As so often, he took quiet charge. "I have a cousin who lives some ten miles North of Bithur. His name is Dara. He has high walls around his compound and no neighbours. The servants are loyal. I was going to wait until it was needed before I made any arrangements, for, though the risk is small, there is always some risk. And servants, though loyal, are more reliable when bribed. But I will put all in train now and then, when you find another lost soul, paradise shall be ready to receive him."

He smiled with a confidence that went some way to restoring my faded spirits and, though Mr Ashley's death still weighed heavy on me, after some hours I fell into a fitful sleep. From time to time, I woke to find Mungo bent over me, soothing me with his hands and his kisses and each time the dreams that had wakened me would fade and by morning I was almost recovered.

Mungo insisted that I not ride out the next day but rest at Saturday House while he made arrangements with his cousin. I promised faithfully that I would ride nowhere and I kept the letter of my promise. Once Mungo was safely out about his business, though, I decided to use my enforced rest to resume what I fancifully thought of as my intelligence activities, though I could think of nothing I was likely to discover that might help my compatriots.

I decided that a sowar conspicuously absent from the field might be the subject of contemptuous remarks and would learn nothing of value. So, instead, I dressed myself in a beggar's rags and slipped quietly through a side entrance and into Bithur.

The village was quieter than the first time I had visited it in this disguise. The fishermen's boats were still there, bobbing on the river while the men busied themselves with lines and nets. The market, though, was almost deserted. Many of the Nana's courtiers had decamped to Cawnpore to fawn on him at his new headquarters. Merchants who could transport their produce to Cawnpore had followed, leaving the street I remembered as being so busy with a faintly desolate air.

I walked about, occasionally knocking my staff against the bowl. After an hour, though, it was still almost empty. The mob might feast on the plunder of Europeans and Anglo-Indians in Cawnpore, but little of that wealth found its way to the villagers of Bithur. Even the porters and idlers who used to swagger the streets or lean against the walls of alleyways in a vaguely menacing way—even they had gone. The owners of the shop-houses, trapped in Bithur by their properties, and the fishermen, whose families had lived beside the Ganges for generations—these were the only people left in the village.

A merchant beckoned me to the shady interior of his shop and cast a handful of rice into my bowl.

"I'd give you more, but times are hard."

"I thank you for any gift and I grieve that you are finding the times troubling. But are these not good times for our people, that the white men are being driven from us?"

The merchant hesitated, stroking his chin before responding. "It is good that the *feringees* go. But their going brings turbulence and when the river is troubled, a boat may be broken."

"So do you feel it were better that these present troubles had not started?"

"Oh, no!" His eyebrows—bushy for an Indian—climbed his forehead as he expressed his indignation at the idea. "I only wish the Europeans had been driven out years ago. Once they are gone, life will be good again."

"Then it is good that they are being driven from Cawnpore."

"Ha! I doubt they are being driven out. Rather I hear that they will stay for eternity in the town." Then he grinned. "*Sub lal hoga.*"

Everything is to become red.

I smiled as best I could, thanked him for his gift, and turned away.

❉

THE NEXT DAY, Mungo having made the necessary arrangements with his cousin, I once again started my search for survivors. It seemed, though, that the luck that I had thought changed with my discovery of Mr Ashley had once again turned and I found no one.

By now it was the middle of June and rumours began to spread that there would be an assault on the Entrenchment on the anniversary of the Battle of Plessey, fulfilling the prophecy that (at least as far as Cawnpore was concerned), the British would be driven out on the hundredth anniversary of their first great victory in India.

Any news of a new attack was, of course, important, but this assault was to be especially significant for me as the story was that the cavalry was to be deployed in force for the first time. I had tried to avoid over-much contact with other sowars, as I feared that any true cavalryman would soon spot me for the impostor that I was. However, I had used the disguise so regularly that by now I was a familiar face about Saturday House and I feared it would be noticed if I was absent from such a significant event.

Although I had always been a reasonable horseman, I rode in a style that reflected the rough riding of my childhood on an English farm. I was not sure that I could hold my own with the cavalry drilled sowars of Nana Sahib's guard. And even if my basic horsemanship passed muster, I had no experience of riding to war. The notion of finding myself in a cavalry charge was utterly terrifying.

Much of the time that I would have liked to have been out looking for refugees was spent in earnest debate with Mungo. His first response to the news was that I should discard my sowar disguise and stay safe at home in his apartment. I turned this idea down flat. I had adopted the uniform because it was the safest way to allow free passage in Bithur, Cawnpore, and all the countryside around. Without it, I could do nothing but skulk behind Mungo's protection until, somehow, the horror of the mutiny was ended or, as I sometimes feared might be the case, I grew old in hiding.

The only alternative to ignominious retreat seemed to be to learn enough of the cavalryman's art to pass myself off not only to the uninitiated, but to the Nana's sowars themselves. It took a full day of argument before Mungo accepted that I could not live with myself were I to give up now. As ever, though, once he had been convinced that I was in earnest, he did everything in his power to aid me. It turned out that another of his invaluable cousins had himself ridden as a cavalryman in the service of a local lord whose little kingdom had long ago been swallowed by the British.

"The skills he learned will be similar enough to the Nana's men." If Mungo was convinced that my idea was insanely dangerous, he had at least decided not to let me see how terrified he was on my behalf. "And you are going to have to tell people you have transferred here from elsewhere. You can hardly turn up claiming to be an old servant of the Nana when none of the sowars here will ever have seen you in their lives before."

"I think that there may be difficulties in my just 'turning up', whatever my story."

Mungo grinned. "Sometimes I forget how English you are, John. This is India, and an India at war. There are no regimental rolls and movement orders. The word goes out and soldiers come. As it happens…" (by now Mungo's grin threatened to split his chin from his face) "one Mahmet Mazullah fell from his horse last week and there is some doubt as to whether or not he will recover. If you study hard with my cousin, you should be ready to replace him when his service ends."

"'Mahmet Mazullah.' A Musalman?"

"Why not?"

"Serving Nana Sahib."

"Serving the Peshwa. Fighting in India for freedom from foreign conquerors."

By now, it should have come as no surprise. The horrors of Cawnpore, the bloated bodies floating in the Ganges, the remains that jackals dug from shallow graves—all these things confirmed the hatred that the populace felt for the foreigners in their midst. Yet it still shocked me that Musalman and Hindoo would put aside their traditional enmity and fight alongside each other to destroy the Christians.

"I had best start studying with your cousin as soon as may be."

❄

THE ANNIVERSARY OF Plessey was now less than a week away and I feared that I could not hope to gain the skills I needed in the few days available to me. I need not have worried. Soon after dawn the next day, Mungo introduced me to his cousin on an empty plain a few miles West of Bithur, remote from any road and away from prying eyes. Amjad (for that was his name) was a wiry man but, though I still found it difficult to judge the age of Indians, I thought him too senescent to be in any shape to teach me. As soon as he mounted the skinny little pony he had brought to our meeting, I realised my mistake. The man was a magnificent rider, relaxed yet secure in the saddle as he galloped his mount in what seemed impossibly tight circles.

After a few minutes, he reined back and cantered toward a lance he had left upright in the red earth. Without pausing, he plucked it from the ground and wheeled again. As the pony turned, the lance was already couched under his arm. He kicked once and galloped straight toward us. My horse shied as Amjad raced just inches past my face and lowered the lance to the ground. A moment later, he raised it. There on the point, was a tent peg he had hammered into the ground before our arrival.

Twice more he turned at the gallop and the lance dipped to the earth and each time he raised it with another peg speared on the tip.

He trotted over to me and passed over the lance.

"You try."

Thinking this a joke, I laughed, but Amjad's scowl showed that he was serious. I looked to where he had speared up the pegs and saw another three forming a neat line alongside them.

I tucked the lance under my arm. It was surprisingly light. I turned my horse but, before I could start toward the pegs, Amjad was shouting at me with a string of criticisms. I didn't hold the lance properly; I had failed to adjust my weight to take account of the new balance point I would need as it dipped; my left hand was loose on the reins. There seemed a hundred other things but these were all I could remember.

I sat on Kuching, feeling more and more ridiculous as he poked and prodded me into what he thought was a satisfactory position. Finally, I was allowed to kick in my heels and start toward the tent pegs.

I had taken barely half a dozen paces before I was subjected to another torrent of complaints. I had shifted my weight again as soon as I had moved, my kick was wrong, the horse didn't understand me, I had allowed my body to slump, I had pulled too sharply on the reins, I had taken my eyes off the pegs…

On my third attempt, I got as far as a canter before the abuse started; on my fourth I almost reached the pegs. By now, Mungo was struggling to keep a straight face. I, blushing furiously under the tan which was now almost as effective a disguise as my walnut stain, tried to hold onto my temper. I was, after all, no mean horseman. I had grown up with the beasts and, if I had not ridden during my sea-faring years, I had more than made up for my lack of practise during my time in India. Yet I had to admit that I did not have the smallest part of the skill of the old man now offering a devastating critique of every aspect of my riding. Even so, I doubted that his comments would be truly useful. Surely his skill was that of a native, born to his way of life. How could a morning spent subjecting myself to being treated like a child at a riding school make any difference to my own abilities? As the day grew hotter, I found, to my astonishment, that I could catch the tent pegs on my lance, if not at a gallop, then at a respectable canter. And my newfound ability to turn my horse back on itself without slowing impressed Mungo to the point where he caught himself clapping, despite Amjad's scowls.

Before noon, we had to stop. The heat had reached the point where neither man nor horse should be in the full sun, and we walked our beasts slowly toward a grove some half mile away, where we sheltered under the trees and Mungo made us a picnic of cold rice with curried fowl and mangoes and figs to make a fine dessert.

Amjad enjoyed his food though, like many older men, he ate sparingly. I took advantage of the break to question him about drills. He was undoubtedly improving my horsemanship but I was still no clearer as to how the Nana's cavalry drilled. Having watched the Company's cavalry on parade, moving seamlessly from 'advance by column' to 'advance in line', responding, as if by magic, to the sounds of the bugle, I was all too aware that I had no knowledge of how to perform these manoeuvres. I was sure that as soon as anything more complicated than following the man in front was required, I would be exposed as an imposter.

Once I had got Amjad to understand my question, he laughed so much that he nearly choked on the last of his figs. Yet again, I had forgotten that the way that Indians organised their armies was totally alien to the British approach to matters military.

"Ride along with your fellows until they order a charge, then draw your sword and charge with everyone else. Your horse will know what to do if you don't." He laughed again.

"What about the lance?"

"If they charge, you won't need the lance. It's for showing off and sticking pigs. The first man you strike with it, it will snap off. And if it doesn't, you can hardly ride around with a body dangling from your lance, can you?"

Mungo passed him water, because we both feared that he would choke if he laughed much more.

"So why have I spent the morning learning to use the lance?"

Amjad spluttered and water splashed onto the baked earth.

"Because showing off is nine tenths of what makes a sowar. But don't worry—once the day cools, I'll show you how to use that fancy sword of yours."

We lazed under the trees, digesting our meal until the worst of the heat was over. Then Amjad was as good as his word. We did not leave the grove but Amjad stuffed a bag with leaves and soil and hung it from a branch. Then, swinging his heavy tulwar, he rode through the trees toward the bag, which was slashed open in an instant.

"Now you try."

My first attempt ended with my nearly falling from the horse as the weight of the sword unbalanced me. Having mastered the whole business of staying in the saddle while whirling my blade around, I twice buried it in tree trunks before I reached the sack. A few more passes rocked the bag to and fro but failed to cut it. Only as the shadows of the trees were stretching long in the afternoon did I finally manage to despatch my enemy well enough to satisfy Amjad. Even at the end, though, he had his doubts.

"Mungo tells me you don't really want to kill anyone," he said. "That's probably just as well."

chapter 7

MAHMET MAZULLAH DIED that night and, in accordance with the custom of the Musalmans, he was buried the next day.

I had intended to introduce myself into the company of the Nana's cavalry that same day but my efforts with Amjad had left me so stiff and tired Mungo said it was better that I rest in his apartment, while he massaged the aches and pains from my body. "Tomorrow will be soon enough," he assured me. I was not certain that his advice was truly impartial, for he was never slow to enjoy the opportunities offered when he massaged me but, in truth, I was too tired to argue and happy enough to allow him the freedom of my body for a day. The next morning, though, I was up early to force myself into the uniform and, trying to look dashing and military, rather than just stiff and uncomfortable, I made my way to the quarters usually occupied by the cavalry.

I was nervous of introducing myself, but Mungo had been right: I just told people that I was there to replace Mahmet Mazullah and no one questioned my presence. Perhaps this was at least in part because everyone had a more pressing matter on their minds. Word had spread that, after weeks of standing by while the infantry failed to take the Entrenchment, the cavalry was now to be given their chance. On 23rd June, the hundredth anniversary of the Battle of Plessey, Nana Sahib had ordered that his sowars should ride against the British and finally drive them from Cawnpore. So it was that only four days after my lesson in the basic skills of an Indian cavalryman, I was to see action against my own people.

My first thought, on finally hearing confirmation of these plans, was that I should warn the garrison, but how could I achieve this in the days that remained? With the cavalry about to be deployed, I could hardly join a raiding party such as I had before and I could think of no other way of getting information to the British, trapped in their Entrenchment.

As ever, it was Mungo's common sense that reassured me.

"The British have calendars," he said. He was straddling me as I lay on the floor and he rubbed oil into my calves, easing the stiffness that remained even three days from my lessons with Amjad. "I think they'll know to be prepared on the anniversary of Plessey."

He was right, of course. The Indians had always been pre-dictable in attacking on anniversaries, or lucky days, a custom that the British had long understood. The 23rd June would see Wheeler's force as ready as, given their situation, they could ever be.

On the Monday morning, the Nana's cavalry was assembled together at Bithur and we rode at dawn to avoid the worst of the heat. We took the road to Cawnpore that, by now, I knew so well. I had thought that the ride would be a sombre affair, with people's minds on the battle that they would face on the morrow, but none showed any sign of fear or concern. Instead, they rode easily, talking and joking amongst each other. Several edged their horses alongside mine to greet me and welcome me to their company. They would ask where I was from and what experience I had. I answered with details of the history I had rehearsed with Mungo. I had come from Dharampur, far enough from Bithur for there to be little chance of falling in with anyone who might claim to know the place. It was in Oudh and, though I had left military life to settle with my wife on a small farm, my anger at the annexation had driven me to join the Peshwa. The story had the advantage that any mistakes in my riding could be excused as carelessness after so long away. The idea that I was an old cavalryman returned to the fray also explained why a man of my comparatively advanced years would still be riding into action.

As we rode, we came across other forces of cavalry. Some were mutineers or deserters from other places where troops had turned on their officers, others were attached to local rulers who, while less significant than Nana Sahib, still had small honour guards they had contributed to the Peshwa's campaign.

We passed through Old Cawnpore and, once in the European quarter, we made our way to the Assembly Rooms where I had met General Wheeler. Could that have been less than a year before? So much had changed. The streets here were wide thoroughfares where parasoled ladies had walked with their beaus away from the native rabble. Now, though, the street had been turned into a makeshift camp for some of the thousands who had flocked to join the Nana. Tents blocked the highway. Indians, in all sorts of uniforms and none, filled every available space. Nana Sahib was to address his men in the Assembly Rooms and everyone wanted to be there to hear their Peshwa urge them to victory on the morrow.

Over four thousand men gathered. Most could not enter the Rooms themselves but stood outside in the street, scorning the shelter of their tents and craning their necks for a glimpse of their leader. They cheered the Nana's arrival and they cheered again and again when they heard shouting from those lucky enough to have found space within the Rooms.

I sat on my horse with the rest of the cavalry, for we thought ourselves above pressing our way through the sepoys and, besides, we did not want to leave our mounts.

We stood there, in the baking sun, for the better part of an hour. At last, with a final exultant cheer, men began spilling from the Assembly Rooms. Many were still in their Native Infantry uniforms (though most had discarded the trousers for loincloths, which were more suitable to the heat.) These joined men from their regiments who had waited outside and from all directions came voices of command as troops formed up. Even my fellows sat to attention and we nudged our horses with our heels until they formed smart lines.

Now Nana Sahib emerged onto the steps of the Assembly Rooms. It was the first time that I had seen him since he established his headquarters at Savada House and I was struck by the change in his appearance. He looked much older and his face, which had been relaxed and easy to smile, was now etched with worry lines that betrayed the cares that had come with his new responsibilities. The glasses were gone and, as his glance darted from side to side to take in the thousands mustered for his inspection, I found myself wondering how much he could see or if the men in front of him were just an anonymous blur. Still, he looked quite grand with a golden sash tied around his waist and a torque of gold at his throat. The pistol and sword tucked into the sash added a martial touch, suited to his new role as army commander and when he raised his hand to acknowledge the salutes (somewhat ragged in many cases but salutes nonetheless) the cheer from his troops was loud enough to unsettle the horses.

Eventually the Nana withdrew back into the Assembly Rooms and gradually the mass of men dispersed, some marching off in tidy columns (a few still carrying the colours of their old regiments), others drifting away in small groups or ones and twos. The Bithur cavalry headed to the European villas where some servants, undecided as to the eventual outcome of the revolt, were keeping faith with their old masters to the extent of watering the patches of lawn around the houses and thus providing some basic grazing for our horses. By now it was late so, after setting small fires on the ground and cooking companionable meals, we made ourselves as comfortable as we could for what might well be our last night on this earth. Some of us settled to sleep on the ground; some commandeered the bedrooms in the bungalows. For a mad moment, I wondered about returning to my own old home to sleep there, but the danger of recognition was too great so, still somehow uncomfortable with the notion of invading my neighbours' homes, I wrapped a blanket around myself and settled for a night under the stars.

We were not to sleep for long, however. Though the cavalry was to attack in the morning on the anniversary of Plessey, the rebel infantry kept up scattered firing throughout the night to deny the enemy their rest. Of course, it denied us rest as well. I lay awake listening to the fitful musket fire—somehow more disturbing than the constant noise of artillery, which I was by now used to. I wondered whether Charles Hillersdon was listening to the same shots and whether he could sleep as he waited for the dawn. Was he even still alive? And poor, pretty Lydia—had she survived childbirth lying on the earth floor?

When I did sleep, I dreamt of them—Lydia, Charles and the children. They came to me, emaciated and bleeding, and asked me why I had abandoned them. I told them I would see them in the morning and, in my dream, I mounted my horse and rode into the Encampment. I had my lance and I galloped at the Hillersdons and the children were on the ground next to a newborn baby and I gathered each on my lance. Amjad was standing alongside Charles Hillersdon and he turned to him and asked if he did not think I had held my seat well.

I woke before dawn, shivering, though it was warm even at that hour. My attempts at sleep had left me more tired than if I had spent the night in useful activity. I cursed myself for not having tried to make contact with the garrison—though with the attack already under way, I could think of no useful intelligence I could have added.

We roused ourselves as soon as there was light to see. The Musalmans amongst us stretched themselves out on the ground to make their morning prayers, while the Hindoos, with me among them, performed our ablutions as best we could with the water available, for the Hindoo values cleanliness of the person.

We took chupattis and dried meat from our saddlebags and ate them as we mounted. Today was not a day for a leisurely breakfast.

The cavalry was to rendezvous at the army riding school, a quarter of a mile North of the Entrenchment. It had been burned down in the early days of the Mutiny and was now little more than rubble, but it remained the last cover available before the plain where Wheeler had made his stand. I wondered if some Indian with an ironic sense of humour had chosen the building where the British had trained their riders to be the gathering place for their nemesis.

We reined our mounts. Now that the moment was come, we sat silently in our saddles. There is an abundance of life in India, which breeds, in its turn, a philosophical acceptance of death. But, faced with the immediate imminence of destruction, even the most stoic of men is liable to pause and reflect on the fate that may await him.

The Nana's batteries had fallen silent as we assembled but now they opened up all at once and the air was so thick with artillery that it seemed for a moment that the Entrenchment lay under the shadow of an unnatural cloud.

Now the bombardment stopped and, for a moment, all was silent. Then came the unsteady notes of a bugle at the lips of a man who clearly lacked experience with his instrument. Cracked as the sound was, though, even I recognised the order to charge. We rode from the ruins of the riding school, forming a ragged line as we emerged onto the plain. For a few moments we were trotting. I drew my sword, already finding it difficult to control the heavy blade against the movements of the horse. I worried that if we lurched I could end up pricking my own mount with the point and I wondered how I would cope at the gallop. Already some of the horses were stretching themselves to their full speed. Instinctively, others joined them. My own horse pushed forward and I could hardly have held him back, even had I wished to.

There was still half a mile to the British defences and we were hurtling forward. Dust rose all around, mingling with the smoke which still hung in the air from the artillery barrage. My ears were filled with the thunder of hoof beats and the cries of my companions.

"Deen! Deen" *For the faith! For the faith!*

We rode on. Now, from the saddle, I could see across the pitiful defences to where my fellow Europeans lay with their muskets ready at their shoulders. Beside them, I saw crouching figures dressed in rags. I did not at first recognise them as the white women of Cawnpore, their finery destroyed, their beauty tarnished. Yet, seeing them steadfast beside their men, ready to reload and pass new weapons to the warriors, I had never thought them finer.

Now we were two hundred yards from the parapet. Now one hundred. Still we rode, with no fire from our enemy. Already, the horses were tiring and the impetus of our charge had been lost but we were almost upon them. Then, when we were just fifty yards from their defences, Wheeler's tattered army opened fire. Three nine-pounders belched flame and smoke. One round of grapeshot found our range. All around me, men and horses were thrown to the ground. Had we not galloped the whole way from the riding school, the speed and exhilaration of our charge might well have carried us to the parapet despite our losses, but the horses were already slowing. As riders tugged desperately at their reins to avoid the welter of bodies beneath our horses' hooves, the animals swung about, causing even further chaos in the line. Within seconds, the charge had turned into a mass of wheeling, panicked horseflesh, riders yelling in impotent rage, scarcely more rational than the beasts they rode.

Ahead of me a horse fell. Its forelegs scrabbled to raise it from the ground but then it collapsed, whinnying its pain and terror. Instinctively, I kicked Kuching on and we jumped the doomed creature, but now all around was chaos. I swerved to avoid another fallen horse, reining back until Kuching stood, flanks heaving, eyes rolling in terror. Again and again, the British muskets fired. All around, it seemed, men were falling to the ground. Exposed to the rebels' fire by the inadequacy of the mud wall that offered their only protection, the British gunners nonetheless stood at their posts and I knew that it would be only seconds before the cannon were ready to fire again.

The charge was broken, the sowars turning and riding hard back the way they had come. I pulled at the reins, turning Kuching toward safety and joined the flight. Before the nine-pounders could fire another round, it was over.

That was the end of the cavalry's attempts to take Wheeler's position. I think we all knew then that the day was lost but, to be fair to the infantry, they made a better showing than us. For now they tried where we had failed.

The Nana's generals had come up with a new plan. They had raided the storehouses along the river and seized the giant bales of cotton that had been left there ready for shipping. Now the infantry advanced pushing the bales ahead of them as mobile parapets. Behind these, the sepoys were able to move in safety, showing themselves only to fire at the Entrenchment before ducking back into cover.

The British were pouring fire toward the infantry but without effect. The cotton bales moved steadily onward and I began to believe that the prophecy of victory on the anniversary of Plessey could yet come true. Those of us who had survived the abortive cavalry charge began to see a possibility of redeeming ourselves. As soon as the infantry reached the parapet, we could follow, moving up behind their cover and then passing through them to bring death and destruction to the enemy camp. Officers ordered us back into our lines and we began to edge forward.

At that point, as we thought that the battle was turning in our favour, we saw smoke rising from the foremost of the bales. As they moved closer to the British guns, so the hot shot was firing the cotton. Minutes later, most of the bales were alight and, suddenly robbed of their cover, the soldiers were at the mercy of the defenders' fire. Like the cavalry before them, the infantry now broke, turning and running back toward us.

So the anniversary of Plessey passed and the British were still there.

No one ever ordered us to disperse. One by one or in small groups, we slipped away. There was no point in pretending that we might charge again. The sun was by now high in the sky and the day too hot for another open assault. The artillery barrage continued unabated but the Nana's troops rested in the shade. There was one small consolation for the rebels. About midday, there was a great explosion within the Entrenchment. It seemed that a lucky shot had struck a store of the defenders' ammunition but the blow came too late and would not, in any case, have been decisive.

Some of those who had assembled for the assault now left the rebel lines but most settled back to the comfortable monotony of the siege. I decided that I, too, would stay in Cawnpore. The events of the day and the valiant defence put up by General Wheeler made me wonder if the defeat of the British was truly inevitable. If they were not doomed, but had, perhaps, even the remotest chance of seeing things to a successful conclusion, did I not have an obligation to fight with them? The men of the garrison were by now physically exhausted after weeks of constant bombardment but I was rested and healthy. Could I not make a useful contribution, especially if I were able to carry in food and medicine?

In the time since my last foray to Captain Moore's position, the eyrie that had been built on top of the unfinished barrack had discouraged such raids. I had seen, during the attack earlier in the day, how one or two men in that vantage point could pick off so many attackers that few were prepared to take the risk of moving into range of Moore's sharpshooters. Reaching the Entrenchment by way of the empty barracks no longer seemed a realistic option. But perhaps, I thought, there might be other possibilities.

I set off to ride along the roads nearest to the Entrenchment to see if there was any sensible path that might allow a determined individual to reach the British position.

By now, the sun was setting and the brief Indian dusk was upon us. To my right I saw some British move out to retrieve any of the abandoned cotton bales that had not been destroyed by fire. With piquets around them to guard against attack, the defenders rolled the cotton back toward their base where the bales made a useful addition to the mud parapet that was their only defence. Despite the guards, the British took a big risk by exposing themselves in the open like this. With hundreds of Indians still lurking under cover following the day's reverses, a massed attack must have killed many of the men in the open—a loss that their tiny garrison could not sustain while any casualties would be negligible to the Nana. It seemed to me that the fight had gone out of the rebels. They no longer believed that they were going to win this battle.

On my left were the remains of St John's, the soldiers' church. This symbol of an alien God had been set ablaze early in the revolt and now the ruined walls were a sad reminder of what it had once been. As I came up with the remains, I saw a group of sepoys, still wearing the uniform of the 1st Native Infantry. They were silently looking toward a storm drain that ran between the Entrenchment and the road. I reined in and, following the direction of their gaze, tried to see what it was that exercised their attention.

Barely visible in the failing light, I could just make out the figure of a native crawling along the drain. Although I could not be sure, he did not appear to be carrying a weapon and, certainly, those who were watching him did not seem prepared for action. Indeed, several had stacked their muskets against the rubble of a wall.

Urgent voices called from the shadows, urging me not to linger in view of the sentries but to ride on.

There was something about the group that made me hesitate. They shuffled like naughty children caught out in a trick. They were nervous but their nervousness did not look like that of men preparing for battle. Besides, with the casualties the 1st Native Infantry had taken that morning, no one would expect them to fight again today.

Rather than ride on, I dismounted and led my horse among the shadows.

Now the sepoys huddled together, casting suspicious glances in my direction. Although infantry soldiers could be unfriendly to the cavalry, I had not encountered such open hostility at Cawnpore before. I tethered my horse to one of the less unstable columns of rubble and approached the sepoys with as friendly an expression as I could muster. I stopped and placed my hands together in greeting. "Namaste."

My greeting seemed to calm them and there were mutterings of "Namaste" quiet in the darkness. There were no Salaams and it seemed that all the sepoys here were Hindoos and my appearance as a Hindoo was in some measure reassuring to them.

"Who do you watch, my brothers?" I asked.

One of the men moved forward. I noticed that the others deferred to him and I guessed him to have been their naik, or corporal, when they served under the British flag. He seemed to have the habit of command though, as the naik wore no rank badges, I could not be sure.

"A brother seeks to enter the fort."

While we spoke, the dark shape of the figure in the drain seemed to move fractionally further forward. The sepoy's answer told me nothing that my eyes could not see for themselves.

"Why does he seek to enter the fort, my brother?"

"He would know the disposition of the British."

The sepoy had chosen his words with care. The man who still moved inch by inch toward the European camp was to report how he found the enemy. To a loyal sowar, this should mean that the man was gathering intelligence that would aid us in our next assault. Try as I might, though, I could think of no information that was needed beyond the number of defenders and the strength of their artillery and we had gathered more than enough intelligence as to those during the debacle of the day. I looked again at my companions. They were Hindoos, who mostly harboured less intensity of rage toward the British than did the Musalmans. And they were mutineers, rather than rebels who had travelled to Cawnpore out of a commitment to the destruction of the Europeans. These men had served with the British for years. They would have known many of the officers now trapped with Wheeler, they would have greeted their wives and, often enough, played with their children—for soldiers as a species are sentimental about children and the Indian sepoy no less so than his European brother. The fact that they still wore their uniforms showed them to possess some residual feelings for their regiment and the life they had abandoned with the mutiny.

I decided to make a neutral response but one which might encourage the mutineers to speak more freely of their intentions.

"The British fought well today."

The naik fixed his gaze on my face, as if trying to discern my expression in the gloom. Still choosing his words carefully, he said, "They fought like tigers. They may yet escape the fury of Nana Sahib."

He had given me my cue. 'Nana Sahib,' not 'the Peshwa.' It was my turn to give some indication of my loyalties.

"I have known many sowars who have fought with the British. They are mighty warriors and, moreover, they know how to use cavalry. If the British had commanded the attack this morning, it would not have failed."

Now the other sepoys began to join in. The British had paid them regularly but the Nana, though generous when pay was issued, could go for weeks without paying them at all. The Company's army had been disciplined and proud, but here they fought alongside the scum of the bazaars and discipline was forgotten. Many of them admired their officers, but here they were ordered into battle by Nana Sahib's advisers who were completely unknown to them.

The complaints were little more than the grumbles that you heard from soldiers everywhere. Listening to the anger in their voices, though, I felt I was listening to men who had deserted the British and were no longer convinced that they had picked the winning side.

"And your friend in the ditch?"

There was a pause in the flow of complaints from the sepoys. The naik spoke in the silence.

"He is to find our officers and ask if we can return to our duty."

"You would join the British in there?"

"You saw what happened today. The Nana's army is weak. The British are strong. They fight bravely and, it is rumoured, they have mined their fort and they will blow it up if the Nana's army enters it. They will die but we will die alongside them."

I smiled to myself in the darkness. It seemed as if the rumours I had started had become common currency amongst soldiery.

The naik went on and I felt he was trying to convince himself as much as me with what he said next. "If a few of us were to join with the British and attack the hill where the Nana hides from danger, then I think the Nana would run. And once he runs, the revolt is over. There are many of the Company's soldiers who feel as we do. There are many who were led into revolt by a few bad men. If they see the British forgive us and allow us to fight for them again, they will join with us. The revolt will be defeated and we will be forgiven and rewarded."

I made no reply but joined them as they watched their comrade moving inch by inch toward the British position. Could there be any hope in their wild plan? Crouched beside them in the darkness, I began to wonder if it could be so. There was no question that, just as the British had had every cause to doubt the loyalty of their troops during the months preceding the mutiny, now Nana Sahib could not rely on them. Most of the sepoys were the sons of soldiers who were themselves the sons of soldiers. Their greatest desire was to serve as soldiers but, like all soldiers, they wanted to be on the winning side. If the mutinous sepoys thought that the British could yet prevail, then perhaps they might desert the Nana just as they had deserted us. And any disaffection amongst the Nana's forces would be exacerbated by the tensions already visible between Hindoos and Musalmans in his ranks.

But even if the sepoys—or many of them—were to rejoin the Company's ranks, could they fight their way out of Cawnpore and across rebel-held country until they reached some place where the British still held out in strength?

For a few minutes, I allowed myself to believe it was possible. The sepoys' envoy would be received by a grateful Wheeler; the native troops would march once more under the British flag; the Nana would be defeated and this nightmare would be over.

From the darkness, I heard a British voice shouting and the crack of a rifle from the Entrenchment. From somewhere between us and the British breastworks, there came a scream, then a desperate sobbing and then silence.

The sepoys looked at each other and then me. Not a word was said and they slipped silently away into the darkness.

I sat alone for the better part of an hour, staring across to where I knew my countrymen would be trying to rest and eking out such rations as they had left. From time to time, there would be the boom of a cannon somewhere in the rebel lines and a crash as shot or shell smashed into the Entrenchment ahead of me.

There, alone in the dark, I doubted that the sepoys' plan had had any real chance of success, but it had been the only hope the garrison had. They were surrounded, outnumbered and outgunned. They had little food and scarcely any shelter. Their defences were no more than mud walls and any day now the monsoon rains would start and they would be washed away. If I joined them, I, too, was as doomed as they. Yet was I not British? Was it not my duty to stand by the men and women of my race even if it was a pointless gesture that could end only in my death alongside theirs? I thought of Mungo's rooms in Saturday House, of his arms around me, his mouth seeking mine. But still some small part of me wanted to cross the open ground to the Entrenchment, to join my fellows there and to die like an Englishman.

It made no difference what I thought. The sepoy's death had shown what fate would befall me were I to attempt to enter the Entrenchment. I had made my decision and abandoned my colleagues to their fate. I could not change things now.

❋

I HAD NO intention of attempting to journey back to Bithur in the dark. Even in normal times, the road was not so good that I would care to risk the health of my horse by riding it at night and the war had brought its own perils. The rebels had opened the jails, releasing all manner of villains. That, combined with the destruction of the usual institutions of police and magistracy, meant that the road could be a dangerous place after sunset.

At this time of year, the night air was no threat to my health. In fact, even at midnight I was more likely to feel too hot rather than chilled and I settled to sleep in the ruins where I had watched the unfortunate sepoy crawl to his death.

I woke at around six. The air was somewhat cooler in the early dawn than it had been when I lay down to sleep the night before, but the sun was already bright in the sky.

I decided that I would stay at Cawnpore until the afternoon, to get some idea of how the previous day's reverses had affected the rebels. Were the sepoys of the previous night an isolated group or were many of the Nana's men ready to give up the siege?

My horse had long since eaten the sparse foliage sprouting amongst the rubble and was now pawing at the dirt in the hope of finding anything edible hidden in the dust. The beast obviously needed food and I was sure that there would be fodder available at Savada House, where Nana Sahib still had his headquarters. A visit there might also give me a clearer view of how things were progressing with the rebels.

I carried on with the circuit I had started the evening before, moving away from the town and turning South with the Entrenchment on my right. I passed the great empty expanse of the parade ground where the vultures were already flapping about the remains of yesterday's dead and then I walked my horse up the little knoll toward Savada House.

The place had a more permanent feel than when I had last been there. Nana Sahib's personal standard flew over his tent, still some way ahead of me. It reassured the people that he was still living among them. Around that pavilion had grown up a little village of tents and shacks. The place was bright with banners— the green of the Musalmans, orange flags of some of the Hindoos, regimental colours from mutinous troops and the heraldry of a dozen minor lords who had pledged allegiance to the Peshwa. Looking at them, I realised for the first time how the reforms that the British had introduced to land ownership had alienated the landowners who were the ancient aristocracy of India and now these petty princelings had found a common cause. And, of course, the poor of the land, who we had thought our reforms had benefited, now flocked to their lords' banners. As my horse pushed its way through the mass of servants and beggars, I was conscious that they were fighting for their right to be robbed by the men whose families had robbed them for generations, rather than pay their dues to a European interloper.

Approaching Savada House, I could not help but think of those Europeans who had been taken before the Nana and hacked down beside this building or of those who even now repined within its walls. This was where the Nana kept the women he had spared and, it was said, here was old Mrs Greenway and her family, who were being held for ransom. It seemed, though, that the Nana now had more prisoners than he could accommodate in the old house. I had seen the looting and destruction that war had brought to Cawnpore and here was the evidence of the new rulers' attempts to maintain some sort of order. A few yards from the house was a crude bamboo stockade, thrown up around a grove of mango trees. Within it, a couple of dozen natives, men and women, squatted disconsolately in the dust, watched over by four men standing with swords drawn. The rebels may have started their revolt by emptying the town jail but they had already produced an alternative.

The mass of humanity became thicker the nearer I came to the Nana's headquarters. This was now the centre of the Peshwa's court. This was the honey pot that attracted everyone who held hopes of advancement in the new India that was to arise after the British left. The men of rank had pitched their own tents round and about but they, in turn, had their own servants and followers. So many people, quite without any proper sanitary arrangements, made for a stink noticeable even to my nostrils, which after a year and a half in India, had generally become inured to the odour of unwashed humanity.

Such was the stench arising from the human population, that I could not immediately distinguish the ammoniac smell that led me to the horses of the cavalry. Once I did, it was easy enough to find some of my fellow sowars. Many of those who had ridden to defeat the previous morning had slipped quietly away but the best of them had decamped here, to be at hand should their Peshwa call on them.

I greeted those I recognised and was welcomed into their ranks. As I had foreseen, they were well supplied with fodder. The Nana employed grass cutters to bring fresh grass for the horses at Bithur every morning and some had obviously been sent to join the other servants at Savada House, for generous piles of grass were scattered about for the cavalry mounts. Nor had the riders neglected their own welfare. A square of canvas had been erected to shelter them from the sun and some carpets and pillows, scavenged from who knew where, provided a modicum of comfort. I tied my horse to one of the posts that had been erected for the purpose and settled down with my comrades to drink tea and, perhaps, chew the odd betel nut.

As the morning wore on, men came and went moving between periods of duty and idleness with the casual lack of discipline that characterised the rebel forces. Usually there were at least four or five of us resting there and the talk was naturally of the events of the previous day. There was reluctant agreement that the cavalry had, as a body, not distinguished itself in the engagement. People could not agree, though, on who was to blame for the debacle. Chimnaji, one of the older men and as near as our little group had to a leader, blamed the failure on men from Oudh, whose martial qualities, he claimed, were much over-rated. Others said it was the fault of some Parthans who had travelled from the North West to join the revolt. The only thing we could all agree with confidence was that Nana Sahib's own sowars had fought valiantly and well.

There was some particular criticism of whoever had caused the bugle to sound the charge so far from the defences. One or two of the younger men suggested that this must have been the result of incompetence by the army's commanders but this led to nervous glances in the direction of Nana Sahib's tent and a shift of the conversation into safer areas.

If the sowars were unhappy with the way that the revolt was going, at least they were not on the verge of deserting like the men I had seen the previous night. But, as with every other army, the cavalrymen had a status denied to the infantry and they would be the most loyal of the Nana's men. Indeed, they were aware of discontent amongst the infantry and they spoke dismissively of many of the men who had flocked to the rebel cause.

"Company soldiers who have half a mind to run back to their old masters; old men who serve their lords loyally but who have never before seen a battle; farmers who bring sickles for want of swords; and every badmash who has a reputation with his fists. They all called themselves the Peshwa's soldiers when they thought the British would be overrun in a day or two. But now they find that they have to fight…Well, it's a different story."

There was much nodding of heads and then Chimnaji started on some yarn about a battle he was in years back. "Now that was real fighting." And then Appa, one of the younger men, tried to top his tale with another and soon everybody had a story to tell and so the morning passed away until it grew hot and time for tiffin and we interrupted our boasting to eat.

Once we had finished our meal, our talk became more desultory until it finally dwindled into silence. The hubbub of the rebel camp was quieted as those around us, from the Nana Sahib himself to the poorest of the beggars beside the road, all gave themselves over to the stupor that Indian and European alike fall into in the hottest part of a June day.

I had just composed myself comfortably in the shade when I was disturbed by the passage of several men hurrying past our little camp in the direction of Savada House. Any movement in the heat of the day was unusual enough but as more and more people passed, I roused myself to see what could be so extraordinary as to rouse people from their idleness so soon after tiffin.

As I approached the building, it was clear that the centre of attention was the makeshift bamboo prison. A crowd, already a hundred or so strong, had gathered but I could not see what had drawn them there. I pushed through, ordering people aside with the arrogance that a genuine sowar would show and in a few seconds I was standing close against the bamboo palisade.

The source of the excitement was apparently a new prisoner. He seemed exceptionally tall for an Indian, though the appearance of his height was accentuated by the emaciation of his body. Indeed, he looked almost like a scarecrow, wearing a turban, a loincloth and a cook's coat smeared with grease. He seemed an unprepossessing fellow and I asked around to see why he was the cause of so much interest.

Most of the people I enquired of had, like me, been attracted by the noise and the gathering crowd and knew no more of the man than I did. However, eventually I asked one young fellow who said that he had followed him as he was escorted into the place and that his guards said he was a refugee from the Entrenchment.

I looked at him with renewed interest. His thinness was now explained but, other than that, he seemed in reasonable health. I was surprised that somebody could have lived in the conditions that must have existed inside that camp and not been more visibly marked by their suffering. This man, although looking understandably nervous, had something about him that suggested an inner strength but I could not put my finger on what it was that gave me this impression.

The crowd was still growing and there was a sense that something must be about to happen. We waited a full fifteen minutes, though, before two of the Nana's guards arrived and, with much shouting and waving of their swords, escorted him through the crowd toward a mango tree that stood a few paces away from the grove, outside the stockade.

In the shade of the tree was a dirty carpet and on it sat an elderly man whose nondescript appearance was belied by the guard standing to attention beside him. I did not recognise him but I knew enough of the protocol of the Nana's court to realise that he must have been a senior official.

The guards gestured the prisoner to stand before him and the old man, after fussing with his spectacles and arranging his writing materials, started by asking him his name and where he came from. He replied that his name was Budloo and that he was from Allahabad.

These preliminaries had excited little interest. None of the audience (still growing by the minute) seemed to know anyone named Budloo and nobody claimed to remember him from Allahabad—a city just far enough away that not many at Cawnpore would have known it. Now, though, the old man moved on to more important matters.

"What do you know of the British fort?"

"Nothing," he said. "Nothing."

"You lie! We know you were in there. Tell us what you know of the condition of the British."

"I was there but I worked as a cook. I was kept in the kitchen and the soldiers watched me in case I ran away. I know nothing outside the kitchen."

Again, the old man called him a liar and the soldiers guarding him swore at him and raised their swords to strike.

A voice from the crowd shouted, "If he was so carefully watched, how then did he escape?"

The old man nodded. "How, indeed?"

The prisoner looked nervously about him as the shouts and threats from the mob grew steadily. It seemed to me obvious that he was lying and desperately trying to think of a credible story. Just as it seemed certain that he would be beaten, he spoke again.

"After yesterday's attack, there were so many bodies that they could not all be buried during the night and the soldiers slipped out of the fort in the morning to throw the last corpses into the well. I bore a helping hand but, while they were busy with the bodies, I slipped away from the well and hid amongst the piles of bricks until I got the opportunity to escape."

Implausible as this story seemed to me, it satisfied the old man who changed his line of questioning. "If you were in the kitchens, you must know how much provision is left and the number of fighting men still alive."

"Well, I will tell you as far as I know. I have often heard the soldiers say, while in the cookhouse, that they can pull on with the provisions for another whole month."

Now, once again, the crowd exploded into anger, with one voice after another denouncing him as a liar. The old man leaned forward pointing angrily with his finger. "We know full well the feringees are starving."

Now the prisoner roused himself to anger. "If you know the situation, why question me? I have nothing more to say to you." At which he hunched his shoulders, and, staring at the ground, lapsed into silence. The guards abused him, calling him a dog and the son of a whore and one made to strike him, but the old man raised his hand to stop them and, adopting a conciliatory tone, asked if he had any other intelligence of the enemy's position.

At this he told his inquisitor, with apparent reluctance, that some two dozen soldiers had died from sunstroke and a very few from shot and shell but that there were sufficient fighting men still left to defend the place and all were determined to fight to the last.

As I heard this, my spirits rose but the news that was so pleasing to me was as displeasing to his captors who again violently abused him. However often they taxed him with being a liar, though, he simply shook his head and repeated his claims.

The insults offered by the guards were joined by those of the natives who had gathered to watch the sport. For several minutes, it was impossible to hear anything that the prisoner might say. On his carpet, the old man shouted for silence and, little by little, the noise subsided and he was able to recommence the questioning.

"Is it true that the European dogs have mined the perimeter of the encampment and will destroy all who enter it?"

It was all that I could do to stop myself from laughing at this further evidence that the rumours I started had grown to the point where so many believed them. Fortunately, this question started the spectators again in their chorus of jeers and abuse and, if my expression betrayed my inner elation, no one gave it any attention.

The prisoner looked puzzled at this question but eventually replied that he was not sure what was meant by "mining" but that he could most positively assert that powder was buried in several places within the camp.

You can imagine my surprise at this. I wondered if my invention might, indeed, be no more than the truth. Yet it seemed unlikely. Had any such plan been intended, I would surely have heard of it in the days when the Entrenchment was being prepared. If that were the case, then the prisoner must be lying to his captors with the same intention of causing fear and confusion which had led me to start the rumour in the first place.

Knowing this, I looked at him with renewed interest. There was something about him that did not look quite right. As I had already noticed, he was taller than the average native and, though he continually lowered his head and often put his hands before him in entreaty, there was that about his manner which suggested a latent pride unlikely to have been found in the breast of a low caste cook.

Although my suspicions were by now fully aroused, the old man and the guards seemed to be accepting their prisoner as what he claimed to be. His inventions about the mining of the fort generated such excitement that within minutes his inquisitor was heading toward the Nana's tent as fast as his aged legs would carry him.

The prisoner was escorted back into his compound and gradually the crowd dispersed. Some settled back to sleep through the heat under the shade of the mango where the prisoner had been questioned. Intrigued as I was by this Budloo, I decided to join them.

The carpet had been rolled up and removed. Dirty though it had been, I would have welcomed something to rest on other than the bare earth but I saw no alternative. I settled cross-legged on the ground where sat or lay the other natives who had chosen this patch of shade.

The prisoner had also decided to rest in the shade and had laid himself out under one of the trees on his side of the bamboo fence. Within a few minutes, it seemed, he was asleep.

I continued sitting in the dust. Despite the shade of the tree, it was hot, even for the summer. There were, of course, no proper facilities for the throng now inhabiting this place and the stench was offensive. I began to wonder if I should return to my cavalry companions who were a little removed from the hoi polloi. The smell from the horses was vastly preferable to that from the mass of humankind and the memory of the cushions the sowars had acquired grew steadily more attractive the longer I sat on the hard ground.

I had just decided that my vigil was pointless when the guards were joined by another rebel sepoy who bustled over from the direction of the Nana's headquarters and immediately started a series of whispered conversations with his fellows.

I moved myself by inches to the very edge of the shade and strained my ears to hear the news that he had brought. Fortunately, as the sepoys grew steadily more excited, so their voices grew louder. One said, "So it will end," and the others hushed him and looked about them.

What might end? Could they conceivably be talking of an end to the siege? My discomfort was forgotten in an instant and I scarcely noticed the heat. My whole being seemed concentrated in my ears as I struggled to catch odd words and phrases.

"…cannot succeed by assault…"

"…mines…"

"…powder magazines set to explode…"

"…hundreds could die…"

"…they cannot be defeated…"

Finally, I was sure.

"The Nana will offer terms…"

I wanted to run, shouting, toward the Entrenchment. The Nana is to offer terms! The siege is to be ended! You are saved! Instead, I had to sit squirming in the heat, trying not to betray my excitement.

I had been so taken with eavesdropping on the sepoys that I had neglected to watch the prisoner. Now I noticed that the cook, though still lying stretched out beneath a tree, was exhibiting the same twitches of excitement as I was. As I stared toward him, trying to make some sense of what I saw, he opened his eyes and caught my gaze. When he realised he was watched, he grew visibly alarmed, and, tugging his turban down over his forehead and hunching his shoulders into his cook's jacket, he seemed to be trying to conceal his features.

It was this very effort to hide his face that made me realise that I had seen it before. But where? I was sure that it was not the face of a cook.

I was still searching my memory when there was yet more movement from the direction of the Nana's tent. A short fat man, perspiring in the heat, approached with clearly unaccustomed briskness. His importance was signified by the smartness of his dress and an escort of not one but two guards. The sepoys at the enclosure promptly ceased their conversation and stood to attention as he wobbled his way to the stockade shouting for "the prisoner Budloo" to be brought before him.

Budloo was already on his feet and, seeing the guards making toward him with expressions suggesting they would not be gentle in carrying out the order, he hastened to stand before the visitor.

This time there were no secret whispers. In a voice clearly audible to all in the vicinity, the official demanded to know whether the Europeans were anxious to leave the Station, and, in the event of an offer being made to that effect, if it would be accepted.

I could swear I saw a flicker of triumph pass across Budloo's features but, as fast as it appeared, it was gone and, with downcast eyes and hesitant tone, he replied that he could not exactly tell. "The women are certainly anxious to get away by any means and to take their children with them," he mumbled. "I think that the soldiers would accept an offer if it allowed their women to escape."

The official nodded vigorously at this reply and turned to scuttle back toward his master.

Intrigued as I was by my growing certainty that Budloo was no cook, I decided to follow the fat official back to the Nana's tent. It seemed that things were moving to some sort of conclusion and the Nana's headquarters was the place to be if I wanted the latest news.

I settled to outside the tent, though to call it a 'tent' does it scant justice. As the Nana had established himself, so the tent had grown into an elaborate pavilion of coloured silks. The glimpses I had of the interior suggested that it was divided into separate rooms. I could, obviously, see only the entrance chamber but even that was carpeted with low tables dotted about and (a reminder, no doubt, of Saturday House) mirrors hanging on the walls.

My presence at the entrance attracted no attention, for there was a continual passage of people entering and leaving as well as a crowd always loitering around in the hope of gathering some crumbs from the rich man's table or just, like me, anxious to hear the latest news and gossip.

Word that something of importance was to pass had clearly spread through the camp, for the crowd of idlers was growing by the minute. Nor was this audience to be deprived of the spectacle they sought. Various officials, gorgeously robed, came and went with earnest faces, pretending to ignore the crowd but, in fact, strutting before them like actors in a second-rate play. Now came a Brahmin, now a mullah; orange robes, white robes, green fringes, red cloth—a veritable rainbow of rank. Even the guards who pushed their way past the onlookers were immaculately turned out in white tunics and turbans of blue or red.

The scent of incense drifted from the tent, going some way to disguise the reek from the unwashed bodies massed around me. From time to time more incense and the smell of rosewater marked the movement of such of the neighbouring rulers who had sworn fealty to Nana Sahib as they hurried from their own tents to their Peshwa's pavilion. I searched their faces for any indication of their mood. It seemed to me that they expected good news but most kept their features masks of disdain for the common folk and it was difficult to discern their feelings.

Now the guards who had set out were returning, beating a path through the onlookers with the flats of their swords. They formed a tight group and, at first, I could not see whom they escorted. Then I caught a glimpse of a white arm, a grey head, the bedraggled remains of a dress. It was Mrs Greenway! It is almost impossible to imagine the shock I felt on seeing this dowager, the respected matriarch of Cawnpore's most influential family, hustled by her guards like some common criminal. Though I had seen the European quarter looted and burned and watched the sepoys firing on their European masters day after day, it was, I think, the pathetic sight of this old woman hurried before the Nana that truly brought home to me the totality of the destruction of European power and all that I had known of British rule in India.

By now, the afternoon was well advanced. There was no more urgent coming and going but I was content to wait on events. The mass of natives around me seemed to share this view for scarcely any moved away while, even now, others drifted over to join us.

For a time, nothing happened. Then there was a sudden eruption of sepoys who ran off in all directions, shouting for horses. I thought for an instant that I might volunteer my own mount and thus maybe find myself privy to any messages the Nana was despatching. My horse, though, was with the other sowars and the messengers were already scattering away from the tent. Besides, if the Nana were sending out new general orders, I would know them soon enough, while any more specific news would best be gleaned by staying where I was.

Again, the crowd settled to wait and I waited with them. A quarter of an hour passed and there was no sign of anything happening. Then came a stirring, an uneasiness, amongst the mass of men around me. I shared their unease, a feeling that some great change had taken place. The heat and the stench were the same as ever but something was different.

I heard a dog barking in the town below and I realised what it was. After days and nights of cacophony, one by one the Nana's batteries were falling silent. By late afternoon, all the rebel firing ceased and only the lazy flapping of vultures' wings broke the eerie silence that lay across the plain around Wheeler's position.

An hour passed. Then two. Still the silence was not broken. Finally, toward evening, the Nana's guards emerged again with Mrs Greenway.

This time she was not hustled along like a criminal but, rather, escorted as if to do her honour. She stood erect, guards on either side, and though her gown was dirty and, in places, torn, she stood up proudly, as if she were robed as a queen.

At some stage during her captivity, her shoes had been taken from her and she walked now on bare feet. Yet, still she stepped forward bravely. The guards walked with her down the little hill. I followed, as did most of those who had been waiting all afternoon for some excitement and who now felt it was only right that they should be able to see whatever show these new events might offer.

Arriving at the edge of the great parade ground, the guards stepped aside and Mrs Greenway started out toward the Entrenchment on her own. With the rest of the crowd, I stopped on the edge of the plain. It was not fear of the English guns that stopped us, I think, but the sense that this plain, where so much Indian blood had been spilt, was somehow alien. As Mrs Greenway walked on, she walked alone, a frail figure in all those acres of empty land.

We watched as she neared those feeble defences that had stood so defiantly for the weeks of the siege. In her right hand, she held what I at first thought to be a walking stick painted white. As she approached the Entrenchment, though, she flourished it in the air and I recognised it as a symbol of envoy, as Europeans might wave a white flag.

Now she was almost at the breastworks. She began to sway slightly, her strength clearly exhausted. Faint on the evening air came cries of command from the besieged garrison and then an officer was clambering over the debris of the defences and catching the old lady as she finally succumbed to faintness and collapsed into his arms. Together the two made their way into the Entrenchment.

"We shall see no more tonight."

Others around me took up the same refrain. Some said we would see no more of Mrs Greenway even if we waited until the next day.

"The Peshwa was holding her for ransom. Surely she is ransomed and now she has gone back to her people. She will not return."

Hearing this, the guards—who stood now with the rest of the crowd—joined in with the enthusiasm of gossips who are privileged to know more than their companions.

"She'll be back. The Peshwa still holds her family hostage against her safe return."

One fellow, bolder than the rest, demanded of the guards why the old woman had been sent to the English in the first place.

"The Peshwa has decided that the English can do no more harm. She carries his message to them. They are to be offered safe passage if they lay down their arms and leave this place for ever."

A murmur of excitement ran through the crowd at this apparent confirmation of the rumours that had been flying around the Nana's camp all afternoon. Even now, I can scarce describe my own feelings. It seemed that there was indeed a God who was merciful to his creation and who was leading his children out of the fire to which I had feared he had consigned them. As night fell, with the suddenness of the darkness in these latitudes, so my fears were carried away by a night breeze and, for the first time since the Entrenchment had been surrounded, I felt sure of their escape.

Most of the men around me shared my mood of relief, though their reasons may have been different from mine. Few will have cared for the Europeans in the Entrenchment but they were tired of the deaths and, I believed, tired of the killing. Now they would have their victory without the need for further bloodshed. Men relaxed, laughing and joking with each other. Sweetmeats appeared from the folds of robes, confections of sugar and fruit that were passed around and shared.

The sun had long set and we watched across the plain by moonlight until a moving shadow resolved itself as the limping figure of an old woman. Mrs Greenway's guards fell in beside her and escorted her back to the Nana's tent and the crowd, deprived of the possibility of further entertainment, finally dispersed.

I made my way back to Chimnaji and the others. My elation was somewhat tempered by the number of trips and stumbles that I suffered in the darkness, but my spirits were lifted by the enthusiasm with which my fellow sowars greeted me on my return. They had heard the rumours, but considered their pride prohibited them from mingling with the common throng to learn more. They were, however, more than happy to benefit from my willingness to humble myself in that way and we sat up around a small fire while I rehearsed the events of the day.

It must have been close to midnight when I finally lay down to sleep. The fire was scarcely necessary, for the night was still warm, but it provided a little light and comfort and I found my mind slipping back to the days before the Mutiny. And suddenly I knew where I had seen the prisoner before. His name was not Budloo and he was no cook. He was Jonah Shepherd, one of the babus in our offices. Now his answers made sense, for his insistence that the defenders were well supplied and the Entrenchment was mined had served to convince Nana Sahib that it would be wise to offer terms.

I resolved that as soon as it was light I should return to the stockade to see what aid I could offer him and, with this thought in my mind, I was soon in the arms of Morpheus.

I roused myself at dawn the next morning. Though I had rested for only a few hours, still I was well refreshed, for the change in the fortune of the Europeans had revived my spirits and I had slept more soundly than for many a night past. I made my toilette as quickly as I could and, telling my comrades that I would scout for more news, I hurried to the stockade to find it empty.

Determined that this time I would not fail a European who had so far survived the tragedy, I enquired of the guards on Savada House as to what had happened to the prisoners.

"The Europeans are here," they told me. "The old woman was returned in the middle of the night and they are safely behind these walls."

"And the others?"

"Oh, them." It seemed that even in captivity, the old caste lines were maintained. The Europeans may be hated now but the guard's tone betrayed the fact that he considered the native prisoners to be of no significance compared to his charges. "They've been taken to the old cavalry hospital, where they can be more safely held."

The hospital was some half a mile away and I decided to collect my horse and ride over there, not only to spare myself the walk, but in the hope that my presence might carry more authority if I were on my hunter. So it was, by the merest chance, that I was mounted and passing near the Nana's tent when an officer appeared in the entrance and, seeing me, raised his voice to command that I immediately attend upon him.

My first thought was that my disguise had been penetrated and I considered fleeing but I saw the mass of men round about and considered that I would have little hope of escape. In any case, the officer's tone was peremptory rather than angry so I rode to him and dismounted.

"Another envoy is to be sent to the British. It is to be an old woman again but we don't want her wandering around half dead like the other one. She is to be transported in a palanquin. She should not be fired on, for the British themselves have asked that we send her, but it is best that there be an escort and if she is to be carried, the escort should be mounted. You'll do."

I had heard the sepoys complain that the rebel officers behaved less well toward them than had the British, but this was the first time that I had personal experience of the way that the army was treated under the new regime. The British might consider themselves a superior race but they had the utmost respect for the soldierly qualities of the Native regiments. By contrast, the men appointed by the Nana to positions of command were, mostly, courtiers and they allowed the contempt they felt for the common soldiers to colour all their dealings with them. I found myself resenting him still more because I was no mere sepoy but a sowar. I still hated the man, even as I recognised how ridiculous I was to allow this to concern me.

Taking care to keep my expression respectful, I mounted again and waited until four men came trotting along the path from Savada House, carrying a litter bearing the figure of a half-caste woman. Her dress, though less dirty and ragged than that of Mrs Greenway, suggested a person of a lower social rank, but she seemed to have fared better in her captivity, being somewhat plump. She may have been the wife of a soldier and, though she was a mature lady, she was far from Mrs Greenway's age. Unlike that matriarch, though, she made no attempt to maintain a show of dignity but half sat, half lay in the palanquin as we set off across the open ground.

As we approached, I saw the men of the garrison strolling around, taking the air as they had done in the mornings before the Mutiny. As they walked to and fro behind their breastwork, I was reminded of how inadequate that defence had been and how they had been unable even to stand erect without exposing themselves to the rebels' fire.

Now the women came out from the ruin of the barracks that had sheltered them, joining their husbands to watch our approach.

The defences were by now so reduced that the bearers were able to carry the litter over the rubble and directly into the Entrenchment, where the passenger was immediately mobbed by the European ladies, content for once to associate with one whose skin was several shades darker than their own. Not that the women of the garrison still had the peaches and cream complexions that they had protected so carefully from the Indian sun. Few now had any bonnets and none sported parasols. As their shelter was destroyed and as they took their places beside the men, loading their guns and salving their wounds, so their skin had been burned almost as brown as that of the babus they had previously despised.

Once our passenger was safely within his camp, General Wheeler himself emerged from what was left of the barracks, accompanied by Captain Moore and some other officers I did not recognise. Moore's attention, naturally enough, was concentrated on the Nana's envoy, but he cast a swift glance over the scene and I saw his eyes swivel back to my face. I gave him the slightest of nods, and as the General and his aides hustled the woman toward the guard post at the gate—one of the most substantial buildings still more or less intact—Moore drifted over to where I was now standing beside my horse. There was no reason why, under these circumstances, a British officer could not speak to one of the Nana's cavalrymen and Moore felt safe to ask my news.

"I'm safe enough, though I've been of little use to you or anyone else. I saw Shepherd yesterday. He has convinced Nana Sahib to offer you safe passage, though now he's been moved to another jail and I'm off there later to see what assistance I can give him."

"The stout chap! We have all feared that he had been lost when he did not return from his scouting expedition."

"He was taken but has persuaded Nana Sahib that you are so strong and well supplied that you can hold out for weeks yet."

Moore gave a short bark of laughter.

"We'll struggle to hold out another couple of days. The men don't mind dying. Most of them are soldiers and it's our trade. But it hurts to see the women suffer like this and to know that they are doomed too. Is he serious about safe passage?"

I thought of the disaster of our cavalry charge, the soldiers I had seen trying to make their own peace with the British, the conviction so many rebels held that Wheeler had mined his own position.

"He's not sure that he can keep his men together for the time it will take to win. No one can believe you've held out so long. I think he's sincere. He will do almost anything to bring this to an end."

"I'll make sure Wheeler knows that."

He turned to join the other officers with the General. Suddenly, I felt desperately alone. It seemed so long since I had seen Mungo. I spent my days and my nights keeping company with men who would kill me if they had any notion who I was. Stepping quickly after him, I reached my hand to Moore's sleeve. "Perhaps I should just stay here?"

Moore did not hesitate. "No. This meeting has to go smoothly and the Nana's envoy must be returned without any fuss. It's our best hope." I think he must have seen the dejection on my face. "Beside, you still have to try to do something for Shepherd."

He strode into the guardhouse. I was left alone with the bearers and a small crowd of English women who looked at me in my native uniform with eyes that held nothing but contempt.

chapter 8

I DO NOT know what happened at the conference Wheeler held with his staff that morning. I have heard some say that it was Captain Moore who spoke most strongly in favour of accepting Nana Sahib's offer. If this were so, I pray my words were not the reason for it. I only know that some two hours after I had arrived at the Entrenchment, I was escorting the woman back to the Nana's pavilion and that the truce, which had started the previous afternoon, still held.

I took advantage of the ceasefire to ride directly across to the old cavalry hospital where I had been told that Shepherd now lay imprisoned. I might have achieved little for those in the Entrenchment but I hoped that I could at least do something to help the prisoner.

When I arrived, I found the door to the jail was open, to allow more air to those inside. A guard squatted nearby, chatting to a friend. When I asked to see the man in charge, he vanished inside, returning a few minutes later with an elderly Hindoo who introduced himself as the subadar. I asked after the prisoners and was assured that all were safe inside. I told him that I was especially interested in the welfare of Budloo and asked if there were any chance he might be released into my custody, but the old subadar was emphatic that this was impossible. "And even if I could," he added, "I don't know that I will be doing him any favour if I let him go. It's all right for you and me—we are armed and have the authority of our uniforms to protect us but for the likes of him, they are less likely to come to harm in here than if they were roaming free on the streets."

There being no obvious way to procure Shepherd's release, I slipped some coins into his palm with the promise of more if the prisoner Budloo came to no harm. The subadar assured me that he would do all in his power to protect him. "For he's a pleasant enough fellow and gives no trouble."

I felt I had done little for him, but I believed the subadar would be true to his word.

My business at the jail concluded, there were no immediate duties calling for my attention. It being now the hottest part of the day, I settled myself under the shade of a tree to rest until the sun was lower in the sky.

Usually I had no trouble in sleeping through the midday heat, even when I was disturbed by the occasional sound of firing. Now, though, I found I could not settle. I tried to tell myself that this was because the day was exceptionally hot (which it was) or that the silence, after the weeks of shelling, was by now more disturbing than the thunder of cannon fire.

In my heart, though, I knew the true reason for my unrest. With the ending of the siege, there was no reason why I should remain a stranger to my own people. I should stay here at Cawnpore and, at the first opportunity, insinuate myself back into the Entrenchment, to leave under the promise of safe passage that the Nana had made to the garrison. Yet, were I to do so, I would never see Mungo again.

I thought of his impish smile, his young, taut body and the pleasure it gave me, his kindness and his caresses. Was I just to walk away from this with no word of farewell?

Nor were Mungo's physical charms the only thing that I would miss if I were to leave Saturday House behind me forever. In my time there, I had come to understand something of what life in India had to offer—its religion, its literature, its art. I thought of the meals I had eaten with Mungo and compared them in my memory with the spicy mess of food that Europeans called 'curry'. Having lived so long in the East, the life that Mungo had shared with me at Bithur was no more alien than the world of the European station in Cawnpore.

I thought of the pleasure that Mungo and I had shared, enjoying our love not only in its sweaty, sticky, physical manifestation but in the quiet hours spent alone, walking through the gardens of Saturday House or in his room where he struggled to teach me to play the sarod. It is true that we were careful not to be overly demonstrative in public, but there must have been those at Saturday House who guessed our relationship. Servants came and went all the time and the laundryman, if no one else, must have been aware that Mungo was no celibate. Yet, at Bithur, this did not seem to be the criminal scandal that it would have been at Cawnpore. A return to my old life would be a return to a world in which I could never be open about the sort of man I was. It would be a world in which I might never truly love or be loved again.

As I tossed on the ground, the shade of the tree providing only the smallest relief from the heat, I knew the only decision I could come to. I had left Britain when I was barely a man but I could not pretend to be other than I was. India was turning against the British and, if they discovered who I was, they would turn against me. It mattered not that I loved Mungo or that I cared for their customs or that I could pick out the unfamiliar melodies on the sarod. I was a European. The Indians, no less than the British, would have me know my place.

After an hour or so of wakefulness, I gave up trying to sleep and braved the heat to make my way back toward the Nana's tent. It seemed to me that with communications now opened between the rebels and the Entrenchment, there would likely be opportunities to pass from one to the other carrying messages for the Nana. In this way, I might escape the rebels and rejoin my countrymen.

As I neared the Nana's headquarters, I was surprised to see almost as many people round about as there had been that morning. I had expected that the heat would have driven them to shelter in the shade and that most would still be dozing but instead the crowd was quite lively.

At first, I worried that something untoward might have occurred and that the truce was to be broken but the smiles on the faces all around reassured me. When I asked what had passed, I was told that at one o'clock the Nana's chief minister—a scoundrel called Azimullah, who many considered responsible for corrupting his lord—had met with Wheeler's senior officers on the open ground before the British camp and that the arrangements for the surrender of the garrison had been successfully completed.

My delight on hearing this news was tarnished only by my realisation that, had I been there as the delegations met, it would have been easy to insinuate myself into Azimullah's escort and so carry out my plan to slip away into the British ranks. Having missed this opportunity, though, I made careful enquiries as to what exactly the plans for the British departure were, so that I could choose the best time and place to escape the rebels.

The first few people I asked all told me that the British were to depart that very afternoon. I was alarmed that they might go without my finding an opportunity to join them, though I reasoned that if the worst came to the worst I could simply ride up to their column as they left and announce myself to Captain Moore. However, without knowing any details of how things were to be managed, I worried that this might not be possible, so I was reassured when others told me that the British had refused to leave immediately but had insisted that transport be arranged before they quit their camp.

"They are to travel down the river to Allahabad." The man who told me this wore the remnants of the uniform of the 56th and his tone suggested that he was not entirely sure that he would not like to be travelling to Allahabad with them. "They are to board at the ghat by Sati Chowra, where the Peshwa is providing boats to carry them away in safety."

I knew the place. Sati Chowra was a fisherman's village, little more than a few huts. It was on the edge of the European station, near to the spot where I had watered my horse on my first visit to the siege. The ghat, little more than a flight of steps to a small stone platform on the riverbank, was a favourite spot amongst the Europeans, cool and tree-shaded, except in the very height of summer. I had often ridden there myself, early in the morning or at the end of the day. There was a little temple overlooking it and young ladies would often tell me how romantic they thought it was. I think part of its romantic appeal was that the river's banks there were very steep and anyone walking at the water's edge would have a degree of privacy not readily found elsewhere in Cawnpore, but perhaps I misjudged them. It was certainly very pretty.

As an embarkation point, it was conveniently situated, being about as close to the camp as the Ganges ran, but my recollection of the river, even when I had taken my horse to drink over two weeks earlier, was that the water was very low. I did wonder how the women were to get across the muddy shallows to a point far enough out for the boats to float off. And even if the women felt that after their weeks in the filth of the Entrenchment they could cope with some mud, there was the more serious question of how to carry aboard the many injured soldiers who would have to be evacuated with them.

The boats would be ready the next day, I was assured, and by the night, the British would be gone.

The atmosphere in the Nana's camp was relaxed, even celebratory. Late in the afternoon, an Englishman appeared on foot, carrying a letter which, I heard, was the formal acceptance of the Nana's terms. There was some cheering as this news spread through the crowd. When he re-emerged from the

Nana's pavilion several men went to put their arms about his shoulders at which he quailed as if he were to be attacked and we all laughed at his discomfiture.

I lay down to sleep that night with an easier mind than I had in the afternoon. The British were safe and my decision was made. The next day, I would join them in time to leave Cawnpore with them.

That night I dreamt that the garrison arrived at the river to find it empty of water. Wheeler was mounted on an elephant.

"There's nothing for it, lads," he says. "We'll have to float them off on our blood." At which the men march to the riverbed and slash their arms open with their bayonets. The blood gushes out and the boats are floating but now the women refuse to board. Lydia Hillersdon turns to me (for I was there, mounted on my horse and still wearing the Nana's uniform) and says, "How can we cross that blood? It will make my dress dirty."

Then the Nana appears, standing on the temple that overlooks the ghat. "If the women won't enter the boats," he cries, "then they must come with me to Saturday House. They'll be quite safe there." He turns to go and where he had been standing, the corpse of Mrs Greenway balances for a moment before falling with a great splash into the river. Her fall disturbs the blood which swells like a great wave, carrying away all the women and wrecking the boats. It runs around my horse, which rears, throwing me into the blood...

I woke, sweating, my heart beating against my ribs so that I thought I might fall down in a moment and die, like those struck by the heat. But it was not yet dawn and the air was as cool as it ever was in June.

I lay back on the ground and composed myself again to sleep. But I resolved that in the morning I would visit the Sati Chowra ghat and see the condition of the boats for myself.

❋

I AWOKE REFRESHED but with memories of my dream still disturbing me despite the promise of the new day. I joined Chimnaji and the other sowars for breakfast. We shared a meal, supplied by one of our number who had requisitioned it from a respectable citizen's kitchen the night before. "Though," he grumbled, "there was little enough there. And the rogue demanded payment. I told him that he'd get paid when we did."

The problem of our pay—or the lack of it—was increasingly difficult to ignore. The token military force that Nana Sahib had been allowed under the British had been joined by thousands of others who had flocked to his cause on the promise of better pay than the British gave their troops. The money looted from the Treasury in the first days of the revolt had meant that, initially, these promises had been kept. By now, though, the money from the Treasury was gone. All that was left was that which Wheeler had been able to spirit away before the Nana's guard barred the doors. That money was in the Entrenchment and forfeit under the terms of the surrender. Nana Sahib needed the money and needed it immediately. Allowing Wheeler to depart with the honours of war was a small price to pay.

Why, then, was I still uneasy? Between mouthfuls of chupatti washed down with weak tea, I tried asking my fellow diners their views of the likelihood of the Europeans being able to get safely into the boats and off down river.

"Why ask me?" The man who had scavenged our breakfast tore off part of his chupatti and threw it onto the fire where we boiled water. "I'm no fisherman." He spoke the word with all the contempt that a high caste soldier would feel for a lowly river dweller.

The man beside me reached across to pour more hot water onto his tea. "So long as the British leave, I don't care what happens to them."

I didn't pursue the subject, but, once we had eaten, I excused myself to exercise my horse and soon I was making my way toward the river.

I decided to take the route that the British would follow, along the metalled road that led from the Entrenchment toward the ruins of St John's church and on to the Ganges. This meant starting at the farthest side of the Entrenchment from where the Nana's camp was situated. The quickest way would have been to cross the plain, a safe enough undertaking now that the guns were silent but, though it seemed a foolish superstition, I could not bring myself to do so. This patch of ground, that had been so long fought across and where so many men had lost their lives (for almost a thousand of the rebels were reckoned to have perished), seemed unclean and I could not bring myself to ride across it. The path I took instead carried me not far from the cavalry hospital where Mr Shepherd was imprisoned and I decided to stop by there in the hope that I might be able to offer him some more assistance or, at the least, to ensure that the money that I had paid to his jailer was having its effect.

Arriving at the jail, I soon found the subadar and enquired after his charge.

He smiled at me, reassuringly. "He is well. He is safe here."

"I hope that soon he will be safe anywhere. His crime was that he was in the Entrenchment with the British," I said. "But the British are to be allowed to leave. Is it possible that he might be allowed to leave with them?"

I had thought my question innocent enough, yet the subadar's smile vanished. He was an old man who looked as if he had been given the job for years of service to the Nana and he seemed an honest enough fellow. Yet now his eyes darted from place to place, avoiding mine and looking, it seemed, for some reason to be elsewhere.

"He should stay here for now. I will attend to everything as soon as I have the opportunity, but for now I have business to deal with."

He turned to go but I put my hand on his arm to detain him. "I am happy to buy your time."

I started to reach for some coins but he shook his head.

"You have paid me already and I will do what you have paid me for. I will make sure your friend is safe."

At that, he positively scurried away, leaving me wondering what was worrying him so much that he would not even take my money.

I rode on, heading up the Course toward the European settlement. All around me, I saw rebel soldiers and civilians strolling aimlessly in the sun, smiling, laughing in groups. All was as it should be in the hour of their victory—so why was I so uneasy?

Here and there, as I neared the river, I saw small groups of soldiers who seemed more earnest than the others. When I reached the ravine that ran down to the ghat, there were half a dozen men squatting beside the burned out ruins of a bungalow and cleaning their muskets. This surprised me, as native troops were never that careful of their weapons and I thought they would hardly bother to clean them if they did not expect to have immediate need of them. They looked up at the sound of my horse's hooves and waved cheerfully. I waved back with a smile on my face but a growing sense of unease.

I eased Kuching carefully down the steep path. When the rains came, there would be a stream rushing down to the Ganges, but now the bottom of the ravine was baked dry in the heat, though the steep sides provided a little protection from the sun.

When I reached the bottom of the ravine, I found myself still a hundred yards or more from the water. Between the bank and the line of boats, presumably intended for the evacuation, was a noisome stretch of mud, strewn with filth. The bodies of two or three dead dogs were visible within a few paces of the platform where I now stood. The stench made it all too clear how the sewage from Sati Chowra was disposed of.

I snapped a branch from one of the neem trees that lined the bank and, standing on the platform, I cautiously prodded at the mud below me. To my relief, it was not particularly deep and I reckoned that the men of the garrison would have no difficulty in crossing it. The women would find it unpleasant but not impossible and the children could be carried to the boats.

Shading my eyes from the sun, which turned the filthy water into a dazzling ribbon of light, I squinted out to those boats. There were around two dozen of them. Some had thatched roofs to protect from the sun but others had only the framework where thatch should be but no sign yet of any covering. The boats were moored on the edge of the deeper water, a few bobbing freely in the current, but most grounded on the mud. Even from here, I could see that they were old and battered. At least—as far as I could tell from the shore—none was actually sinking. I had seen boats like these on the Ganges before—ungainly things around ten yards long and ten feet wide. They were difficult to steer and each would need a crew of four or five men, but I saw far fewer than that scrambling about the vessels, apparently trying to make them ready to sail.

While I watched their preparations, I heard the sound of naked feet slapping on the stone steps behind me. Turning, I saw a group of porters carrying baskets on their heads. Arriving on the platform, they stepped unhesitatingly into the mud and waded across to the line of boats. I was relieved to see that I had been right—they made the journey with little difficulty, though one spilled some of his load, rice flour pouring down his shoulders and into the mud.

I would have stayed longer, but at the end of the line of porters was one of the Nana's officers who, seeing me there, told me brusquely at I should make myself useful on the other bank. I had no idea what he meant, but it was clear that he expected me to make my way there. It seemed wisest to avoid suspicion and I set off immediately up the ravine.

Back on the road again, I puzzled over the order I had just been given. All the time I had ridden under the Nana's colours my duties, and those of all the sowars I had spoken with, had been confined to this side of the river. Why should the Nana now be deploying cavalry on the Oudh bank? Although the garrison had hoped for relief from Lucknow, the rebels' scouts were confident that there were no troops on the way and I could think of no other threat from the East.

I decided that rather than return directly to the Entrenchment, I would ride North along the river to the bridge of boats which connected Cawnpore to the Lucknow shore.

The bridge had not been cut and, indeed, was barely guarded. This made sense in view of the absence of any threat from this direction, but it made me even more confused as to why cavalry was being dispatched to the Eastern bank.

There was no equivalent city to Cawnpore on the Oudh side of the river, so there was no proper road along its bank. There was a track, though, used by boatmen and the people who lived in the little villages which one came across every mile or so. There were bushes and some small trees growing between the bank and the river. This close to the Ganges, they remained in leaf even in the dry season, sucking river water from deep beneath the ground. Even the grass grew lush and tall. The greenery was a welcome change from the arid ground around the Entrenchment, where the trees on the Course were the only growing things above the height of a dandelion. Through the leaves, I could see the sunlight shining on the river. After Cawnpore, it was close to a rural idyll.

I relaxed, enjoying the comparative cool of the morning, the heat tempered further by the faintest whisper of a breeze off the water.

I rode on for a mile or two until I saw, through a gap in the vegetation, the Sati Chowra ghat. It was a little downstream of my position but I could make it out quite clearly with the boatmen still busying themselves about the line of craft in the stream. I turned my gaze back to the path ahead. At first, I saw nothing untoward, but then a glimpse of scarlet caught my eye. There, concealed amongst the bushes, was a group of rebel soldiers.

I hesitated for a moment. The men ahead were clearly trying to hide from sight and I wondered if it might be best to turn back. But I was wearing the Nana's uniform and I had been ordered to this point. On balance, it seemed best to ride on and see how matters would develop.

As soon as the rebels were sure that I had seen them, they stood up from cover and I found myself facing a score or more of men clustered around two cannon. A dozen muskets pointed at my chest. They were clearly not pleased to see me.

One man, who appeared to be in charge, though he wore no rank badge, stepped forward to challenge me. "Who are you and what are you doing here?"

"I am Anjoor Tewaree," I replied, giving the name I used in my native guise. "I am a rider in the Peshwa's own cavalry and I was ordered here by an officer at the ghat." I gestured through the grass and bushes at the platform, which lay directly opposite the guns.

The man looked at me as if I were some low-caste beggar. "Whoever told you to come here is a fool. We have no need of horsemen on this side of the river."

"My apologies." I had nearly said, "My apologies, Sir," but I choked on the honorific. Clearly, this was an officer of some importance on a special mission for his Peshwa, but I was still in dressed as one of the Peshwa's own sowars and I would never willingly acknowledge the superiority of any lesser type of soldier. "If you are sure you have no need of me, I will return to Cawnpore where there may yet be fighting to be done."

The fellow sneered at me. "Yes, it's probably best you return to the city. After all, when we have finished our work, the Peshwa may still have some small requirement for your services."

I decided not to linger, but to turn at once and ride back the way that I had come. Not for the first time, I blessed the rebels' poor communications and inept officering which had turned so many of their attacks into chaos.

Still, whatever their military inadequacies, these men were quite able to fire a cannon and the sight of their artillery had unnerved me. I struggled to find an innocent reason for its be-ing in that position and aimed so squarely at the line of boats that was to be used in the evacuation. Yet, it was difficult for me to believe that Nana Sahib, for all his faults, intended treachery. Clearly, the men that I had seen relaxing around the rebel camp did not anticipate anything untoward. At the same time, a secret plan to attack the British boats would explain the nervousness of the jailer and the sight of soldiers apparently preparing for action.

Perhaps, I thought, some elements amongst the various factions that made up the rebel forces had decided to act independently, carrying on their attacks on the British after Nana Sahib had promised an armistice. Certainly, the men I had just seen looked to be Musalmans. The followers of the Prophet had shown themselves much more ruthless in their hatred of the Europeans than had the Hindoos.

If there were a plan to attack the British and if this was a conspiracy amongst just some of the rebel soldiery, then perhaps the best course was to go to the Nana and warn him of what was afoot. But if the Nana knew of the plan, then going to him would achieve nothing and might, by exposing me to questioning, result in the discovery of my true identity. Perhaps, instead, I should warn the British they might be walking into a trap. But, even forewarned, what could they do? The terms of the surrender meant that their artillery had already been handed over to the rebels. Rebel soldiers had entered the Entrenchment to take possession of the guns and any pretence that the Europeans were in any condition to maintain their defence was exposed as a lie. They were now entirely at the mercy of the rebels. Indeed, it was their very helplessness that made me question whether treachery was really planned. For why commit an act of such barbarity that it would be bound to lead to future reprisals when the Entrenchment would inevitably fall in the next few days anyway?

By the time I reached the bridge of boats and my horse's hooves were clattering across to the Cawnpore bank, I had decided that the first thing was to rejoin my fellow sowars to see if they had any intimation of treachery.

I returned by the road that I had come. I noticed in passing that the jail was firmly shut and a guard stood with his musket at ready at the door. It seemed that, whatever the jailer did or didn't know, he had decided to watch his charges more carefully than he had in the past.

By now, I was seeing threats everywhere and I could not judge what was real and what my imagination. It seemed that there were somewhat fewer men on the road, though, as ever, the place was still busy. And it may be that those that were about were less careless in their manner than they had been only a few hours earlier.

Yet when I rejoined my fellows, they were as relaxed as ever. I was sure they did not suspect me of being anything other than I claimed for, if they had, my life would have been forfeit. So when they suggested riding down to the Entrenchment to see the Nana's men bring away the treasure that Wheeler was handing over, I was confident that they knew nothing of any plans other than for an orderly surrender.

As had been the case even at a height of the conflict, we sowars passed the midday hours taking a leisurely tiffin in the shade. It was late in the afternoon before we made our way down past the ruins of the half built barracks and over the crumbling defences into the European camp. The Nana's men had yet to arrive to take away the treasure but we were not the only rebel soldiers to visit the camp. Natives were coming and going with impunity. Some were there to gloat but others had come to see if old friends had survived the siege and to offer them such comfort as they could. Many of the officers' servants had remained in the city, trying to protect their masters' property and now appeared to report what had been saved and what was lost.

The Company's European soldiers watched with their muskets at the ready. From here and there came the sound of bayonets being sharpened on grindstones. Clearly, many there were not convinced the fighting was over. The sight of the skeletal figures of their womenfolk, in their ragged clothes and bare feet, showed that however brave the fighting men, there could be no more serious resistance while they were encumbered with so many civilians.

A boy of no more than five or six ran up to where we sat, still mounted. He stared at me. I feared he might recognise me, but he just stared at each of us in turn and then asked, "Did you kill my Daddy?"

Before any one of us thought to answer his mother, seeing where he stood, called urgently for him to come and he turned and ran to her. But for every child boldly searching the ruins for wood for the cooking fires or grabbing at the arms of natives they recognised among the visitors, three or four others would be clinging to their mothers, looking nervously at the world from behind what remained of their dresses.

"It is a bad thing," said one of the sowars, "when men make war on children and their mothers."

"It is truly a bad thing." I looked around and realised that almost all those I could see were, indeed, women and children or enlisted men. I called to one of the soldiers watching us.

"Where are your officers?"

"Lieutenant Bridges is in the Main Guard, sir."

The 'sir' had slipped out before he could stop himself and I saw him blush with shame. It was the natural deference of the defeated foot soldier toward the mounted victor, yet it marked, I knew, a change in the relations between the races in India. Things would never be quite the same again.

"I don't ask for your lieutenant, man. I want to know of your captains." I hoped that if Captain Moore were at hand, I might yet make an opportunity to talk secretly with him about my fears.

"All the officers of rank that are fit have gone to the river to inspect the boats."

I turned to my companions.

"Would you like to see the boats that will carry our enemies from Cawnpore?"

There was some shrugging of shoulders and they decided they would not bother. "We will see them go soon enough. There is nothing to be gained by looking at boats now."

I shrugged in my turn. "I am curious to see how this will be managed, and if there will be any role for us sowars. I shall ride down to the river to see."

I set off, leaving the others to return to the Nana's camp. I took the metalled road that ran North from the Entrenchment and carried on past the ruins of St John's Church and the Artillery Bazaar until I found myself back on the road I had followed that morning. The soldiers I had seen cleaning their weapons were no longer there. Indeed, the place seemed strangely empty.

Before I reached the ravine, the unnatural quiet was broken by the sound of men and beasts waiting on the road. A few of the Nana's sowars who had been absent from our camp that morning stood with their horses, alongside two elephants and their mahouts. The first of the sowars to see me was young Appa, who greeted me with a laugh. "So you've decided to join us and do some work, have you?"

"This is work? A trip to the Ganges? And then you can't even be bothered to climb down to the river."

"The Peshwa has sent some fine gentlemen to show the English their transport. They're down at the river now. But we know our place. It's up here with the beasts."

I laughed. The idea of a sowar knowing his place was absurd.

Appa joined in my laughter. "Truth to tell, the path is steep and the company uncongenial. The British are insisting that they will not leave today and that we should provide proper transport to bring them to the river. I am sure that they will complain about the state of the boats, too. The Peshwa's courtiers are the right people to soothe them." He spat on the ground. "If it were up to me, I'd have them walk to Allahabad or stay in their wretched fort and die."

"But you are content that they should have safe passage to Allahabad?"

He shrugged. "So long as they leave Cawnpore and do not return, I care not where they go."

I was relieved to hear him say so. Some troops may be planning treachery but it was clear that most of the sowars expected the rebels to hold to their word.

We waited, exchanging tall tales of our exploits during the siege. After about twenty minutes, we heard the sounds of the British returning up the ravine. Even before we could see them, it was clear that Appa was right: the British were unhappy with the arrangements. Raised voices echoed off the rocks. "…disgraceful…inadequate…deceived…" Occasionally, as the British voices paused for breath, I caught the soothing tones of the Nana's courtiers.

They were still complaining when they arrived at the top and continued to grumble as the mahouts ordered the elephants to kneel so that the officers could scramble up to the howdahs on their backs. There was not enough room for them all and a few walked beside the elephants where they continued to wrangle with the Nana's men. Captain Moore was one of those who walked and I heard him complaining that the boats were not ready to sail and the provisions were inadequate.

Beside him, a courtier continued his attempts to reassure. "You can see the boatmen are working to get everything ready and more provisions will be loaded. Not only flour, but sheep and goats also."

It was clear from his face the Moore did not believe him but, though he continued to complain, he had the appearance of a beaten man. The dashing soldier I had met in the half finished barracks was gone. The captain now was gaunt, his features worn with fatigue. The battle had been lost and I could see that in the end he would accept whatever the Nana would give him.

I pushed my horse alongside him as he walked. I had hoped

to catch his eye but when he was not looking at the man he was talking to, his gaze was fixed morosely on the ground. With his cavalry escort all around and the Nana's agents in our midst, I had no chance of a private word. The best I could do was when one of the other officers started his own complaints and Moore was left alone for a few moments. Bending in my saddle, I had just time to whisper a few words. "There may be treachery. They have cannon aimed at the boats." Then the Nana's man turned back to Moore and I had no chance to say anything further.

I watched Moore's expression to see how he responded to my news but, though he looked up at me, his face registered no recognition. He seemed past the point where he could respond any further to the blows that fate was dealing him.

As the sad little procession made its way back to the Entrenchment, I discussed loudly with the other riders whether there was any possibility that the British might be attacked as they tried to leave. As I had expected, they expressed shock at the very idea but I hoped that at least some of the officers might hear the word 'treachery' and be alerted to the possibility that all was not as it appeared.

By now, I was almost certain that at least some of the rebels planned to violate the terms of the surrender. The attractions of my present guise were growing greater. I could remain as a sowar and, if the evacuation proceeded safely, slip away from the rebel army later. I feared that if I revealed myself now, I could find myself with the other Europeans walking into a trap as they boarded the boats.

As soon as we arrived back at the Entrenchment, Moore was away to consult with Wheeler, who even the natives knew was by now so broken that he remained commander in name only. The Nana's cavalry had no reason to linger and obviously expected me to return with them, so I had no opportunity to pass any private messages, even if there were faces I recognised to pass them too. I had to content myself with uttering bloodthirsty threats to every white face we passed, in the hope that they would at least realise that the armistice was not as secure as they might imagine. I did notice several of the men responded with suspicious glares but, as I passed for the last time through the devastation of Wheeler's defences, I found myself wondering, yet again, what choice they had. The British would trust Nana Sahib to keep his word because the alternative was annihilation.

At least, I thought, I could make sure that one man escaped. As we drew back to the rebel lines, I told my companions that I had a cousin in the jail and I must go and enquire after his health. It says much for the state of lawlessness that by now prevailed in the region that it was accepted without question that one of their leader's own cavalry might be related to a felon. Indeed, by now I doubt that there were many native families left where at least one person had not fallen foul of one faction or another amongst the new rulers.

The door to the jail was still barred, now with two guards on duty. One went and got the old subadar. I bowed to him, my palms pressed together in front of me.

He gave me a small smile, grim but not unfriendly. "Each new day gives us the possibility of wisdom. Are you wiser than you were this morning?"

I returned his smile. "I know you have my friend's interests at heart."

He nodded and, as he did so, moved casually away from the door and out of earshot of the guards.

"I do, though he does not know it. He heard this afternoon that the fort is to be evacuated and he claims he is not Budloo but Mr Shepherd and one of those who have been fighting against us. He would have me tell the Peshwa of this, so that he might rejoin his friends." There was a long pause. "I have told him that I am too busy to run such an errand."

I bowed again. "I am sorry that your duties keep you so busy but perhaps all will be for the best."

"I pray every day that it might be so." He cocked his head on one side and looked quizzically at me. "It's strange, isn't it, that you should have known him as Budloo, if that is not truly his name?"

"Perhaps his name really is Budloo and now he lies in the hope of his release."

"It is possible. But, there again, in these days it may be that many people are not who they claim they are."

His old eyes glinted with amusement and I knew he sensed my discomfiture.

"Do not worry," he said. "Enough people have died, both the innocent and the guilty. And I fear there will be more blood spilt yet. I would not add to the deaths if I can avoid it."

I reached again for the money I kept in the pouch on my belt but he shook his head. "I will not have you think I acted for money. I am an old man and it is time I think of gaining some merit before I die."

I bowed a third time. "I am sure that the gods will look kindly on you for what you do now."

"Well…" He chuckled. "I hope some of them will."

I watched him walk back to the jail and vanish within. I was sure I had just been talking to a good and honest man. But I was now certain that there were those in authority who were neither good nor honest.

The day was drawing late. Wheeler would evacuate the next morning. Until then, there was nothing further I could do.

Mounting, I set off back to spend another night camped with the horses. As I rode, I looked across the plain at the shattered remnants of the Entrenchment, and the rebel piquets, keeping up their half-hearted guard. I tried to fix it all in my mind. Whatever happened, tomorrow the garrison would leave and things would never be the same again.

chapter 5

THE NEXT MORNING we were awake before dawn. Looking from the low hill over toward the Entrenchment, we saw the lights of a dozen or more little fires. I imagined the women I had seen in the past dining on banquets prepared by an army of native servants now crouched over their cooking fires, making chupattis for the journey ahead of them.

By dawn, the Nana's transport had arrived in Wheeler's camp. We watched from above while a motley array of elephants, palanquins and carts started to take on board their human cargo. A line of rebel troops stood sentry around the convoy, supposedly offering some security to their defeated foe. However, as we watched, hundreds, perhaps thousands, of the rebels who had been surrounding the camp entered into the Entrenchment to see the British leave and to mock them in the hour of their humiliation.

"Shall we ride down there?" Appa asked.

"No." Chimnaji's voice was definite. "We are men of honour. We have no business there."

So we stood watching the spectacle as the weary defenders, some so wounded that they had to be carried to the carts, gathered in dreary procession. There must have been about four hundred men, women and children who set off to the ghat that morning. At the front came the elephants carrying the officers and these made a fine show. Looking at them, it was possible to believe that I was watching an army leaving with the honours of war. Behind them, came the palanquins, mostly carrying women and children. The common soldiers and those whose position in society could not obtain them a place in the palanquins followed behind in the carts. Even then, there were those left who could not be accommodated in any of this transport and they followed the rest on foot. They dragged themselves along as best they could while the mob drew close about them, yelling insults and striking at them with their fists.

I watched with the others for almost an hour, and still the stragglers had not left the Entrenchment. I turned to Chimnaji, saying that I would watch no longer. He nodded his understanding and I mounted my horse and rode off in the direction of the jail.

Most people were in the Entrenchment, either to watch the British depart or in the hope of finding loot—although I could not imagine what might be left there to steal. This left the roads quiet and, once clear of the Nana's camp, I was able to gallop my horse toward the ghat.

I was not sure exactly what I intended to do, but if treachery were planned, then at least I would be at the riverside to take such action as I could. There was no point in my taking the path to the ghat that I had followed the previous day. The road would be packed with Wheeler's people and the natives who had come to watch them pass. I decided instead to head for the river slightly to the North, by way of the village of Sati Chowra itself.

I misjudged my path and arrived at the river a little upstream of the village, which announced its presence with a noisome stink of fish and filth, though the place was a quarter of a mile away from where I stood. The line of boats stretched upriver from the ghat to level with Sati Chowra and I had a clear view of them without moving any closer to the ravine. The vanguard of the evacuation had already arrived at the river and British officers were splashing through the mud, trying to get the boats into the water. Whether the river had dropped overnight or the boats had been pulled further toward the shore, I could not say, but almost all were beached.

At the first of the boats, I could make out a small figure in gold braid that I recognised even at this distance as General Wheeler. The elephant that had brought him to the river had waded out to the boat and the mahout was now guiding it against the vessel which it pushed gently away from the shore until it was bobbing safely in the stream. The officers in the other boats were not so fortunate as to have pachydermous assistance and they were still struggling to get their vessels afloat. More officers and men were pushing through the mud from the ravine. A few women had already joined them, though they were slower than the men, hampered by what remained of their dresses. All was chaos and confusion but there was no sign of any attack.

I dismounted and stood beside the river. Looking at the height of the sun in the sky, I judged it almost nine in the morning. It would take an hour or more to load all the boats and get everyone into the stream. I could watch the progress of the evacuation from where I was—close enough to act if action was required but far enough away to be inconspicuous.

I looked across to the Oudh bank. There was no sign of the gun crews that I had seen there the day before but anything could be lurking in the greenery.

On this side of the river, my view of the bank was obstructed by the huts of the village. The ravine and its little platform were entirely hidden from view but I could see the temple that was perched just a little higher on the bank above the ghat. I could see some natives sat there, the sun catching red cloth and gold braid. I imagined the Nana's generals and officials there to gloat.

A movement just beyond the village caught my eye. For a

second I thought I saw a glimpse of red there too, but I looked again and it was gone.

My horse sensed my nervousness and whinnied softly. I imagined another whinny from further along the bank but then a group of monkeys, disturbed from their rest in the ravine, came bounding along the higher ground behind me, chattering and screaming.

Every sound had me jumping. I looked out again at the boats. Two had been pushed clear of the mud and men were climbing aboard. All was proceeding according to plan. I willed myself to relax. I thought of Mungo and his smile, the green of the gardens at Saturday House. Out on the river, the men continued to clamber aboard the boats, some were helping wounded comrades to clamber aboard. The first of the women were pulling themselves clear of the mud, dresses hanging heavy with filth.

I began to think I had been imagining the danger. Everything would go smoothly. No one else need die.

I had just convinced myself that my fears were groundless when, from somewhere in the direction of the temple, came the sound of cannon fire. I started forward and, seizing my reins, I mounted. Yet there was no sign of artillery falling on the boats. No water spouted in the air. There were cries of alarm, certainly, but no screams of pain.

Aboard the boats, though, all was confusion. The native boatmen, who had so far taken little part in proceedings, suddenly threw their oars into the water and leapt from the craft to splash through the mud toward the shore. In the panic and uncertainty that immediately gripped those trying to board, it took a few moments before people noticed the smoke pouring from the thatch of several of the boats which the boatmen must have fired before fleeing.

Hardly had I realised that the initial cannon blasts had been a signal, than the rebels opened fire in earnest. Grapeshot and cannonballs fell around the boats, mud and spray drenching the vessels and their occupants.

Now I saw that my eyes had not deceived me. From where they had been concealed the other side of the village, scores of sepoys rose and ran toward the temple, firing their muskets. At the same time the sound of shots and screaming made me realise that more were attacking down the ravine itself.

Although the cannon fire had caused terror on the river, I had seen no one hit. By contrast, the sepoys' attack was immediately effective. As their musket balls struck home, I saw men fall on the boats. For a moment, all I heard was screams and the sound of firing, but then British voices shouted over the din as the officers rallied their men. Some of those on board were set to beating at the burning thatch with their coats while others returned fire. The British musketry brought down several of the sepoys who were forced to concentrate their efforts on returning this fire, allowing the men still in the water to keep pushing at the boats in their desperate efforts to get them afloat.

Now another cannon came into action. Shot was falling from four separate places and the rebels had found their range. Boat after boat was struck and this, combined with the flames billowing from the roofs, made escape impossible. The men and women who had so recently clambered aboard now threw themselves over the sides. The wounded, who had been painstakingly lifted into the boats, were abandoned and, as the vessels blazed, I could hear the screams of those trapped aboard.

Most of those fleeing the wrecks jumped out on the side furthest from the shore, hoping thus to shield themselves from attack. Alas, the flimsy vessels provided scant protection from cannon ball and grapeshot.

The rebels had by now formed themselves into a long line along the bank, firing repeatedly into the smoke. I looked on helplessly. I wondered whether to make a charge along the line. It might be possible, I supposed, to kill one or perhaps even two before they turned their muskets on me and I joined the English dead.

By now, a few of the boats had floated free and the sepoys were following them down river. Almost all the other vessels had been abandoned and their passengers floundered in the mud between boats and riverbank. With the boats out of action, the cannons ceased to fire and it seemed for a moment that the survivors were to be left to make their way to dry ground as best they might. Anticipating this, I started forward to assist them to the shore but, as I did so, I saw rebel horsemen start out from the other side of the village where the sepoys had concealed themselves before their own attack. While I hesitated, they rode into the shallows and, leaning low in their saddles, began to hack at the people struggling in the mud. Desperately, the survivors from the boats who, as the sepoys drew off, had started to struggle toward the shore, now turned back to the river, hoping to hide themselves in the smoke. Their attempts at escape were unavailing. The horses were coming at a canter and, one after another, they were struck down. Watching, and listening to their screams, it seemed to me that many of the riders had allowed their blades to lose their edge for some people were struck four or five times and fell back, still living, to drown in the muddy water.

I could watch and wait no longer. Urging my own horse forward I joined the fray. Busy at their bloody work, I doubt any of the rebels noticed an extra rider.

My plan, such as it was, relied on the notion that any rabble of men engaged in attacking a body of women would include a few who would seize some of the females for their private pleasure. I therefore hoped that I might be able to bear off at least one of the young women without it being seen as anything other than an undisciplined attempt to satisfy my lust. Indeed, as I splashed into the mud, I saw one or two of the men in the melee ahead of me sheath their swords and reach down to seize one of the struggling creatures in the water.

Those boats that had not been destroyed or pushed free into the river were now being systematically pillaged by rebels.

On the vessel nearest to me, I saw men shoot down two children no more than eight years old before turning on the adults who they were robbing even as I approached. By now the water was almost at the height of my saddle and my horse was struggling to keep moving through the mud, but I came right up to the boat just as the ruffians were attacking the last of the survivors—a young, dark complexioned girl who was trembling with terror. They were searching her roughly, tearing at what was left of her gown, and I was sure that once they had robbed her of whatever money or valuables she had secreted about her person they would kill her as they had all the others aboard.

Drawing my sabre, I shouted to the nearest rebel that the girl was mine and that he should throw her to me. For a moment, he hesitated but there is always something commanding about the presence of an armed man on horseback, especially as he is holding his weapon within an easy arm's reach of your throat. I think, too, that the man was also responding to authority in the way that Indians of lower caste will do. Whatever his reasons, he obeyed, seizing her around the waist and tossing her into the river. Caught by surprise, she was unable to find her feet and was carried along in the water while I pushed my horse to catch up with her, finally grabbing her and pulling her over my saddle as she reached dry ground and tried to stand.

I now found myself with a frightened and angry girl trying desperately to wriggle free and landing several blows about my person with her fists and her feet. I had, unthinkingly, imagined that I could simply tell her in English that I was a friend and that she would then trust me to save her. Foolishly, I had failed to take account of her fear and confusion and the natural terror my appearance roused in her. Her struggles, though, were ineffective, for she was lightly built and the privations of the siege had reduced her strength to the point where her blows caused me no harm.

By now, we were almost level with the ghat. The platform and the steps were covered with bodies and soldiers were searching the clothing of the dead for any loot they might still be able to recover. I turned my horse away, having no desire to push through either the living or the dead. The looters were shouting and cursing as they tore at clothes where jewels might be sewn into the hem or concealed in undergarments and they had attained the degree of excitement where they might well turn on the girl even though she was notionally under my protection.

I turned instead back toward the village. None of the other sowars tried to stop me or even seemed to think my behaviour unusual. Indeed, one or two grinned broadly when they saw the young woman struggling in my grip and made imaginatively obscene suggestions as to what I might do with her.

What I actually did with her was to carry her beyond the village and, once we were alone on the track back to Cawnpore, to put her on her feet on the ground and try to explain the situation she found herself in.

"I'm trying to help you. If you don't want to be helped, I can leave you here. The first man to find you will kill you. He may dishonour you first or he may be merciful and kill you quickly but you will die. I'm British. You have to trust me if you want to live."

I had to say this several times, for the poor girl was in a terrible state of shock. She had survived the Entrenchment and had believed herself saved when the rebels' treacherous attack brought her again to the edge of death. Her friends and her family were being cut down around her and she herself was about to join them when she was carried off by a mounted ruffian. No wonder she struggled to take in what I was trying to tell her. I was only surprised that she had not entirely lost her reason.

Once I had made myself understood, the girl's first reaction was to break down in hysterical weeping. I stood beside her, quite uncertain as to what to do, nothing in my experience having prepared me for such a circumstance. At length, though, she recovered herself and I was surprised by how calmly she seemed to accept her situation. She told me that her name was

Amy Horne and that she had seen all of her family slaughtered. She said she would place herself entirely in my hands and asked what I intended to do.

At least I was no longer in the situation I had found myself with Mr Ashley for I had a plan ready. "I will take you to a place of safety," I said. "There you will be concealed until this revolt is over and the British have returned."

She looked at me with deep brown eyes that had seen too much suffering but now showed, not fear, but a calm calculation of the possibilities for the future. "And what if that day should never come?"

"It will come," I said. "I'm sure of it."

She made no reply but appraised me with another look and I knew that she recognised my words to be a lie.

I lifted her from the ground. We had a long way to ride and I suggested that she sit astride the horse. Perhaps once maidenly modesty would have caused her to object but women who had survived the siege had lost their concern for superficial propriety. The rags she wore did not constrict her legs and, emaciated as she was, she was easily able to sit before me on the saddle.

We had been riding for an hour when she began to sway dangerously from side to side. Fortunately, we were not far from a grove of mango trees and I rode toward them and dismounted, lifting her gently down from the saddle. As I put her on the ground, her legs buckled and I had to catch her before she fell. I cursed myself for my stupidity. The poor girl was exhausted and in no state to ride further without food and drink. I would have liked her to have a chance to rest as well, but I feared to stop for more than half an hour, so I had to be content with giving her water from my flask and dried beef that was carried in my saddlebag.

She sat, pulling her rags around her to maintain her decency and, while she sipped from my flask and chewed at her meat, I encouraged her to talk about herself, for it seemed to me that she would recover from her ordeal more easily if she could share her story with another.

"What brought you to Cawnpore?"

She started to laugh and I feared that she would fall prey to hysteria but, swallowing, she controlled herself.

"Would you believe that my father brought us here from Lucknow because he thought it would be safer? We arrived only in April." She began to sob. "He's dead now. And my mother. There were five children beside me and now…"

She was weeping uncontrollably by now and for a while she could not speak. I sat beside her on the ground, not knowing what to say or do. At last, I put one clumsy arm around her shoulders and she leaned against me and, slowly, the sobbing eased.

Amy and her family had been billeted in a bungalow near the St John's Church and had only moved into the Entrenchment when the mutiny broke out. There she and her family had sheltered under a veranda, which had been their home for three weeks.

"They died every day." She was shaking with the horror of it. "One day an officer rested from the sun next to us when a shot struck him full in the face, taking his head clean off. His body just stayed sitting there, his hands falling by his sides, the blood gushing from between his shoulders like a fountain." She described how those around her had died one after another. Sometimes whole families would be found lying dead side-by-side. "I tried not to look at it, but the smell! My God, the smell! And the flies. Flies everywhere."

Both Amy and her mother had been wounded in the head and her five-year-old sister had her leg fractured by a falling block of masonry. They were so hungry that the children had been reduced to eating a horse that had died outside the Entrenchment and been dragged in by the troops. Her mother had gone mad. That Amy herself had remained sane seemed little short of a miracle and I was determined to see her safe.

As soon as she was recovered enough in mind and body for

us to remount, I rode on. We headed North, skirting Bithur and making directly for the shelter we had been promised we could find with Mungo's cousin, Dara. I had met him only once, when he first volunteered his house as a place of refuge, but I had trusted him immediately.

My confidence in him was repaid. His gatekeeper may have looked askance at the sight of one of the Nana's riders arriving at the compound with a half naked young woman mounted before him, but he clearly had orders to admit me without question. The gate swung open and, moments later, Dara came bustling out to greet me. "I am glad that you have need of me, for it means that you have saved at least one person from this disaster. Our gods teach us that, though there are times we must kill, life is sacred and we have a duty to protect it whenever we can."

As a respectable householder, Dara had Amy whisked away to the women's quarters as soon as he set eyes on her. I was not entirely comfortable at the idea of abandoning her but Dara was firm that I could not penetrate his zenana. "It is a place reserved to women and your friend will be safe there. It would be quite improper for you to enter. Beside," he smiled, "judging from her appearance, I think the first thing that the ladies will do is to bathe her and provide her with new clothing. I am sure you would not wish to intrude on that."

I had to accept his argument. In any case, I felt it was best not to linger. I did not want curious minds to wonder where I was spending my time. So I drank the tea I was offered, nibbled at some sweets presented on golden trays and, as soon as was decently possible, I was back on my horse and headed South.

※

IT WAS LESS than a week since I had left Bithur, but when I opened the door to find Mungo waiting in his room, I fell upon him as if we had been parted for many months. Holding him in my arms, I felt somehow cleansed, as if his presence washed away some of the horror of what I had just witnessed. The eagerness with which Mungo pressed his body against mine suggested that he too had felt my absence.

"You should have come back after the battle or at least sent me word. I heard that the cavalry were driven back. Can't you imagine how worried I have been?"

"I'm here now. I'm safe."

He pulled me tighter to him, his fingers tracing the line of my spine as if he thought it might have changed since last he saw me. "You're safe and the fighting is over."

"For now, at least."

Mungo pulled away, searching my face for my meaning. "How can it not be over? The Peshwa is to review his troops in Cawnpore tonight, in celebration of his victory."

"And do you know how that victory was achieved?"

Mungo could tell from my voice that there was something amiss but his honest face showed he had no idea of what had happened on the river.

"The Europeans must have realised that they could not beat off the cavalry again, so they surrendered." He tried a smile. "You see, your efforts won the day after all."

I could not smile back and his face turned serious. "In any case, I suppose you should be at the review."

He was right. I was supposed to be a soldier of the Nana and, after what I had seen, I had no illusions as to my fate if my true identity were discovered. Nor was I the only one with an identity to protect. Shepherd must be in more danger than ever. I could only pray that the old subadar had kept faith.

"Yes, I need to be there. I must show myself with the others—and I have someone under my protection and I must see that he is well."

Mungo obviously wanted to know about his person and I told him in as few words as possible of Mr Shepherd's disguise and my efforts to buy his safety. I was undressing as I spoke, for I wanted to get myself clean before I rode back to Cawnpore and it was already afternoon. I had little time to waste if I were to take my place in the Nana's victory parade.

Mungo insisted on 'helping' me bathe, so I spent much, much longer than I had intended being cleaned and scented and generally cosseted before I was allowed to put on a clean uniform (Mungo having secreted one away while I was in Cawnpore) and presented myself at the stables to find my horse, too, had been pampered. At least, as the two of us set out on the weary road back to the battlefield, we started with the benefit of cleaned and rested bodies.

Even so, by the time I rejoined my fellow sowars I was weary in the extreme. My fatigue meant that I did not find the grand review as impressive as I otherwise might have, for all of the Nana's troops were arrayed on the plain, which now took on its original purpose as a great parade ground. There were mutineers from Cawnpore, Lucknow, Allahabad, Azimgurh and Nowgong; Benghalis, Golundazes and Nawabees as well as a great mob of zemindars—landowners who had pretended loyalty to the British but who had turned up with gangs of armed followers once they thought the Nana's cause would be triumphant. In all, there were some tens of thousands of men parading. A 21-gun salute was fired for the Nana after which he made a mercifully short speech, praising us for our great courage and bravery and promising us a lac of rupees apiece as a reward for our labours (although I was not alone in doubting that we would ever see the money).

We woke late the next morning and took our ease. We talked, of course, of what had happened the previous day. The others in my company had been as shocked as I by the massacre. Chimnaji was especially upset.

"I have ridden for the Peshwa for many years and I can scarcely believe that he could be involved with such a thing. To promise safe passage and then to strike down your enemy when he is defenceless. It is not an honourable way to wage war." He shook his head and there was a murmur of agreement from our little assembly. "At least the women and children were spared."

This news caused me not only astonishment but some indignation, for I had seen them being cut down, but I did not want to admit that I had been present at the massacre so I simply asked if he was sure that it was true.

"Certainly it is, for I saw them brought up here and locked into Savada House with the other European prisoners."

The news that at least some of the women and children had escaped filled me with joy. I decided that I would try to visit all the prisoners that afternoon and I set off with high hopes of being able to bring some succour to them but, alas, I was to be disappointed. Savada House was, as ever, well guarded and I was told in no uncertain terms that the prisoners were allowed to see no one.

"But one of the ladies employed my sister's nephew as her houseboy and when she went into the fort, he was left without his wages. I would see her to ensure that arrangements are made to pay him."

The guard laughed. "No one here will be paying any of their debts. They have nothing but the clothes they stand in— and those are little better than rags. Tell your cousin to help himself to anything he wants in the house and take that for his wages. Not that I doubt he has stolen from them already."

Rebuffed, I made my way to the cavalry hospital where Jonah Shepherd was still a prisoner. When I arrived, though, the old subadar was not at his post and I was rebuffed there too. A young guard I had not seen before claimed to be in charge and refused me entry.

"The old guy is too soft on them." He spat on the ground between us. "I've ordered your cousin chained up. He's a dirty traitor to the Peshwa and he'll have no visitors while I'm in charge."

He spoke with the arrogance of a young man revelling in his first taste of authority. I could see that bribery would not help me here. The guard was enjoying his moment of power and the control it gave him over the lives of his prisoners. All I could do was return to my place with the other sowars and trust that the old subadar would return soon.

We had been told that Nana Sahib would return to Saturday House the following evening, when there was to be a great ceremony acknowledging him as Peshwa. Until then we had no duties and we were all grateful for a day of rest after the excitement of the last week. I took the opportunity to explore the remains of the European Quarter. One or two of the houses had escaped looting. I think these were where servants loyal to their old masters had remained in their homes. Now, with the Europeans gone, the servants had fled too. Everywhere was desolation.

Near my old home a Labrador, someone's favourite gun dog I guessed, trotted hopefully toward me. Its coat was glossy and it looked well fed. Again, the work of loyal servants was evident. Now, it had been abandoned like the homes. I threw a stick and, as it ran to catch it, I turned my horse and rode away.

I returned to camp with some delicacies pillaged from abandoned kitchens. There was tinned fish, a jar of marmalade, a tin of Bath Oliver biscuits and even a jar of Gentleman's Relish. The other sowars thought my taste eccentric but all were happy to sample the food with me, though some claimed the flavours (especially the Gentleman's Relish) too alien to be enjoyable. I welcomed the feast as a reminder of what seemed a long-lost life, but I had to be careful not to seem too familiar with the food, lest I rouse my comrades' suspicions.

The next day, to my relief, I found the old subadar back on duty.

"I am sorry I was away. A family matter."

"I hope it is resolved now."

"All is well now. At least, all is well with my family. As for your friend here…" He gestured toward the jail. "I must confess that he is becoming a thorough nuisance. He's heard that there were Europeans who escaped the killing and he wants to be put with them."

"Is that why he has been put in chains?"

"Not really. I am afraid that while I was away my young colleague became rather—shall we say, overenthusiastic. Don't worry. I will ensure that they are removed today."

I thanked him.

"You have been generous to me and I am generous to your friend. But he thinks I am cruel in keeping him a prisoner here. He still insists he is a European and should be at Savada House with the others."

I had seen how the Nana had dealt with the Europeans who had fallen into his hands at Sati Chowra. I understood that if Shepherd thought his family might have survived he would be desperate to join them but, like the subadar, I thought he was safer kept in jail as Budloo. "He is no more a European than I am." We both smiled at this. "He should stay here. And, if he is to stay longer with you, it is only right that you are rewarded for your care of him."

Gold passed from my hand to his. The subadar bowed his gratitude and I returned to camp believing that I had at least been able to assist one prisoner, even if I had not been able to reach the others.

IN MID-AFTERNOON, WHEN the worst of the heat was over, we mustered to escort Nana Sahib back to Saturday House for his inauguration as Peshwa. He moved in state, sitting in a gilded howdah, while we cavalry formed an escort around his elephant. Following us came many of the troops who had marched in his victory parade. By no means all the troops left Cawnpore, though. The most enthusiastic rebels remained and I noticed the green flags of the Musalmans conspicuous among those who stood and watched our departure rather than ride with us. Even without them, though, our train was miles long. I did wonder if the tail had left Cawnpore by the time we arrived at

Bithur. Riding at the front, as I was, I never saw the back of the procession.

Once the Nana was safely deposited at his home, we sowars were dismissed, allowing us time to smarten ourselves up for the ceremony. I prepared alongside Mungo, who was bubbling with more than his usual enthusiasm.

"It will be a splendid ceremony. To think that I will be one of those who see him finally made Peshwa."

Tired from my journey and having sat through one evening of ceremonial already that week, I could not summon up the same enthusiasm. "He's been telling everybody that he's the Peshwa already."

"And he is!" Mungo's face flushed and I had to remind myself that it was his own family honour he was defending. "But he said he would lay formal claim to the title only once he had won it in battle. And this night his reign will be inaugurated. How can you say that the fighting is not over?"

"I know the British. They will not let this pass."

"But they are few and we are many. They have left Cawnpore. Surely they would not be such fools as to return?"

I tried to reassure him with a smile but I had broken the mood.

"Anyway, we should not linger here." Mungo was all business now. "I must be seen at the celebration, honouring my master's new role. And you should tidy yourself up and be there too."

We did not speak again of whether the fighting was over or of whether the British would return. I bathed and Mungo and I both scented our bodies. He relaxed enough to laugh at this, rubbing scented oil into my hair and then massaging me in my private places and I laughed too and pretended that the events of the past days had not come between us.

As night fell, we went out into the gardens. I think every servant in the place must have been pressed into working there. I wondered how Mungo had escaped fetching and carrying but I supposed that a Peshwa has more than enough people to do that sort of thing. Two great pavilions had been set up. One already housed the ladies of the court, so that they could see the celebrations through a screen without exposing themselves to the gaze of men. I glanced at it curiously. Hidden in there were the late Peshwa's widows, whose disinclination to see any sister slain had saved at least some European lives. I remarked to Mungo that they may have been unhappy to hear of the massacre of women and children at the ghat.

"I have heard a few were killed in the fighting, but when the Peshwa heard that there were women and children there, he ordered them spared."

"Only after a score or more had died."

Mungo bridled as he had in his room. "I tell you that the Peshwa has shown mercy. The women and children are kept prisoner and no harm should come to them."

I could not bear another argument. "I'm sorry. It's difficult in the heat of battle. I'm sure the Peshwa was as merciful as he could be. "

At once, Mungo's tension was gone and he smiled at me with the smile of the innocent boy that he was. "You see, you need not have worried. Really, you could send that girl you carried away back to Cawnpore. She'd probably be better off with the others."

I tried to keep my face from showing the horror that I felt at this suggestion. I had seen the Nana's treachery at first hand and I did not intend to trust Amy to his uncertain mercy. Fortunately, the sight before us made it easy to change the subject to something less likely to generate discord.

"I had thought the Peshwa's pavilion at Cawnpore was splendid but this is even more amazing."

Mungo beamed as if the pavilions before us were his own property. "It is as it should be for the inauguration of the Peshwa. It will truly be a wonderful thing. You'll see."

The gardens were already filling with people. There must have been several thousand there. Mungo pushed through with the easy authority of a courtier. I always thought of him as my friend—a young man easy in his manners and pleasant to know. It was always a shock to me when I saw him in situations like this, where others quickly deferred to his rank.

Thanks to him, I was seated in one of the best positions when Nana Sahib's procession entered. It was led by elephants in all the crimson and gold trappings. Behind them followed bullock carts, palanquins and led horses. Mixed in amongst the animals were men dressed up as horses who pranced about, kicking and playing antics. The most curious part of the procession was the platforms for the dancing girls. These were made of bamboo over which was spread an awning ornamented with crimson and gold and silver. On each travelling throne sat a native musician playing on a kettledrum and before him danced two girls, swirling with all their might and skill. The platforms were carried on the heads of men in the procession and had a curious and singular effect. The situation was a very unsteady one for the dancing girls, one of whom became giddy and tumbled down upon the heads of the crowd of people below.

The Nana himself was, of course, riding on the state elephant. He sat in a howdah covered in red cloth and liberally decorated with gold. Arriving at the pavilion, he dismounted and was carried the short distance to his throne on a litter. He sat while Hindoo priests charted and anointed him with oil. Representatives of the Musalman community were present too. They watched the Hindoo ceremonies without enthusiasm but, just by being there, they endorsed Nana Sahib as a ruler acceptable to both of the faiths.

The ceremony lasted an hour or more. At its conclusion, the new Peshwa rose from his throne and raised his arms in benediction to the crowd. The noise of cheering from the thousands of men assembled there was such as to render thought, let alone conversation, almost impossible. It went on for several minutes and as soon as the cacophony started to diminish, fireworks burst into the air from all around the garden, supplementing the noise of the crowd with their own bangs and whistles.

Mungo turned to me, his face lit by the flashes of red and blue in the night sky.

"You see, John. It is a new beginning. The British have gone. Everything is going to be alright."

※

THE BRITISH HADN'T gone, of course. In fact, the news from Allahabad was that the British now controlled the town. They had assembled an army there and were marching toward Cawnpore. The new Peshwa had to leave his palace and hurry back to lead his troops again. From his headquarters, set up in the Old Cawnpore Hotel, he sent out orders, passed laws, appointed officers and generally conducted all the business of state associated with his elevated title, though in the chaos of those times his writ did not run more than a day's ride from the city.

The women and children from Savada House were moved to a small house near the Nana's headquarters, as if he felt more secure with his hostages nearby. I went to see the building for myself. It was pleasant enough, having been the home of some European's mistress in the days when such liaisons were more public than they are now. But it was small—only about forty feet by fifty feet—and quite inadequate for the 180 or more souls now crammed into it. I know that the Nana had the prisoners fed, for I saw servants going and coming with food, but I think they must have been hungry. Sometimes they were allowed to take the air, outside the house and I saw some of the women once. They were a pathetic spectacle, thin to the point of emaciation and clad in rags. They limped pitifully up and down the patch of ground allowed them, for most had no shoes and several had obviously been wounded, either in the Entrenchment or at Sati Chowra. I would have approached them to offer comfort, or treats of food and drink, but they were carefully watched and no one, not even soldiers of the Nana's guard, was allowed to draw near to them.

There were still vast numbers of rebel troops in Cawnpore. Some were waiting for their pay, some were waiting for orders and some had just decided that staying where they were and looting the remains of the city was preferable to marching off to somewhere like Delhi where there was fighting to be done. Now, ten days after the celebration of the driving out of the *feringees*, the shirkers and the idlers were gathered up with the remnants of the mutinous regiments. The Nana's generals had recognised the danger and I was kept busy with my fellow so-wars, carrying despatches from the hotel here and there about the city as the rabble of the Nana's followers was shaped into an army that might resist a British advance.

After almost a week of frantic activity, the Nana had eight thousand men under arms in something approaching a disciplined force. By now, the British were reported to be closing on Cawnpore so, on July 14 (my commonplace book tells me it was a Tuesday) we were told that the next day we were to march out to meet the enemy on the road to Allahabad.

With everyone on the lookout for deserters, there was no question of my not rejoining Chimnaji and the other sowars to head South with the rest of the troops. I sought my erstwhile comrades out that evening, and we camped together overnight. Some of our company were in a sombre mood. They remembered the struggle that the garrison had put up when hopelessly outnumbered and outgunned and they were not looking forward to meeting a British column that was well prepared for battle. Chimnaji worked hard to raise the mood, though, with tales of great victories in the past and a store of jokes and anecdotes about the life of a sowar. By the time we were lying on the ground, waiting for sleep, we were all, if not happy, at least prepared for the day ahead.

In the morning, Chimnaji suggested that we leave ahead of the main force. It would take hours for the army to muster together and, he pointed out, if we set off to scout ahead of the troops, we could ride out in the cool of early morning, rather than wait in the sun while everyone else was organised. We were all happy with the idea so, early on the Wednesday morning, we rode a way out of the town and then camped in the shade.

It was not until the middle of the afternoon that we saw clouds of dust advertising that the Nana's army was on the move. We scouted quickly to make sure that the British army had not arrived while we were dozing and then we rode back along the road until we met the rebel force. Salutes were exchanged, we reported the way ahead clear and took up our rightful position as the advance guard of the column.

We led the way for about ten miles to a place called Aherwa. It was a village of no importance but it was well situated beside the road, allowing a force placed there to prevent the movement of troops Northward. Accordingly, it was here that the Nana decided to make his stand.

The cavalry were to be held back in reserve, so I was not at first clear how our force was to be deployed. Only as I saw the troops spread out ahead of us did I realise that the Nana's generals were finally getting to grips with the basics of proper strategy. Apart from us in his cavalry, Nana Sahib deployed all his troops in a wide arc across the road, with one end of his line anchored on the Ganges so that he couldn't be outflanked on that side. The whole army was screened by mango groves and five mud-walled villages that hid his artillery.

It was an impressive plan. The land here was lower than the country further South so the army was concealed in a dip in the landscape. The British would not see the rebel force until they were practically on top of it. Having fought their way so far, they would be unlikely to retreat but would attack straight down the road. When they were within the curved line of the rebels' army, the Nana's force could open up with their artillery, wreaking havoc on the British ranks. It was a simple trap but nonetheless likely to be effective.

Now, at last, I had some information of real value to the

British. As importantly, the confusion of movement inevitable when inexperienced commanders tried to position that number of troops, gave me an excellent opportunity to carry that intelligence to them.

I did not try to slip away unnoticed. Rather I rode openly from place to place, as if carrying despatches from one part of the army to another. I was able in this way to reconnoitre the whole of the line, confirming my view that the Nana's strategy was sound. Once I reached the end of the line, I simply carried on until one of the mango groves that were so useful in concealing the rebels from the British now served to conceal me from them.

The delays in leaving Cawnpore, the inevitably slow progress of a large body of men and the time I had spent scouting the rebel positions all meant that by now dusk was falling. I waited an hour until full dark and then eased my way in a wide loop back to the Allahabad road.

Once safely away from the rebel lines, I settled to a night of fitful sleep and, as soon as there was light enough to ride, I headed on to meet the British.

I had removed my turban and made a bundle of my uniform jacket, so when I ran into General Havelock's scouts, they did not shoot me before I had time to greet them as friends and tell them that I had urgent information for their general.

"Have you, indeed? And who the hell are you, when you're at home."

I opened my mouth to give my name and then I hesitated. As soon as I was known as John Williamson, I would be gathered back into the bosom of the European community. What then of Mungo, waiting trustingly for me to return to him? What of Amy Horne? Even Jonah Shepherd's life was safer for as long as I could pay his jailer to make sure he came to no harm.

I had a whole life as Anjoor Tewaree. I had friends and responsibilities. I had someone who loved me. It was, I knew, a life that couldn't last. One day I would have to return to the world I had known before Mungo, but not today. When Anjoor Tewaree departed this earth, he would not be sacrificed to a brutal trooper like this fellow.

"I am Anjoor Tewaree," I said. "I have intelligence of the enemy's position and it is vital that I give it to the General as soon as may be."

While we were talking, an officer had ridden over and now demanded to know what was going on. I gave him a quick summary of my news and he recognised its importance immediately. Ten minutes later, I was standing before General Havelock.

The British were making a quick breakfast of biscuit and beer, anxious to be on the march. The General must have eaten already, for he was on his feet when I was brought before him. Short, like Wheeler, he seemed to stand constantly at attention, brimming with an energy that belied his white hair and the evidence of age in his craggy features. He scarcely deigned to look at me but barked questions about the exact placement of artillery, the numbers in each of the units and the morale of the men. He asked about fodder for the horses (we had none but that close to the Ganges would have no trouble foraging) and the condition of the ground (firmer where it drained into the river, marshier on the other flank). There was question after question and I was not sure that he really attended to my answers until he bent down and, with a stick, sketched an astonishingly accurate map of the rebel positions in the dust at his feet.

"Is that right?"

"Yes, sir, you've got it exactly."

"Good man. Well done." And he just turned away.

I hesitated for a moment and the trooper who had escorted me hissed in my ear. "You're dismissed, you little runt. Now bugger off."

So that was my meeting with Old Phlos, as the soldiers called him. I could see why he wasn't popular with his men. He was a brilliant general, though. He led an attack right down the edge of the Ganges, so that he could flank Nana Sahib, for all the rebel strategy. It was a huge risk, relying on my assurance that the ground was firm close to the water and pushing his men into a space where there was no room to manoeuvre if things went wrong.

Perhaps it was not really such a risk. Havelock's men knew about the massacre. They knew that there were still women and children held by Nana Sahib in Cawnpore.

I had to ride back to the rebel lines, galloping my horse, apparently fleeing from the British. I rejoined my fellow sowars and said I had been out scouting and the British were coming. With all the confusion of the night before, no one suspected anything.

Then the British came. They charged at us with a fury that we had never seen before, never even imagined possible. The charge was led by the Highlanders, their kilts incongruous against the Indian landscape. They came with artillery and they came with musket fire but it was their bayonets that carried the day. Seventeen inches of cold steel in the hands of an angry Scotsman is not to be taken lightly. One village after another fell and our infantry were in retreat.

We sowars were ordered to cover the sepoys as they fell back toward Cawnpore. We formed up in a block but the British cavalry came on us like madmen. I heard their captain shouting his orders: "Point, point, no cuts!" and then we were fleeing to the jeers of the soldiers behind us.

We made one more attempt at a stand around a 24-pounder that had been held in reserve on the Cawnpore Road. Nana Sahib himself rode among us, followed by musicians beating drums, clashing cymbals and blowing bugles. I was on the flank with Chimnaji, determined to redeem ourselves after the last rout. It seems odd, looking back, but, at the time, my determination to stand up to the British in battle seemed quite normal. I had been in their camp at breakfast, telling them how best to defeat the rebels and now here I was with the rebels, doing my best to defeat them. I can see that it's absurd now, but at the time, riding alongside men I had come to like and trust, it seemed perfectly natural. In any case, I think that most men have an understandable desire to fight back when someone is trying to kill them. And the British were certainly trying to kill me.

At first, we were successful, pushing forward with our artillery smashing into the British and the rebel fighters taking heart at seeing the Nana himself fighting with them. Soon, though, our attack lost momentum. Our guns were pouring grapeshot into the enemy ranks but they just kept coming. They were like men possessed. It seemed that however many we killed, more came at us. After a quarter of an hour of this, we were losing heart. Then the British sent up a sudden cheer and charged for our 24-pounder. Minutes later, we saw Nana Sahib flee the field, riding hell-for-leather on the Cawnpore road.

That was the end of the battle. We all broke for Cawnpore.

I MADE SURE that I rode back to Cawnpore more slowly than my comrades of the Nana's cavalry. Now I had shown myself as a good soldier I had bought some time to deal with my private business.

Cawnpore was in an uproar. The streets had always been busy, but now I could hardly move for people rushing about in a panic. As soon as the first of the retreating rebels had reached the town, the whole population realised that the British could not be that far behind. Everyone was trying to flee. The streets were jammed with every kind of cart. Horses, camels and mules were everywhere, kicking passersby and each other, adding their cries to the din and contributing more than their share to the stench that pervaded the place. Some enterprising soul had even found an elephant to press into service, though how he intended to use it as a pack animal, I have no idea.

At first, I was quite amused by all the panic. After all, I had nothing to fear from the British and the rebels had surely brought their trouble on themselves. Then I saw among the crowds babus who had been hiding from the rebels for weeks, a shop keeper who I knew had been loyal, even some of those servants who had come to bid their masters farewell when the Entrenchment was abandoned. What had these people to fear from the British? I knew the troops might be out of hand when they first arrived. There would, doubtless, be looting and some wanton destruction. But those natives who had stayed loyal were in less danger from the Company than they were from the Peshwa. Trapped between the two camps, they nonetheless stood a better chance if they stayed where they were.

I stopped one man who was struggling under the weight of the bundle on his back. I recognised him as one of the Company's babus, but I was confident that he would not recognise me.

"Why are you fleeing? Do you think you have anything to fear from the British?"

He looked at me as if I were mad. "They will surely kill every one of us."

"Because of the massacre at the river?"

"No, you fool. Because of the killing of the women."

Despite the heat, I felt a chill shiver across my body.

"What killing?"

"How can you not know? The killing that the Peshwa ordered yesterday."

Yesterday. While I was camped with Chimnaji and the others, relaxing in the countryside. I turned to the babu in a fury, demanding to know what had happened.

I drew the story from him, with much stuttering and hesitation. I think he saw madness in my eyes and thought that I might turn on him and destroy him.

The previous morning, he said, orders had come to the guards to destroy all the European prisoners. No one seemed entirely sure where the order had come from originally, though the soldiers were told it was a direct command from one of their generals, who went by the name of Tatya Tope.

"The soldiers said they would not do it and Tatya Tope

came to the house himself and said it was their duty but still they said it was unmanly to cut down women and children and they refused. So they brought in men from the bazaars who went into the house with tulwars."

The screaming had gone on for an hour. The leader of the five swordsmen had twice had to emerge for new weapons as his blades shattered.

In the dawn of the day I had arrived back at Cawnpore, men had entered that dreadful charnel house and cast the bodies down the well that lay beneath a banyan tree. According to the babu telling me the tale, not all those inside the house were dead but, dead or dying, all were thrown together into the well.

"There were some children who lived and ran about trying to find any person who might save them but no one came to their aid and, in time, they were cut down and thrown into the well with the others."

He was crying when he finished his tale, though whether in sympathy with the victims of the rebels' treachery or for fear of what would befall him, I could not tell. Certainly, he was right to be afraid, for, like him, I knew that the British would be merciless. The massacre at Sati Chowra had been bad enough but at least some of the victims had been under arms, even if they had slaughtered the innocents alongside them. But the women and children who had been held prisoner were just that. They were prisoners, unarmed, helpless and harmless. I thanked the Lord that I had not listened to Mungo and that Amy Horne was still safe in the countryside.

"What of the Indian prisoners?"

"What Indian prisoners?"

"There are prisoners in the old cavalry hospital. What of them?"

The babu shrugged. "They will still be there. It was only the Europeans who were killed."

I tossed the man a few annas, as much because I was relieved as for any service he had rendered me. Then I headed off, as quickly as I might through the mob in the streets, to see that Jonah Shepherd was still safe where I had left him.

There were fewer people about near the makeshift jail. It was not that people there were calmer, but on the outskirts of the town there were not so many houses and most of those there were had already been evacuated. Outside the old cavalry hospital, though, men were hurrying back and forth, throwing their belongings onto a cart. I saw the old subadar supervising and went to greet him.

"You are leaving as well?"

Some of his usual friendliness had gone but he answered me politely. "I don't think we want to be here when the British arrive."

"What of the prisoners?"

He spread his hands in the universal gesture of a man helpless to change the situation.

"I cannot release them. I have my orders and if I release them I could lose my life."

"Then surely you should stay to guard them."

This time, as he spread his hands he shrugged as well. "We are leaving now. If the British arrive, then these men will be released by the British. There is nothing that I can do to stop that and I will not be blamed."

There was some truth in this idea, but it could be days before the British came across this jail and paid any attention to the men inside. Days when they would be without food or water and at the mercy of anyone who happened by them. The British would not be able to restore order to Cawnpore overnight. It was likely to be a very dangerous place for a while. The jailer, though, was not going to be concerned about this. Once the British had entered Cawnpore, the prisoners would no longer be his concern. Until then, he was going to keep them locked in.

I tried another tack. "What if the British do not come?"

The subadar had been struggling to remain polite but now he allowed his irritation to show. "Do not take me for a fool.

The Peshwa's forces have been defeated. Nothing lies between the British and Cawnpore. They will be seeking revenge for all they have suffered here. They will surely come."

"They could delay. They may not find the prisoners until too late."

The subadar nodded. "That is possible. But if they do not come, I will return to my post and the prisoners will still be here."

I produced ten rupees—a fortune for a man like him. "Just let them go before you leave."

He hesitated and I could see the indecision on his face. Then he shook his head. "I cannot do it. I cannot betray my trust."

"But if you can't return, then you would be happy for the prisoners to be freed?"

"If I can't return, they can no longer be my responsibility."

"Suppose you do not return today. Can the prisoners be freed tomorrow?"

"If I am not here tomorrow, I am sure they will be freed."

I counted out another five rupees. "Leave me the keys. You have my word of honour that the prisoners will not be released until tomorrow. I will wait here and, if you return, I will yield the keys back to you."

It was a compromise that allowed the old man to retain his honour.

Five minutes later, he was gone. My purse was fifteen rupees lighter, but I held the keys in my hand.

I RESTED IN one of the houses abandoned in the rebels' flight. It had high ceilings and offered some comfort and shade.

As I waited, I was sorely tempted just to open the jail and release everyone straightaway, but I decided I should keep my word. There had been too many broken promises in Cawnpore. But I did allow myself a liberal interpretation of 'tomorrow' and it was still dark when I set off back to the jail.

I had taken a candle from the house. I doubted that the owners would need it again. By its fitful light, I traced my way to the cavalry hospital and unlocked the door.

Inside was one large room, undivided by any partition. The sound of the door opening had awakened the prisoners who appeared agitated and cried out for food and water. In the dark, I could not see how many men were held there, but it seemed a great number of voices cried out to me from the blackness.

For a moment, I stood in the doorway. The candle flickered in the foetid air and it was as if the wavering light brought the prisoners a realisation that the door was open and that I was all that stood between them and their freedom. A moment later, with cries of joy, they were running out of the building. I had barely time to move from the doorway or I would have been trampled as hundreds of men pushed their way through.

I called over and over again as they ran by. "Budloo! Budloo from the Entrenchment!" No one paused. I began to think he might have passed without hearing me. In desperation, I even risked shouting his true name. "Jonah Shepherd!"

I had almost given up hope when, amongst the last to leave that miserable place, hobbled a figure that I recognised from his questioning at Savada House.

"Jonah Shepherd."

He stared at me in the candlelight, his face blank, his eyes on the edge of madness.

"I'm English, Mr Shepherd. And I've come to save you."

I GAVE HIM water and a little food and warned him to move away from the town as quickly as he could.

"I think our army will arrive today, but until they take control, this is a dangerous place to be. You are weak and in no position to defend yourself. You need to move away from the town. Head toward the British. They are coming on the road from Allahabad. Make your way in that direction."

Shepherd looked at me in confusion. "But aren't you coming with me?"

I admit I hesitated. But I was still responsible for Amy Horne. And when the British moved Northward—as I was sure they would—Mungo would need my protection, as he had protected me.

"No. I must stay here. But I will be safe. I fear that my capacity for deceit is greater than yours." And I have a friend who has assisted me in that deceit, I thought to myself, but I did not share this with Shepherd.

It was still almost full dark but there was starlight and the faintest glimmerings from the rising sun in the East. Perilous as the road might be by night, I wanted to be away as soon as may be. With the Nana's armies gone, any small pretence of law and order would already be breaking down. And though I hoped the British would bring some sort of peace, I thought that any business to be conducted at Saturday House was best done with before their arrival.

I set off, for what I suspected would be the last time, on the road to Bithur. Fortunately, by now I knew the way well enough to find my route in the darkness. The streets were littered with more than the usual amount of detritus. An army in retreat abandons much of its gear and all but the most valuable of its plunder. Still, my horse found a clear path through the rubbish and we moved slowly but surely through the town. There were no people about to disturb us at that hour, although the occasional sound of splintering timber and more than one or two screams in the distance suggested that there was still loot to be stolen and scores to be settled now that the rebel army was no longer there.

Once out of the town and clear of the shadows of the houses, the path was easier to see. By now, too, the glimmerings in the East were already growing brighter. The dawn would soon be on us. I pressed my heels to my horse's flanks and we were soon moving along the highway at a brisk trot.

Dawn comes quickly in the Orient and I was not halfway to Bithur before it was full daylight. Before the revolt, the road here had usually been quiet as it passed through the countryside, but there would be farmers in the fields and the smoke from breakfast fires rising from villages in the distance. Today, though, the countryside as far as I could see was still and silent. Everyone would have seen the Nana's army fleeing North and would know by now that they were on the cusp of change. So they hid in their homes to wait and see what their fate would be.

I pressed on. I had some vague hope that I might catch up with the rebel army. I did pass the odd straggler—men whose wounds slowed them and who had been abandoned in the Nana's flight—but it was clear that the main body of the rebels had pushed on as fast as they could. Well before I reached Saturday House, I knew that they had already abandoned Bithur.

At first sight, everything at Saturday House seemed normal. There was the slightest of breezes and the leaves on the trees lining the avenue that led to the house rustled a little. Otherwise, there was silence and it took a few minutes to realise that the little sounds that you might expect to hear weren't there. The faint clack of hoof on stable stone was missing. There came no whispers of conversation on the breeze. There was no sound of shouted orders or the footsteps of servants hurrying to obey them. There was the occasional cry of a peacock and, as I came nearer, the gentle splashing of fountains, but otherwise there was nothing.

The gates of the compound were open and no sentry challenged me. The sound of my horse's hooves seemed unnaturally loud as we clattered toward the stables.

The stables were quiet too. Every horse had gone. I had never seen them empty before. It seemed that the Nana's army had taken every beast that might carry a fleeing soldier.

At first, I had thought that the stable lads had fled with the army but after I had called two or three times, a nervous boy of thirteen or fourteen appeared from the corner where he had been sheltering and took the bridle from my hands and led my horse away.

"Take care of him!" I called. "I will not have him stolen by some ragamuffin who would flee after the others and who wants to spare their legs."

The boy looked at me as if he were about to burst into tears. "There's none left that would steal your horse, sir. All have fled."

"All?"

"All the men, sir."

I turned, leaving him still standing at my bridle, and hurried into Saturday House. Down corridor after corridor, my feet echoing on marble floors. The hour struck as I was near the corridor of clocks and the sudden din in all that silence near unmanned me. I carried on through the maze, which was now as familiar as any place I'd lived, and soon I was at the door of Mungo's apartments. I opened without knocking, sure that I would see naught inside but the evidence of hurried packing.

Instead, I saw Mungo.

He was sitting cross-legged on a carpet placed in front of the door. He held no book or paper for writing. No painting occupied his eyes and there was no little sculpture for those long fingers to play with. He just sat, waiting. And when I opened the door, he raised his eyes to my face and his eyes were filled with tears.

"I thought you might not come," he said.

Then, after a while, he said, "I should have known that I could trust you."

chapter 10

MUNGO DESCRIBED THE panic of the previous day. The army had swept past Saturday House, pausing only long enough for Nana Sahib to collect up his treasure and have it loaded onto barges on the Ganges. He and his closest family had set sail up-river with about a hundred soldiers to escort him. The rest of the army had vanished Northward and Westward. Saturday House had been gripped by panic. The guards at the gates had joined the army's flight. The courtiers had commandeered every horse, cart, elephant and camel in the place and had set off in pursuit.

"It is because they killed the women," Mungo said. "They say Azimullah and the generals made the Peshwa do it so that he could not surrender to the British. They thought it would make him strong. But now they are all weak and fly, as children do who have stolen into their father's rooms and broken the ornaments there and now hear their father returning. They know the British will be merciless."

"But you stayed."

"I knew you would return here. And where you are, there I belong. How could I flee and leave you? Where could I live if not with you?"

I held him then, for I do not know how long. I held him as

a drowning man clings to the rope that holds him to the shore. I had loved before but I had never been so needed.

At last, I broke off from our embrace to address the practicalities of our situation.

"People have been wise to flee. The British will come here and, when they do, their vengeance will be terrible. We must leave."

Mungo nodded enthusiastically. Now that I was with him, he seemed happy for us to leave together.

"The girl I saved is still with your cousin. We should go there. It is far enough from Bithur that it may well be spared. In any case, the worst of the violence should be over by the time the troops have finished with Saturday House."

"How will we get there? All the horses are gone."

I looked at his lithe figure. I had always loved the way he looked. Now I could see a practical advantage to his slimness. "I have a horse. We'll both ride that."

Relief flooded Mungo's features. "Very well, I'll pack."

"No. We shouldn't waste the time and we won't be able to carry much anyway. Your cousin will have enough for us to cope. We shouldn't be there long."

"Just a few things."

I started to argue but realised after a couple of minutes that it would be quicker to let him take a favourite tunic and a book he treasured than to waste the time disputing.

"And then there are these." Mungo was leaning over a chest on the floor where he kept some clothes and a few gold bangles.

I imagined the clocks ticking in the corridor. "We don't have time for these trifles, Mungo."

"These are no trifles."

I looked over his shoulder. The bangles were narrow and the work, to my inexpert eye, of no great value.

"They aren't worth anything, Mungo. Leave them."

But then I heard a click and Mungo's hand was darting into a cavity in the base of the chest. It came out holding a small bag, from which he shook three diamonds, each about a quarter of an inch across and a ruby of a similar size.

He grinned up at me. "Perhaps these are worth taking?" He slipped them back into the bag, pulled the drawstring tight and slung it from his neck under his tunic. "Now we go, yes?"

We hurried to the stables, Mungo almost skipping ahead, as if convinced that now I was here he was out of danger. I was less confident, but the same scared stable boy was quick to return my horse. Though the beast was tired, he had benefited from the brief rest, food, water and a rub down. Refreshed, Kuching was easily able to carry Mungo's weight along with mine and, as we set off slowly Northward, I began to share his optimism.

It was early afternoon, the hottest time of the day at the hottest time of year. We rode at an easy pace but, even so, our horse was struggling after the first half hour and I was worried that, although I was by now well used to the climate, I could be struck down by the heat, which killed so many Europeans exposed to the midday sun. I decided it would be wise to shelter in one of the occasional groves of trees that broke up the landscape. If the British did send scouts North immediately, they would surely spend some time in searching Saturday House. Now we were clear of Nana Sahib's palace, I thought that there was less urgency to our flight.

We left the horse loose to forage for grass in the shade. There was no danger of it wandering into the open country in the heat of the day. We lay down and rested.

After a few minutes, Mungo rolled against me and I held him in my arms.

"John, now that the British are back, what do you intend to do?"

I did not answer at once. A few weeks ago, my flight to Saturday House and Mungo's protection had seemed just a precaution while we waited for the situation in Cawnpore to settle down. But these past few weeks had seen my life so changed I could hardly believe that once I had breakfasted in the Club, worked in my office with Hillersdon and Simkin and dined in the evening with the ladies of the Station. All these people were dead now. With them, it seemed to me, a way of life had died and, perhaps, a part of me had died with it. Could I ever return to that world?

"I don't know, Mungo. I really don't know."

He lay still against me and I knew it was not the answer he had wanted to hear.

"And what of you?"

He forced a smile. "You have seen the diamonds."

I could hardly have forgotten them. Since he left Saturday House, they were the sum total of his wealth and he wore the little bag around his neck almost all the time.

"And I have my family. Dara will give me shelter for as long as I need." He paused and his expression grew more optimistic. "And you, too. You can stay there with me. You will be welcomed as one of my family."

I knew that what he said was true. Family ties were close and I knew that Dara would offer me the same protection as he would Mungo. Perhaps it would be for the best. Perhaps I should settle down as a zemindar—just another of those thousands of landlords whose livelihoods I had been so busy trying to tax away while I worked for the Company.

It was an idea not without its attractions. The attractions grew when we finally rose from our rest and completed our journey. We were welcomed into the compound where Dara lived with his extended family. The main building, with its separate wing for the women, housed him, his two brothers and their sons. I don't think I ever worked out exactly how many sons there were. Around a score of boys and young men, ranging from a toddler to a strapping youth in his early twenties, were forever coming and going about the place. Another son had his own separate house in the compound where he lived with his wife. There were separate, smaller houses for the servants and the farmers and their servants who farmed the fields closest to Dara's home. Mungo explained that a zemindar like Dara would never take direct responsibility for his land but that the farming would be left to the tenants. Many of these people were not relatives, but the man who farmed closest to the compound was another of the network of cousins that bound these families together.

Mungo and I were given a room in the main house. Dara did not seem concerned about our relationship. He was much more worried about my request for a private interview with Miss Horne. It was not until we had been there for two days that Mungo was able to convince him that, as Europeans, it would be acceptable for the two of us to meet and then Dara only allowed it on condition that Mungo acted as chaperone.

When I finally did meet Amy Horne, I scarcely recognised her. The frightened, starved, half-naked girl I had rescued has been replaced by a calm and assured young lady, dressed in native clothing beneath which, as far as I could judge, was a well-fed and healthy body.

"I find you in better health than when last we met, I hope."

"Thank you, sir, you do."

"And you are happy here?"

Her face, unremarkable in repose, was beautiful when she smiled, as she did now.

"Very happy, sir. Everyone has been most kind."

"You know that the British are back in Cawnpore?"

The smile vanished. "I did not know. There has been talk, of course." She paused, chewing her lower lip. "I think that the others must have known but have kept this from me."

"I imagine that this must be good news for you."

She rallied, trying hard to summon an appearance of delight to her features, but she was too palpably honest a girl to succeed.

"We think it will soon be safe to carry you to Cawnpore to rejoin your people."

At this, all attempt at dissemblance was abandoned. Indeed, I feared she might burst into tears. "Please do not send me away. What would I go back to? I have no people. My father was neither a Company servant nor a soldier. No one will care that he has died and I have no family living."

I endeavoured to set her mind at rest. "You are a pretty girl, Amy. I am sure that someone will take care of you."

She blushed. "Sir, it will be known that I have been living with the natives. It will be assumed that I have been dishonoured." She must have seen something in my face for she hastened to reassure me. "No such thing has happened, sir. I have been treated with every kindness and I believe that the women here love me as my sisters did when they were living. I would be protected from any insult. But you must understand, sir, that no one in Cawnpore will believe this. No man will have me now."

I did my best to reassure her that this could not be the case. All I achieved, though, was more tears. In the end, I released her back to the women's quarters.

"It's a poor show, Mungo," I said, once she was safely out of earshot. "For I fear that she is right."

Mungo shook his head in astonishment. "But she is young and very beautiful. I am sure that one of Dara's people would be happy to marry her."

"But not any of her own people, I'm afraid. I don't know what we are to do, for with no family, no income and no prospect of marriage, her condition once she leaves here will be pitiable."

"Then she must not leave here."

I was surprised by Mungo's comment. It was one thing for me, a man, to have chosen to live among the natives, but it was unseemly to see this imposed on an English girl. My irritation at his suggestion must have shown and Mungo resented it.

We ended up arguing for some time. By the end of our altercation, both of us were in an ill humour and all that had been agreed was that the girl would have to stay for the time being. That was hardly a concession on my part, for with neither rebel nor European army clearly established in the countryside, transporting Miss Horne to Cawnpore would have been, in my view, too much of a risk to expose her to.

So life continued, with we three refugees enjoying Dara's hospitality. I had occasional interviews with Amy. She was by now physically recovered from her ordeal, but Dara said that the women told him that she would often wake screaming. They had all grown to love her and had coaxed out more details of her life in the Entrenchment. It seemed that, young as she was, she had done everything she could to help the men and women around her, looking after her younger brothers and sisters while her mother descended into madness, and always willing to assist with the nursing of the wounded soldiers.

"I think," said Dara, "that European women can be braver than their men."

For Mungo and me, our stay was, in many ways, a simple holiday. I did worry, from time to time, that our idling might eventually cause offence within the household but then I observed that idleness was endemic amongst the zemindar class. The day-to-day running of the farms was the responsibility of the tenants though they, of course, did no actual labour themselves. The work was done by labourers who lived on a few annas a day. The tenants lived quite well themselves but the majority of the profits came to Dara, whose efforts consisted mainly of attending to his accounts and adjudicating on the odd dispute amongst his various tenants and sub-tenants.

"You are unfair, John," Mungo argued when I remarked on this to him. "When you worked for the Company, did you tend the fields?"

"Well, no. But the Company administered the whole country. We made laws and enforced them. We built roads and kept order. We did our best to protect the weak from exploitation."

"And Dara and the other zemindars do the same. Do you think there were no roads in India before you came? Did we not have laws and were they not observed? The zemindar acts as your magistrate did, adjudicating disputes. When men are needed to guard the country or keep the peace, the zemindar provides them."

I thought of the landlords who had joined the Nana's army, each bringing their own followers to swell the ranks. I thought of the beggars I had seen fed, the bloated household of the Nana Sahib with all the retainers whose survival depended on his generosity. I thought of myself and Mungo, fed and cared for because Dara had a responsibility for his family.

Mungo watched the working of my face while I thought these things.

"You see, John. You think the Company changed so much. But really, we Indians just exchanged one zemindar for another."

IT WAS A few days after this that the British sent a force North from Cawnpore on the road to Bithur. Word spread from village to village, through that network of family connections and casual gossip that has served the Indians for their news for longer than there have been Europeans in the country. One of the first acts of the rebels had been the destruction of the telegraph, but I believe that, even had the wires still been in place, news would spread on the native grapevine faster than it could ever be transmitted officially from Company outpost to Company outpost. In any case, before we took our tiffin at midday, we knew that the British had marched out that morning.

It will have taken them hours to reach Bithur. A military expedition moves slowly, even in the absence of organised resistance. Even so, by that evening we were being told that the soldiers had got to Saturday House. By then such servants as remained had evacuated the building so we had no news of what occurred inside, but I could imagine the destruction. Still thirsting for vengeance, the troops will have rampaged through the place, stealing anything they thought of value and, as often as not, destroying all they could not steal. I imagined the mirrors smashed, the idols desecrated, the books in the library torn and scattered on the floor. The corridor of clocks would not be disturbed by their din again.

That night neither Mungo nor I could sleep. The British would have rested at Bithur. The question that kept us awake through the night was whether would they turn back to Cawnpore or press on Northward?

An hour after dawn, the word from the field hands—who had it from a farmer's son who had it from a beggar who had it from who knows where—was that the British were making their way back South. Our relief was short lived, though. Soon after came news that, while the main force had headed South, a small column was pushing on Northward.

By mid morning, we did not need news to tell us where the British were. Smoke from burning buildings on the horizon made all too clear the direction of their advance—and they were heading directly toward us.

Tired as we were after our restless night, we could not sleep through the heat of midday. We knew that the British would rest at noon and march again as the afternoon cooled. What we did not know was whether they would continue Northward or turn to rejoin the rest of the army.

Labourers working on Dara's land watched the soldiers, ready to bring news as soon as they moved. Meanwhile, we could do nothing but wait.

The first of them returned at around three in the afternoon. The soldiers were making North.

Dara gathered his household together (by which I mean the men, for the women remained secluded) and announced his intention to abandon his home. "If we flee now, we will stay well ahead of the British. They may burn and pillage for another day, maybe two, but then we can return."

It was Mungo who objected to the plan. "Cousin, you do not have to abandon your home and expose your women to the dangers of the countryside. The British are not barbarians, killing and destroying without reason."

"Mungo, we can see the burning from here. They are destroying the farms. Burning the villages."

"But we are not their enemies."

"You are of the Peshwa's household. I am your cousin. How can we not be their enemies?"

I had remained silent, leaving Mungo to debate with Dara, but now Mungo turned to draw me into this argument.

"We have John here with us. He can speak to them and tell them that we have not fought against the British but rather that we have protected him."

"Can you do this?" Dara asked.

"I can speak to them. I will do my best."

"They will listen to John," Mungo assured his cousin, "and we will be spared."

"Is Mungo right?"

I hesitated. I remembered seeing British sailors in Borneo killing without compunction or mercy. The troops that were heading in our direction would know all about the massacre. They would be angry and looking for revenge.

Dara spoke again. "Is Mungo right?"

It would be alright. I would speak to their officer. They would listen and leave the place unharmed.

"Will we be safe?"

"Yes," I said. "You will be safe."

It was late in the afternoon and the day was beginning to cool when the troops arrived. There were about thirty of them, marching slowly but steadily in a neat block with a young lieutenant riding beside them.

As they approached the compound, I walked out to meet them with more trepidation than I allowed to show. My European clothes had been abandoned, so I was dressed as an Indian, though I left my head uncovered. I had given up using walnut juice some weeks earlier but my skin still carried the stain and my constant exposure to the sun had left me well tanned. Given my natural dark colouring, it was not immediately obvious that I was a European.

I walked slowly toward them, my arms raised, shouting, "I'm British," over and over again, as loudly as I could. Even so, the platoon halted and rifles were pointed in my direction before two men were detached to bring me to the officer.

As soon as my escort had me in hand, the rest of the men started to move forward again. I was led forward by the arm and the soldiers seemed to think of me as much as a prisoner as a free citizen of Great Britain.

As soon as I had been secured the platoon moved forward and, by the time I had been brought before the officer, the front rank was already pushing into the compound.

The young man looked down from his horse. "You say you're British."

"I am British. I'm John Williamson."

He looked at me blankly and I realised that, with the European community in Cawnpore all dead, there was no reason why the name should mean anything to him.

"I'm the Deputy Collector."

The lieutenant snapped a salute and dismounted.

"I'm happy to see you well, sir. My understanding was that all the Company's officers in Cawnpore were killed."

"Well, as you see, I survived. Thanks largely to the protection offered to me by the men in that compound that your soldiers are forcing their way into now."

He turned to see the last of the platoon vanishing inside the compound walls.

"I will ensure that they are gentle, sir."

He pushed his horse forward to follow the men but, before he reached the gate, I heard the sound of shots from inside. He kicked his horse to a trot and I started to run after him. There were more shots and then I heard him cry out, "Cease your firing! Sergeant, rally the men."

By the time I arrived, some sort of order had been restored. The doors to the main house hung off their hinges. In front of them, a line of troops, bayonets fixed, stood on guard. Two bodies lay on the ground in front of them. Servants clustered sullenly in front of their homes. It looked as if they had run out to protect their master when the troops forced the doors of the house and had paid the price. Looking at them as they faced the troops, I feared that they might rush forward again.

"Wait!" I shouted in Hindoo. "All will be well if you wait."

The men shifted and muttered amongst themselves. They clearly remained unhappy and suspicious, but by now they knew me and I felt my words might have some effect. I had no time to wait to be sure, though. The lieutenant had left his horse at the entrance to the house and I hurried catch up with him.

Inside was chaos. Doors were open, the low tables had been kicked over, soldiers seemed to be everywhere and I could hear shouts and screams. The worst of the noise seemed to be coming from the direction of the women's quarters so I made my way toward them.

I have explained that the women's quarters were separate from the rest of the building and that the men, except for Dara, did not enter unless special permission had been given. There was but one door that linked these rooms to the rest of the house and that was generally guarded by a servant. It was not that Dara thought anyone might enter without permission but more that the proprieties might be observed. Unfortunately, faced with British soldiers demanding entrance, the servant had elected to stand his ground and he had been struck down. As I arrived, the lieutenant was crouched over him. He looked up as he saw me approaching.

"He'll live." Then, gesturing toward the door. "What's through here?"

"The women's quarters. For God's sake get your men out."

The poor lad was really very young. He looked around as if

hoping to find inspiration in the corridor where we stood, but before he could do anything there was the sound of women's screams from the zenana, followed by European oaths and the noise of booted feet running back toward the door.

Four soldiers appeared, coming full tilt toward us. Their faces were blotched red with fury.

"He's got one of our women in there. A British girl in his bloody harem!"

The lieutenant gawped at the man, who ran on into the house.

"You need to stop them!"

"But…" He looked puzzled. "I say, what do they mean about an English girl?"

"I saved her. She's been sheltering here with me."

He was still gawping. He was obviously new to India. Brought up on stories of the exotic East, he saw no difference between the careful propriety of the zenana and the erotic fantasy of the harem. The idea that Amy Horne's most exotic activity in the past weeks was a little embroidery work would have been utterly incomprehensible to him.

"Get your men under control!"

It was too late. He was too inexperienced and the men had their blood up. If he did not understand the finer points of the position of women in the household, his men knew nothing and cared less. They had found a pure English lass at the mercy of the foul Indian fiend and the rage that they will have been nursing since they learned of the massacre was now allowed full rein.

I heard shouts from room to room and the sound of splintering doors and breaking furniture.

"Avenge our women!" was the cry which swept through the platoon. I started to follow the noise but the lieutenant grabbed my sleeve.

"Don't try. They'll kill you too. There's no stopping them when they're like this."

His face was white but I think he was no coward. He might have been young and inexperienced but he knew the temper of the British soldier. He had allowed himself to lose control. Now all that could be done was to wait for their fury to burn itself out.

✳

IT WAS PROBABLY only about ten minutes before his sergeant began to drive the men to the door but it felt much longer. Two corporals were sent back to the zenana to escort Amy Horne back to what they doubtless thought of as civilisation. I watched as she was brought out. Tears were pouring down her cheeks and she was screaming at the men to let her go. Behind her, I could hear the keening of the women.

They dragged her past the bodies that lay in the entrance hall. I recognised Dara and two of his sons. The others had been beaten so badly they could have been anyone.

There was no sign of Mungo.

"Best if you leave with us, sir."

"I can't. I have to…"

I had to find Mungo, was what I wanted to say, but I didn't feel I could explain.

"We'll wait a few minutes, sir, but then you'll have to come with us. I'm sorry about the way things turned out but I can't leave you here." He tried to smile. "I can't have them say I found the Deputy Collector and then lost him again."

I started back to the room I had shared with Mungo. I tried to ignore wreckage all around, the smeared blood on the floors, the last of the soldiers pocketing such small valuables as they could loot before their sergeant rounded them all up. One was hacking a sapphire from a statue of Ganesh that sat in a niche in the wall. Another was holding a drawstring bag. He grinned at me. "Diamonds," he said. "And a ruby."

I was on him before I had time to think, my hands at his throat. His comrade seized my coat and tried to pull me off but I was a man possessed. Now the soldier behind me was striking at my head and shouting for help, but I scarce felt his blows. All that mattered was my fingers, tightening on the throat of the man below me.

There was the sound of running feet. Men pulled at my arms but still I did not release my grip. The face below me was purple. The eyes bulged. The lips were turning blue.

"Mr Williamson! Williamson! Let him go!"

Gradually the lieutenant's voice penetrated my brain. Suddenly I felt the pain where my head had been struck and the force of the men pulling at me. My fingers released his throat and I was pulled to my feet.

The sergeant was kneeling beside his man.

"He's alive. Just."

The lieutenant started to speak but something in my face stopped him.

I shook the men off and turned to walk away. No one tried to stop me.

As I walked, I became aware of the lieutenant walking with me. I let him be. It seemed easiest.

I knew what I would find. I didn't know the details, of course, but I knew that Mungo would have been wearing that bag round his neck. No one would have searched his body while he was alive.

He was lying on the floor. There was no blood. I was glad of that. I think his neck had been broken. He lay there, as if he had just fallen asleep. His shirt had been ripped open and the skin still glowed as it had when he was alive.

He was so beautiful. I knelt and lifted him to me and kissed his lips. I did not care that I was watched.

The lieutenant said nothing. He waited and when I laid the body down, he took me gently by the arm and guided me out.

I did not cry. I wanted to but I did not.

Someone had found me a horse. It was not mine but I didn't care. They helped me mount.

The platoon moved off. South, toward Cawnpore.

"It's alright," said the lieutenant. "We're taking you home."

chapter 11

THE NEXT FEW weeks passed in a daze. Cawnpore was still at the forefront of the fighting, with the rebels expected to counterattack at any time. It was no place for a civilian. I was evacuated to Allahabad. Amy Horne was whisked away somewhere. I don't know what happened to her, though I heard she eventually arrived in Allahabad too.

Physically, I was in good shape but the doctors said I was suffering from nervous exhaustion and the effects of the heat. I suppose that sounds better than to say I had a broken heart.

The British won the war, of course. Looking back, it seems inevitable that they would have, but it didn't seem inevitable at the time. For a few weeks in Cawnpore, it seemed that the world was about to change. Maybe in some ways it did. The East India Company was wound up and India became part of the British Empire. The same officials remained in charge but the British Government was able to maintain a tighter control on how things were done. There was some liberalisation of the way that the natives were treated. Annexations were to end. The Government recognised that the best way to maintain control in India was to develop an Indian middle class which would act as a cushion between the bulk of the native population and their European rulers.

The babus, like Mr Shepherd, many of whom had risked everything by their loyalty to the British, were among the principal beneficiaries of this policy. At last they were to have the chance to rise up the ranks of what was to become the Indian Civil Service, instead of being condemned to toil always at the lowest levels.

These changes, though, were all to take time to implement and, meanwhile, with the fighting over, there was still a country to run. And though the Company men were now servants of the Crown, we still had to do the same old work. The Summer of 1858 found me back in Cawnpore. The Company offices had been much damaged during the revolt, but repairs had been effected and the place was still familiar. I was not to sit in my old room, though. Mr Hillersdon's death had left a vacancy for Collector and, once I was judged recovered, it was felt that I should be allowed a run at the job.

The press of work required in the rebuilding of the country can easily be imagined. The late starts, long lunches and early ends to the day, which had so characterised the office when I first arrived, were no more. Indeed, we were under the necessity of holding office for eight or ten hours daily, inclusive of Sundays, and such a thing as a holiday was never heard of. At first I welcomed the work as distraction from my grief, but as the months passed I began to find concentration difficult. A phrase in Hindi, a glimpse of a young man whose face brought to mind that of my beloved Mungo, the smell of herbs in a cooking pot: all these things might suddenly bring to mind my time in Saturday House and I would be lost in reverie until an anxious colleague would bring me back to the business in hand with enquiries as to my health. Sometimes, I sat at my desk, unmanned, tears streaming down my cheeks. No one ever referred to these incidents but I know they talked about me behind my back. I do not think they were cruel, but I know the gulf that had always separated me from them had grown wider.

I could not remain as Collector, of course. A new man arrived as the worst of the summer heat gave way to the more bearable weather that presaged the bliss of the winter cool. He was very kind. I should not really have remained as Deputy Collector, but there was much to do and he felt that the work helped me by keeping me from dwelling on what had passed. In fact, everyone was very kind, as one is kind to a dog that has been beaten. Their kindness was distant. I cannot blame them for, of course, they did not know the one unbearable truth that was at the centre of my distress. I had loved Mungo more than I realised and his death had left me diminished. I had thought that leaving Borneo and the love I had known there was hard but this was a thousand times worse. I had loved him with the passion of an older man for a younger lover. It was the flowering of a lifetime of experience, intoxicated by the excitement of youth. And, for so long, I had dismissed it as mere lust, denying what I only now realised was the marriage of two souls.

My youth has long departed. Mungo had warmed my middle years and made me feel young again. Now all that was over. I was suddenly an old man.

I struggled on to the end of the year but I was tired. Tired of India, tired of the life I had lived there. It was time to go home.

The Collector was very good about it. I was a survivor of Cawnpore, after all. He spoke a lot about strain and nervous collapse. He said I shouldn't feel guilty. He said that the Company would pay my passage home and arrange a pension for me. He was very generous.

So, almost exactly three years after I had arrived in Cawnpore from Calcutta, I retraced my steps. It was a melancholy journey, for it lacked the sense of excitement and discovery that I had felt on my arrival. The country, too, was melancholy, at least in the early stages of the journey, for the British had not been gentle in their destruction of the rebels and we passed village after village that had been put to the flame. Among the men rebuilding their habitations, almost all were very old or very young. On some trees still hung the remains of the ropes where a vengeful army had hanged all the men of fighting age who could not account for their actions during the rebellion.

At Allahabad, instead of travelling on by road, we took to

the river. I travelled in a very fine sixteen-oared pinnace, containing two excellent cabins, fitted up with glazed and venetian windows, pankhas, and two shower-baths. Even on this final journey, the Collector had insisted that I travel with an appropriate number of servants, so there was a separate dinghee for the cook and provisions for the voyage, and another for a valet and my baggage. I had been pressed to take another so as to carry more servants but I had drawn the line at this. There was, after all, a full crew on the pinnace and they would more than adequately see to my needs on the journey South.

So we flew down the river on a powerful wind. We passed Mirzapur and Patna, Berhampur and Cutwa. I am told the journey is very beautiful but I was in no mood to appreciate it, although I did enjoy the smoothness of carriage in the pinnace, compared to the rigours of travel in a buggy.

By the time we reached Nuddea, the tide was perceptible and I began to brighten at the prospect of arriving in Calcutta and transferring to the vessel that would take me home.

We arrived in Calcutta on February 12th. The view of the shipping was beautiful and I enjoyed it, although the crew dashed among the other vessels with fearful velocity.

I was put ashore in Calcutta and stayed two days in the same hotel where I had rested on my arrival. During this time a Government agent found a vessel with accommodation suitable for my return trip, so, with only the briefest of delays, I was settled aboard the *Earl of Hardwicke*. A steamer towed us down the river on the morning of 15th February, and the pilot quitted us on the 17th, from which moment the voyage actually commenced.

I will say nothing of the passage. It was long, and we broke our journey at the Cape and at St Helena, arriving in the Channel early on 3rd June 1859. I determined to leave the ship at Plymouth and I, together with a large party of other passengers, was taken off by the pilot vessel.

So it was that, after so many years, I found myself once more in the county where I spent my youth. It was a balmy day and, as I walked up from the port, roses were blooming in the hedges. I breathed in their smell. It was the smell of England.

I was home.

editor's notes

WILLIAMSON'S ACCOUNT OF events at Cawnpore is generally in agreement with other published accounts. There are a few details that do not fit the public record. In some cases, it is clear that the public record was edited to avoid awkward questions. (Amy Horne's account of what happened to her between her capture and her eventual reappearance in Allahabad would be a case in point.) In other cases, it seems peoples' recollections of what actually happened when they were caught up in these traumatic events may not always be precisely accurate.

The principle facts about Cawnpore would, until the mid-Twentieth Century, have been known to every British schoolchild. Wheeler's force consisted of around 60 European artillerymen with 6 guns, 84 infantrymen and about 200 unattached officers and civilians and 40 musicians from the native regiments. In addition, he had 70 invalids who were convalescing in the barrack hospital and around 375 women and children. They were besieged in a wholly inadequate position from 6th June 1857. From 6th to 25th June, the Entrenchment was under continual bombardment by day and sometimes by night. Faced with overwhelming numbers of enemy cavalry and infantry, the tiny defence force nonetheless managed to hold out until they were offered safe passage in return for their surrender. General Wheeler, by then a broken man whose son had been killed during the siege, accepted the terms. Many people think that he was strongly influenced by the views of Captain Moore, who had taken much of the responsibility for the defence as Wheeler's health had deteriorated. Williamson's account confirms the general belief that Moore was a man of exceptional vigour and courage who did much to maintain the spirits of the garrison.

The rebels broke the terms of the surrender and the massacre at the ghat became part of the history of the British Empire. Williamson's description of the massacre is consistent with other accounts. Amy Horne was carried off by a sowar, although she afterward claimed that the man had been a Muslim. Reading Williamson's account, it is easy to see why Miss Horne may have been discouraged from telling the whole truth about the incident.

The massacre of the women and children at a house generally referred to by the English as the Bibighar, happened almost exactly as described to Williamson. The reason why Nana Sahib ordered such an atrocity is not clear. Some people believe that he hoped, by killing the last surviving witnesses, to escape responsibility for the earlier massacre. Others consider that he was trapped into it by hardliners within his court who wanted to make sure that he would not be able to make peace with the British. Nana Sahib's role throughout the events reads strangely to a modern Western onlooker. It may well be best explained in the terms used by Mungo. It is quite likely the Nana Sahib was trying desperately to maintain a position where he could claim to be favouring either side until it was quite clear who was winning. Many local leaders in India at the time changed sides and the British were often prepared to accept as allies people they had every reason to think had been plotting against them when it looked as if they were going to be defeated.

Williamson's depiction of the battle against Havelock fits the known facts. Havelock's victory was in part down to intelligence received from a native spy called Anjoor Tewaree. Williamson's account provides a valuable insight as to who Anjoor Tewaree actually was.

We do not know for certain what became of Williamson after his return to England. In 1861, a John Williamson is recorded as having bought the Grange, a substantial house in the village of Bickleigh, just North of Plymouth. The parish records show no trace of him in the years before that and whether it is the same John Williamson, we have no way of knowing. He seems to have been a well-respected member of the community, as he was churchwarden from 1863 until his death in 1872.

Williamson was obviously not in a position to know exactly what became of all the people that he met at Cawnpore. However, the fate of many of them is a matter of historical record.

CHARLES HILLERSDON was struck by a cannonball in the Entrenchment. Some reports put his death on June 7, others on June 13.

LYDIA HILLERSDON survived childbirth but was killed by a cannonball on June 9.

LADY WHEELER and her daughter ELIZA WHEELER died with the General at the ghat.

MARGARET WHEELER is believed to have been one of the only survivors. She was captured by a Moslem soldier whom she later married. She lived quietly in Cawnpore, finally admitting her identity to a priest shortly before her death early in the 20th century.

CAPTAIN MOORE died at the ghat.

NANA SAHIB returned to Cawnpore to lead a counter-attack on the British but failed. After a succession of military defeats, he fled. It is widely believed that he died in Nepal.

JONAH SHEPHERD survived to publish an account of his adventures. He came close to death on several occasions and was saved more than once because his jailer refused to allow him to plead before the Nana that he was with the Europeans and should be released with them. He ascribed his survival to the direct intervention of God and, as a result, in his later life his enthusiasm for proselytisation verged on religious mania. Williamson's narrative suggests that his survival may have had a more secular explanation.

AMY HORNE survived and, despite the prejudice she feared she would be exposed to, married.

There are several contemporary accounts of the siege of Cawnpore. Captain Mowbray Thomson's book, *The Story of Cawnpore* is available online through Google Books. Jonah Shepherd's book, *A Personal Narrative of the Outbreak and Massacre at Cawnpore: During the Sepoy Revolt of 1857* is available through Nabu Public Domain Reprints.

Sir George Otto Trevelyan's book *Cawnpore*, published in 1866, draws heavily on Thomson's account but does provide other useful background.

Andrew Ward's book, *Our Bones Are Scattered* (1996), provides an astonishingly detailed and comprehensive account of the events in Cawnpore. For a broader discussion of the events in India, I would recommend Julian Spilsbury's *The Indian Mutiny* (2007). For a more accessible account, you could try John Harris, *The Indian Mutiny* (1973).

Williamson's experiences do, at times, show remarkable similarities to the accounts given by Fanny Parkes (*Wanderings of a Pilgrim in Search of the Picturesque*) published in 1850 and now available free through Google Books and Vivian Dering Majendie (*Up Among the Pandies*) published in 1859 and recently republished by Leonaur Ltd.

TCW, London, 2012

about the author

TOM WILLIAMS LIVES in London, where he has written about boring things like insurance for much of his adult life.

A trip to Borneo eventually resulted in his first novel, *The White Rajah*, based on the life of James Brooke of Sarawak. One thing led to another and eventually he wrote *Cawnpore*. Historical novels have become something of a habit and he is now finishing another book, this time set in Argentina around the time of the Napoleonic Wars.

When he is not writing, he enjoys skiing, skating, and dancing the tango, preferably in Buenos Aires. In between, he has exciting conversations with his bank manager about how this is to be financed. Your purchase of this book (assuming you did purchase it) has made a financial adviser very happy.

Lightning Source UK Ltd.
Milton Keynes UK
UKOW030407140212

187232UK00001B/12/P